SHERLOCK HOLMES
AND THE
SCARLET THREAD OF MURDER

By
Luke Benjamen Kuhns

Paperback ISBN 978-1-78092-785-5
ePub ISBN 978-1-78092-786-2
PDF ISBN 978-1-78092-787-9

Published in the UK by MX Publishing
335 Princess Park Manor, Royal Drive, London, N11 3GX
www.mxpublishing.com

Cover layout and construction by
www.staunch.com

Dedicated to each and every person who plays the game for the game's own sake.

The Scarlet Thread of Murder

A Sherlock Holmes, Martin Hewitt, & D.I. Edmund Reid Mystery

Prologue

I don't believe that I, Doctor John H. Watson, shall ever run dry of the fantastic tales in which I accompanied my great friend, Mr Sherlock Holmes. We had a remarkable and long-lasting career that began in the late Victorian era and continues even in our elder years. Sherlock Holmes, who now lives in Sussex, is still as sharp as ever. I often look over our old cases and wonder which of our tales I should disclose next. Some I do not believe will ever be released, unless I myself have passed from this life. However, it was on a summer day in June 1920 that I came upon a series of notes that had not been touched since late 1890.

Sherlock Holmes, you see, was not the only detective in London. There were many others. What made Sherlock Holmes unique was his singular position as a consulting detective. There was another in the profession who went by the name of Martin Hewitt. His adventures were chronicled by a journalist named Brett, and though they were not as popular as those adventures I shared with Holmes, Mr Hewitt was a brilliant detective with a powerful mind. Holmes' client list boasted members of the Yard, his brother, and personages of even higher position, while Hewitt did extremely well amongst the general public when Holmes was otherwise engaged or unavailable. And while Holmes often scolded the efficiency of Scotland Yard, there were some officers who shone bright. One of whom was D.I. Edmund Reid of Whitechapel, one of his most notable tasks being his work on the Ripper Case.

In 1890, these three men found themselves tangled in a web of intrigue. It is important to note that the events that transpire in this narrative are compiled from the notes of myself, the journalist Brett, and D.I. Edmund Reid. They have never shared their stories with the public, but they did share their notes with me, making it my responsibility to disclose the outré events that we endured.

Chapter 1
D.I. Edmund Reid
Disaster in Whitechapel

August 1890

Very few things have so shaken my faculties as the events that began one late-summer's day. As the Detective Inspector of Whitechapel, it creates a certain immunity. One feels prepared and braced for horrors, both weird and wild. Whilst I sat at my desk at Leman Street, buried in piles of paperwork, I found myself suddenly moved by a heart-stopping boom. The windows shook, and I could hear panicked shouts in the street. It did not take long to realise the cause of the incident: an explosion on the underground railway. I jolted from my seat and took my hat as I raced outside. I could see a cloud of smoke rising above the buildings. It was coming from the Whitechapel and Mile End station.

Two officers and I arrived first on the scene. A terrible sight lay before us. More people than I could count had come to watch as smoke poured out of the station entrance. Survivors were stumbling out of the station: men, women, and children, coloured grey and black from the heavy smoke, collapsing upon the street.

My men immediately began attending to the fallen. I could hear the choking screams of the people still inside, unable to find their way out. I covered my mouth with a kerchief and raced inside to help the desperate. The heat within the station was immense, as if walking through a wall of fire. The smoke blocked my vision, making it nigh impossible to quickly assist those in need. I stumbled into someone, a woman; I took her by the arm and led her out. She wrapped her arms around me.

"You are safe now," I informed the woman.

Her skin was darkened by the smoke and dirt. Something fell from her person—a silver oval pendant. It opened upon hitting the ground. Inside, I noticed a picture of a crown. She took it and clutched it tightly while she coughed.

"Thank you, thank you!" she gasped.

I motioned for an officer to take her, and I went back inside. I found the body of a man on the floor, but he did not move. I hauled the corpse outside and laid him upon the ground; to my horror, not only had the body been trampled, and bones protruded from his flesh, but his face was severely burned, the skin charred and peeled back.

More officers and the fire brigade arrived as I looked over the charred body. The smoke began to clear as the fire brigade battled the remaining flames. In total, it was over four hours before all the bodies were moved and some form of peace restored.

"Detective Inspector," called Officer Kipling, swiftly approaching me. "We need you to come see something." I followed him down into the wreckage. Looking over the scene, it was clear the train had pulled in on time; while passengers were embarking and disembarking, the engine had exploded. The two carriages nearest the engine were affected most by the blast and were now twisted heaps of metal and charred wood. The remaining carriages had been knocked off the tracks and were blackened from the fire. Officer Kipling leapt down into the wreckage, and I followed. "You see this?" he said, showing me the epicentre of the destruction. "This was no accident. This was a bomb."

As I looked up and down the line of carriages, the chain reaction of explosions which had followed was utterly devastating. I found myself drifting, thinking about the innocent who were carelessly slain as I gazed upon the destruction.

"Sir... sir?" Kipling's voice called me back.

"Yes, an explosion," I confirmed. "I can see that."

"Suppose it was Jewish rebels?" Kipling asked. "They've caused a lot of trouble lately."

"It could be the Irish, or Scottish, or Welsh!" I snapped. "For all we know, it could be the Americans!"

"Americans, sir?" Kipling questioned.

"My point, Officer, is that we know not who it was. Don't assume blame upon anyone until you have all the facts."

"Yes, sir. Sorry, sir." Kipling hung his head a moment.

"We need to get this cleaned up… get Mr White down here first. I want him to take a look before we start removing the scrap," I ordered.

"Right away, sir." Kipling darted off out of the abyss.

I continued to look around the dismantled carriages. I observed the bodies that remained. They were horribly charred, unrecognisable—clothes and flesh ripped open, like a hot knife through butter. A foul stench was trapped in the station, a smell fit only for the seventh circle of hell. The scorched bodies and burning coals stung my sinuses.

It would take some time to identify the remains and contact relatives. I thought back on Kipling's remarks: this could be Jews, or even Irish rebels. Either way, this was no mistake; the explosion had a purpose not yet known. An extremist at the engine, perhaps?

Whitechapel—these streets run wild with moral insanity. Here whores are gutted like pigs; men from the highest ranks of society transform into drunkards and rapists as they indulge in opium and give in to their animalistic urges. It feels as if God himself had turned his face away, leaving me, and a band of men, to battle the devils that haunt this modern Sodom and Gomorrah.

Within the hour, Kipling returned. With him was Mr Vigo White, a man of average height with fiery red hair and wild sideburns. He walked towards me; I could see his beady blue eyes surveying the wreckage. He wiped his mouth in amazement at the destruction. Lifting a pair of spectacles from the arch of his pointy nose, he rested them atop his head, pushing his ginger locks back.

"I found him, Mr Reid," Kipling called.

"Thank you for coming," said I, stretching out my hand towards Mr White. Setting his case upon the ground, he took my hand.

"Of what service may I be?" Mr White returned as his observations continued. "Looks like quite the mess."

"Indeed, it is. We found traces of an explosive. I want you to have a look at it and see if we can gather any clues from what is left behind—a maker or seller, perhaps."

"Don't you have other people who could do this?" White asked. He took his spectacles into his hands and rubbed them clean with a cloth. He returned the cloth to his grey tweed jacket with exaggerated care. "I don't even work for the Yard."

"You don't work for anyone; you're a vagabond," said I.

"I have my experiments and a more than generous lump sum every six months," said White with a smirk. He enjoyed his anonymity. He lived in the shadows, and we left him to it unless his assistance was needed. For all his bizarre behaviour, his skills and scientific knowledge were paramount to me.

"You know our resources are limited. None of my men is as skilled as you," I paused. "Why do you question my call for aid?"

"No reason, I just like hearing that I'm needed." White grinned, picking up his case. "Show me where this bomb is—or was."

Setting his case upon the ground, he opened it up. Inside were various scientific tools, bottles with strange solutions, a small burner, and glass tubes for collecting samples. He descended onto the tracks and waded through the wreckage to examine the origin of the explosion and gingerly collect samples. White knelt by the remains of the explosive and began to examine them. The explosive casing was virtually non-existent. Shrapnel was all that remained. Strange burn marks of various colours of red and orange trailed away from the central blast. I watched White drift into his own world, as he often did during his examinations. He mumbled, sighed, and chuckled as he took samples and packed them into the tubes.

After a few minutes, White shot up like a bullet and cried, "Sweet Mother Mary!"

"What?" I asked excitedly. "What is it?"

White turned to look at me, stepped over the wreckage, and climbed back onto the platform. His hands were black, but that did not stop him from rubbing his forehead, leaving residue.

He leaned in close to me and whispered, "I've seen these types of explosive burn marks before."

"Where from?"

"You're not going to like it," he warned.

"Tell me, White."

"I knew a chap once, a Jewish mechanic. He had a design for an explosive that was small in size but with a fierce impact. His work always left these kinds of red and orange burns."

"Who is this mechanic?"

"Look, Reid, I'm not saying he did this. It is possible that someone stole his plans."

"The name! Tell me his name."

White hung his head and ran his blackened hand through his red hair. "The man's name is Abraham Lamech."

"Lamech, you say? The Jewish anarchist?"

"Say that again?" came an unfamiliar voice. White and I turned to see a man approaching us, carrying a pad and pencil. He wore a brown-and-blue tweed suit, a red waistcoat with a gold watch chain, and a brown fedora. "Did you say Lamech is responsible for this attack?"

"I shan't be saying anything. Who are you?" I demanded.

"He's a piss-taker, Mr Reid. A scribbling monkey for the papers."

"Care to comment on this attack, Mr Reid? You suspect Lamech? Will you be arresting him? What is your evidence?"

"Officer Kipling!" I shouted.

"Will you be taking this to Abberline? Or are you afraid of the Jewish threat?" The reporter carried on asking questions.

"Kipling, get down here at once!" I ordered again.

"You are avoiding the question. Why, Inspector Reid? Are you trying to cover something up?"

I gripped the reporter by the collar and pulled his face close to mine. "Now you listen here. I don't know how you slipped in, but whatever you think you hear or know is all hearsay. I will not have scum like you twisting words and making false reports so that you can sell papers."

"Still bitter about Ripper getting away, Inspector?" I shoved the reporter back; he nearly fell to the ground. Kipling came towards us.

"Officer, throw this man out of here. And make sure everyone knows his face. I don't want to see him sniffing around here again!"

Chapter 2
Doctor Watson
The Goblin Man

Autumn 1890

It was a bright and sunny autumn day. The windows of 221B were
open, which allowed a pleasant breeze to flow through the rooms.
The sound of carts and horses' hooves banging on the cobbled
road filled the background, along with the occasional loud-spoken
man or laughing woman. I found myself gazing out our bay window, watching the business below. Holmes was in a dark mood.
The previous week, he had concluded work on a high-profile case
for a well-known foreign dignitary, which had seen him rise to
new heights within his field. As a result, he was flooded with letters from prospective clients across the country. However, he took
little interest in this sudden flurry of requests for his services.
With open letters piled high around his chair, all of them pleas for
help, he sat with his chin resting on his knees.

"Watson!" he called. I turned from the window to see him
throw his head back and rest it on the back of the chair. His arms
hung over each side like an exhausted child, and a deep sigh left
his lungs.

"Find something of interest?" I asked.

"Quite the opposite, I'm afraid." He sighed again. He leapt
from his chair and walked over to the mantel. He rested his long,
thin arm across it and repeatedly tapped his middle finger upon
the wood. "Dull, Watson, just dull. All of these letters." His head
turned back and forth as he looked at the pile. "Ah! Take this
one." He walked back to his chair and picked up a note. It ran this
way:

Dear Mr Holmes,

I require your services. My wife has left me and given no indication of where she has gone. Help me find her.

Sincerely,
George Peabody Jones.

"Is there nothing of interest in this woman's sudden disappearance?" I asked.

"Women disappear all the time, especially when they have spent time in the company of people like George Peabody Jones."

"Are you familiar with this man?" I pressed.

"I am, Watson. He's a fiendish man, a banker. He is unaware of my knowledge of him, but he is a member of a spiritualist club that often partakes in immoral indulgences fit only for the ancient city of Corinth. It is likely his wife left for good reason, probably to escape his lunacy."

"Well," said I, "not all of these letters can be from such indulgent individuals, surely."

"No, no, they are not." He threw the letter down and collapsed into his chair. Legs sprawled and fingertips steepled, he continued, "But they are all void of interest. A missing ring here, a problematic will there, men and women wanting to cover their petty scandals. I'm not a repair service, Watson. Give me real problems, give me real work! Don't hound me with these minuscule problems that Scotland Yard's most ineffective officer could handle."

"I'm sure something will crop up. It always does," I assured him. He nodded and rolled his eyes. Just then, the bell rang.

"Half a second ring!" said Holmes, sitting up straight. He slouched back into his chair. "Probably someone with a missing pet."

I could hear footsteps coming up the stairs. I walked to the door and opened it before our guest could knock. It was a man around 5'5". He had blonde hair and blue eyes, was dressed in a well-pressed black suit, and held a top hat.

"Are you Sherlock Holmes?" asked the man in a thick Scottish accent.

"I am Doctor Watson…"

"Yes, the chronicler!" the Scotsman said with a nod. "Where is Mr Holmes? I must speak with him."

"I am right here," said Holmes, who was now standing with hands clasped behind his back. "Come and have a seat, and do try and calm your nerves, Mr…?"

"David Daniels," our visitor replied.

"Mr Daniels," said Holmes, extending his arm, "please, sit."

I fetched our guest a glass of brandy as he settled on the long couch. Taking it quickly, he downed the liquid and asked for another. After obliging, I replaced the bottle and sat opposite Holmes as our guest dried his mouth with his sleeve. After several deep breaths, the man appeared more composed.

"Now," Holmes began, "what brings one of London's most successful businessmen to our bohemian abode?"

"You know of me, I see," Mr Daniels said. "But I would abandon my fortune, my business ventures, all my success to escape this horrific fate that has befallen me." He took several deep breaths. "Mr Holmes, I have found myself terrorised by a ghastly creature; a creature known only as the Goblin Man."

I looked at Holmes, but his expression remained firm.

"Have you heard of him?" Mr Daniels asked.

"The Goblin Man?" Holmes questioned. "Watson, hand me my index, would you?" I did as he asked. Holmes flipped through his papers. "Ah, yes. Reports of a Goblin Man have been present for some time. He is reported to work in dark alleys. He chases his victims, binds them, strips them of their possessions, and leaves them. Reports, though often given by women of questionable nature or drunken men, say he has a large nose…"

"Big green eyes," interrupted Mr Daniels, "yellowish skin covered in boils, ratty clothes which consist of a dirty cotton shirt, a red velvet waistcoat, chequered trousers, a long natty jacket, and a battered top hat. His hands are like ice, and his fingernails are long and sharp and black as coal."

Holmes and I gazed upon our guest. His description of this Goblin Man sent chills down my spine.

"He sounds like the stuff of fairy tales, something the Brothers Grimm might have crafted," I said, breaking the silence.

"You've seen this man then, have you?" asked Holmes.

"I have," Daniels admitted. "He is my tormentor. He is the demon that stalks me in the night, chases me till I can no longer run, but he never hurts me or takes anything from me. He has touched me once, no more. I feel him always behind me. His presence lingers when awake; sleep is a struggle, for the Goblin haunts my dreams. Mr Holmes, I need your help. I need you to stop this Goblin Man."

"And you believe this Goblin Man to be of supernatural origins?" I asked.

"Heavens, no," replied Daniels, "but he is a foul creature whether birthed in hell or not. He is very real. What I can't understand is his fascination with me; am I the only one he does this to? What have I done to deserve this torture?" His eyes drifted from Holmes, and he stared into the fireplace. "I thought myself an honourable, God-fearing man; maybe I'm not." Our guest trailed off into silence a moment. "Can you help me?" he asked, looking straight into Holmes' eyes.

"I'm going to need more details, Mr Daniels. When did you first encounter this Goblin Man? Tell me everything."

Mr Daniels leaned back, his hands in his lap. "It began a fortnight ago. I was returning home after a long evening of drink and gambling at my club. The time was around midnight, if memory serves. A misty fog rolled in the air, and the streets were deserted. Moving briskly with my head down and my coat collar turned up to keep dry, I did not pay much attention to my surroundings. Strange chattering and quiet giggles could be heard from behind, but when I turned around, no one could be seen. My first thought was that someone from one of the local public houses was fumbling home. Then a horrendous screech echoed through the air. That's when I saw it." Our guest turned pale. "Standing under the yellow glow of a street lamp was the Goblin Man. His shoulders moved up and down as he breathed in and out.

"'Who are you?' I called out, but there was no response. Taking a few steps backwards, I turned and quickened my pace. My home, which is on James Street, just off Lancaster Gate, was near. Quick steps followed me. The Goblin was chasing after me. I began to run for fear that this maniac might kill me! My terror was amplified when I realised I was leading this monster to my very doorstep. So I darted down a small path between two rows of houses. Without warning, I found myself flung to the ground. The Goblin pounced on top of me, digging his knee into my back. He wrapped his cold hand around the back of my neck and squeezed tightly." Daniels placed his hand around his neck as if the mere memory of it caused him to relive the horror of the event. "I lay there motionless for some time."

"'What do you want?' said I. The man suddenly stood up and backed off. I quickly rose to my feet and faced my attacker. It was dark, but I could still see him clearly. He was not... natural-looking. His face, that is, was that of a monster. 'Who are you?' I stammered. Like a beast, the Goblin flailed his arms and let out a piercing scream. I began to run again, but he did not follow me. When I felt safe, I proceeded home. Nerves shattered, I collapsed the moment I got inside my door. I stayed home the entire next day and attempted to recover. I reported this incident to the authorities, but no others had been reported before mine. In fact, the officer said there hadn't been a Goblin case since a few years back. They stationed a few extra officers within my area and assured me they'd do their best to find this man." I noticed the slight twitch of a smile upon Holmes's face at this statement. "Well, nothing happened for a day or two. Then about four days after the first encounter, I stepped into my back garden and was horrified when I saw the Goblin Man sitting upon the stone fence. His hand dangled between his legs, and his head was bent down. I raced back inside and grabbed my revolver. When I came back, he was gone!"

"And what time was this?" Holmes asked.

"It was about nine o'clock at night. I sent a wire to the police, but of course they did not prove much help at all.

"A week after the first encounter, I found myself back at my club. This time my revolver was with me. I looked constantly behind me during my walk home but saw nothing. It wasn't until James Street that fear consumed me, and I saw the Goblin Man a short distance ahead. I reached into my pocket, withdrew my revolver, and began to fire. Utter panic took me when I realised my revolver was not loaded! I had loaded that gun that very morning, but now it was empty! The Goblin Man held out his hand, and he dropped several small objects on the ground. They pinged as they hit the ground, and I then realised what they were. They were my bullets! How he got them is a mystery. He then chased after me. We ran for what felt like hours. He didn't appear to wish to catch me this time, as if he derived some kind of enjoyment from the chase alone. I ran, Mr Holmes, I ran and ran until I could run no more. I fell over with aching legs and a pounding chest. After recovering my strength, I managed to make my way home. My incident was told to the police. They said they would have an officer on my street every night between nine and midnight. Their inability to do anything thus far did not ease my fear, but whom else could I turn to? Thankfully, for the sake of my sanity, the next four days passed uneventfully. On the fifth day, after this third encounter, I had prepared myself for bed, and when I stepped into my room, my window, which overlooks the back, was open. A cold wind crept in and rustled the curtains. I walked over to close it, but something caught my attention. I turned, and, sitting in the armchair, was the Goblin Man! I dropped my lamp, and it shattered on the floor. Thankfully, nothing caught fire. There, in the darkened room, the Goblin Man approached me. I could feel his breath on my face. It stank, like the smell of death.

"'What do you want? Why are you tormenting me?' I pleaded.

"'Don't you know?' the Goblin Man replied.

"'No! I don't know, so tell me, damn it!' I shouted.

"'Shouts won't bring you any aid,' he said in a slow, serpent-like voice.

"'Leave me alone! Is it money you want? I'll pay you, just leave me alone!' I told him.

"'Money? I don't need your money. Just know that I'm always going to be here. You can't escape me.' I turned to hit the Goblin Man, but he was too fast. He ducked, missing my swing, and threw one of the bed sheets over my head. By the time I had untangled myself, he had escaped through the window and was gone. I told this to the police, yet again. They found no clues within my room. But I can bear it no more, Mr Holmes. This man is real and he must be stopped. Can you help me?"

Holmes sat in silence a moment or two. "Have you wronged anyone?"

"Pardon?"

"In your line of work. You have your hands in several operations. You invest in many companies—shipping, manufacturing, a few others. I need to know whether you have, in all your business dealings, ever wronged anyone. It's better to tell me now than have me discover it later," said Holmes coolly.

"Oh, well," stammered Mr Daniels, "I am an honest and ethical businessman."

"Then you may very well be the first in history," Holmes returned.

"Business is not about making friends, Mr Holmes. It is about making money, and I am particularly good at it. But I can say there are no harsh feelings between me and any of my investors."

"Any business partners?" Holmes asked.

"Well, I lost my most recent partner," said he.

"How so?" I asked.

"Do you recall that explosion in East London?" Daniels asked. "The one that tore through the station. My partner, Thomas, was on the train that went up. He was a damn good man, a damn good businessman!"

"I'll take the case, Mr Daniels," said Holmes. "As I am sure you are aware, my rates are fixed, and Doctor Watson will be accompanying me on my investigation. I will need full access to your house, your room, and I hope that you retained the bullets that this Goblin Man took."

"Why, yes, of course!"

"Very well, I have some things to take care of and some tidying up to do. We will call upon you tonight, Mr Daniels." Holmes stood and walked to the study door. "Good day."

Mr Daniels stood and held the rim of his hat with both hands as he passed by Holmes. "Thank you, Mr Holmes, thank you indeed! I will see you later."

Chapter 3
Martin Hewitt
The Problem at Davenport House

Autumn 1890

This was a singularly unique affair, one that happens once in a lifetime. One autumn evening, when Martin Hewitt and I had found ourselves coming home from the public house, The Hare and The Hounds, we were greeted in the street by a stranger. A woman. She was tall and slender, wearing a dark blue dress with a floral design. Her black hair was tied up, accentuating the severity of her face. Her sharp cheekbones, wide green eyes, and pointy nose dazzled us. She looked upon us intensely. I admit that for a moment, there was a light feeling of intimidation at the strange beauty that she possessed.

"Are you Martin Hewitt?" she asked in a gentle voice.

"I am," said Hewitt, stepping forward and extending his hand.

"I need your help," said the woman, placing her hand into his.

Hewitt brought it to his lips and kissed it. "Well, why don't we step inside so we may talk? Perhaps with a warm drink?"

"Very well," she replied.

She followed us up the stairs and into our chambers. I offered her a seat and quickly set about boiling some water to make tea. Hewitt sat with our guest, and I observed from a distance.

"Now, what is your name?" Hewitt asked.

"Mrs Clara Edwards," she replied.

"Well, Mrs Edwards, what can I do for you?"

"I am here on a most important request. Someone very dear to me has gone missing. I have no clue where they have gone or why they have just abandoned us. I was hoping that if I gave you enough information, you would be able to find my missing associate."

"Mrs Edwards, you can drop the act," Hewitt smirked. His fingertips danced on the armrest of his chair. "I know very well that the person you seek is no associate of yours, but is rather a husband, or a lover." An expression of complete bewilderment fell upon Hewitt's client. Her face went flush, and she stirred in her seat. Hewitt remained cool and calm as he continued: "I can also see you are around three months with child, and feel it safe to assume this abandoner is the father."

It started with a quiver of the lower lip; soon, a stream of tears flowed like two great rivers from her green eyes. "How can you possibly know any of this?" she begged, an explanation through her sobs.

"Your dress, for one, is bulging ever so slightly around your stomach. You are not a rotund woman, yet I can see swelling in your fingers where your wedding ring has tightened. Furthermore, your fingernails; I can see a brown dust under them, and, judging from the aroma obtained when I kissed your hand, you are taking Tabloid Opium for your morning sickness. So the logical explanation would be that you are with child. How do I know that you are looking for the father? Well, you said 'they abandoned us' rather than 'they abandoned me'. You also went out of your way to conceal their gender. So you may drop the act. I will help you, but only under the umbrella of complete and total honesty."

She held her head low. The kettle screamed. I quickly prepared three cups of tea. I brought them in on a tray, with a bit of milk and sugar on the side. Mrs Edwards lifted her head as I approached. With the assurance of the warm drink in her hand, she told us her tale.

"His name is Phillias Jackson, a struggling businessman. He has all the charisma one could need, but he lacks the finance to succeed in anything. His profession changes weekly; it feels like he could never stick to one line of work. He has passion, though, a raw sort of attitude towards life, which was what attracted me to him."

"And your wealth attracted him to you?" Hewitt interrupted. "Or your husband's wealth, I should say."

"My husband is dead, Mr Hewitt," she said with a bite in her voice.

"Yes, but not three months ago."

"And how do you know?" she demanded.

"Mrs Edwards, or rather, Mrs Goodtree, I recognise you from the papers. Your husband, Thomas Goodtree, died in that terrible explosion at the Whitechapel station," said Hewitt. "Now, it will be much easier if you tell us the truth from the start."

Her eyes widened. She had a childlike look of surprise on her face. She was caught out completely, with no more places to hide.

"Yes, yes, I can see that. Thomas was a good man, but he was so wrapped up in the shipping business that he paid little attention to me. I never cared to be rich; I simply wanted a happy life. So when I met this passionate man, Phillias, I gave in to my desires. Thomas cared little about what I did or where I went, so he never knew. He spent all this time with his business partner. I worked to get Thomas to take Phillias into their business and introduced them. But then I fell pregnant, and we discussed what we would do. We agreed to run away together with the money we had and start a new life somewhere. Then one day, he sent me a note saying he had some other business to take care of out of town and that he'd be back in a week or two. That was two and a half months ago. He never came back, nor have I heard from him. He's just gone! I've lost my uncaring husband, and the one man who did care is missing. I don't want to make a public ordeal of this, Mr Hewitt. That is why I've come to you. More than anything, I need closure. If he's dead, I need to know."

"Were there ever any feuds between your husband and Phillias?" Hewitt asked.

"Never. The times I saw them together, they acted like gentlemen."

"And when did you see them together?"

"Not often. But as I said, I introduced Thomas to Phillias, and for a while, he did do some work for them. Neither man complained about the other, at least not to me. I have no reason to think there was any issue between them at all."

"Where did he work for them?"

"Thomas and his partner had a factory on Nine Elms. Phillias managed it."

"Very well. And as you have no idea where he went, I think it would be best to look around Mr Phillias's home for a clue to his whereabouts. What is his address?"

"I'm not sure. He never disclosed it to me. We only met in hotels."

"Dear me, Mrs Goodtree, this is quite the mess. At what hotels did you meet?"

"Fashionable ones. The Savoy, most recently. The Langham Hotel and the Midland Grand on St. Pancras."

"Would you know anyone that might know where he lives?"

"Thomas's partner, David Daniels, he might know. He lives on James Street by Lancaster Gate."

"Can you give us a description of Phillias?"

"He is tall, about six feet. He had a lovely face." Her eyes began to well, but she fought back the tears.

"Please, no romantics," Hewitt interrupted. "Tell it straight."

Our guest took the rebuke on the chin. Straightening her posture, she continued.

"He is six foot with peppered hair," she continued, "he has a rugged face, and he rarely shaves, so he usually has a thick layer of stubble. When I last saw him, he had a moustache. I could always find him in a crowd, as he wore a bowler hat with a card pinned to it." She paused a moment, and her lips quivered. "The card was a Queen of Hearts, and on the backside, the side facing the hat, was a photograph of me. He calls me the queen of his heart, you see."

"His eyes and face, any unique markings upon them?" Hewitt asked.

"His eyes are a swirl of colour, a brownish green—very earthy and wild. On the left side of his face, just before his ear, is a mole. His frame is thin, but strong. His nose is slightly arched in the middle. He often has bags under his eyes from late nights working, and his cheeks are sunken as he never eats enough. He does have a small scar on his right hand and one on his left index finger. He was cut badly, so the scar is quite visible."

"What type of dress?"

"Gentleman's dress. A blue waistcoat was his favourite. A black frock coat and grey trousers with a green-checked pattern."

"Very well. Brett, you and I will go see what we can find out from Mr Daniels. Where can we find you, Mrs Goodtree?"

"Chester House, Elsworth Road, near Primrose Hill."

"Ah, yes. I know it."

Mrs Goodtree rose, as did we. I walked over and opened the door. She stopped in the doorway and turned back. "Find him, Mr Hewitt. I can't bear this child without my sweet Phillias." With that, she rushed down the stairs and out of sight.

Chapter 4
D.I. Edmund Reid
An Anarchist's Playground

August 1890

Kipling and I left the Whitechapel and Mile End stations and headed towards Brick Lane, where Lamech and his Jewish anarchists were known to camp. The Mariah battered along the cobbled streets, the driver shouting abuses at the filth that either stumbled into the road or felt the necessity to stand there. I looked at my watch; the time was nearly three o'clock. I realised I had not eaten since I left my home and my bride, Emily. By now, she would have heard of the explosion, and I could only imagine her panic for my well-being.

I saw the piercing steeple of Christ Church ahead as we drew nearer and nearer to Lamech's dwelling. Kipling sat across from me, gripping his baton; his knuckles were white, and his face grimaced.

"Steady, Kipling," said I. He turned his eyes from the cabin floor towards me, and a half-smile broke on his face.

"Yes, sir."

"No need to be. We are simply going to have a conversation with Lamech, not break down his doors… yet." I grinned in an attempt to ease his tension.

The Mariah came to a jerking halt, thrusting Kipling and me backwards and forwards. The driver called to say that we had arrived. I looked up and down the street. There was an eerie quiet that loomed in the stale air. Our only company was the foul stench of urine and other bodily remains that swam in the gutters. We ducked down an alley and approached a black door. I pounded upon it until it was jerked open. A short man with dark hair and a thick beard answered. His eyes met mine with disapproval and disdain.

"What do you want?" he asked in a thick Polish accent. He raised his arm and leaned on the doorframe, and I saw that his arm was speckled with tattoos. Upon his wrist, I noticed a small symbol—the Hebrew Alpha symbol, and on the underpart, connected by a chain, the Omega symbol.

"I need to see Lamech. I know he's here," I demanded.

"This some sort of joke?" the man demanded, his face turning red.

"I'm not joking," said I. "Now, where is he?"

"Lamech is dead, you bastard!" he shouted. "Don't act like you don't know!"

"Dead?" I retorted, taken aback by his news. "What is the cause?"

"You, English, and your fake ignorance. You can't pretend you know nothing of this."

"I assure you we do not."

"How did he die?" Kipling asked.

"What is this man doing here?" roared a voice from inside. A tall, lanky man with wide-set eyes and a large nose sprang towards us. His wrist bore the same tattooed symbol. It was a sign showing which group he belonged to.

"We are here to speak with Lamech, but your friend here tells me that he is dead," said I.

"I know you, Inspector Reid. You think you can cleanse Whitechapel. Rid it of vermin like us!" shouted the tall man. His hand was jerking, and I noticed him playing with a silver ring bearing the Star of David. "I will not have your presence here!"

"I do not need your permission. Now, if there has been a death, I want to know the cause. Should I suspect anything, it will not cost me any great trouble to rally my troops and arrest you all for illegal imports, petty theft, and other random acts of violence."

"Mr Reid, maybe one day you'll follow through with your threats of arrest," the tall man replied. He turned and walked away, saying, "Show him in."

We followed the short man down a dark hallway, and then up a narrow stair and into an attic. The room was covered in Jewish symbols. A desk was piled with newspapers, letters, and several thick Torah scrolls. A strong aroma of incense hung heavy in the room. In the far corner sat two women on the floor, their backs to us. There was a body laid out in front of them. The tall man stood in a corner, smoking a cigarette. The women turned to look at us. One was elderly and frail-looking, the other young and fair-skinned.

"They are his mother and sister," the short man informed us.

"I am Ruth," said the young woman. "This is Naomi." Ruth pointed towards the older woman.

"I am sorry for your loss," I said, removing my hat.

"Can you tell us what happened?" Kipling asked.

"We do not know," Ruth said. "He was fine until last night. He felt ill, talked lots of nonsense, as though he was dreaming but still awake. Then he fainted."

"When did he breathe his last?" I asked.

The young woman looked at me sternly. "Is it always straight to business with you, Mr Reid?"

"May we have a look at him?" Kipling asked softly. I was impressed with Kipling's tact, and the woman appeared softer towards him. Ruth nodded and we approached.

"He departed from us an hour ago," Ruth said. I looked upon the face of Abraham Lamech. There was a strange shading under his eyes and a sort of yellowish tint to his skin. His body expelled an aroma that was not one of death. It was something else. A toxin, but I could not be certain of which one.

"Was he with anyone last night?" I pressed.

"Not that we are aware. He went out for a drink."

"At what time?"

"Haven't you pressed enough?" the tall man said from his corner, still fiddling with his loose ring. "I think you can leave us now."

"I think not. His manner of death was no accident. He was poisoned."

"He went to the inn around the corner. The White Stag," Ruth said.

"Quiet, woman!" snapped the tall man.

"They need to know," she returned softly, but her eyes gave him a piercing stare.

"Do you know who he saw there? Was he meant to be meeting anyone?" I asked. They were unsure. "Has he had any plans to bomb the Whitechapel and Mile End station?"

The women were silent.

"You come here accusing a dead man of this?" the short man said.

"He did it, or someone wants us to think he did. An explosive very much like the ones we know he has used in the past was the cause of the tragedy today. Many are dead. If he had nothing to do with this, it's important that we learn who did, but it all points here."

"We know nothing of it," the tall man said. The short man looked uneasy.

"Cooperation will go a long way," I returned. The room remained silent.

"We'll cooperate when swine like Lord Myers stop trying to force the Jews out of the city!" exclaimed the short man. The other shot him a fierce glance.

"I'm not here to discuss matters of prejudice, nor the thoughts and actions of Lord Myers. I am here about the underground station. We will need Lamech's body for autopsy."

*****

Kipling and I came to an agreement with Ruth and the others regarding Lamech's body. I sent Kipling back to the station to make arrangements for the body to be retrieved while I carried on to The White Stag. The streets were still quiet as Lamech's followers mourned his passing in silence. Soon enough, the sound of glasses clashing and the murmur of sloshed men could be heard here and there. I approached the public house, and the smell of stale beer rushed into my lungs as I set foot inside. Glares of disapproval followed me as I walked up to the bar.

"Your name, sir?" I asked the bartender.

"Jeffry," the man managed to mumble.

"Lamech was here last night. Who was he with?"

He wiped out a glass with a dirty towel. "Don't know what you mean, guv'ner," he said, and put the glass onto a shelf.

"Give us some gin," said a man at the bar. Jeffry grabbed a bottle and a glass and filled it for him.

"I know he was here," said I. "You can either help me, or I can have a look at your books. I know you've made arrangements with local whores for the use of your rooms."

"You'd like to know who they bring back. That'd be the real crime." Jeffry grinned.

"I do not care that others in authority have looked past this. I will not do the same. What I can promise is this: help me, and I will give you time to move your whores before we storm this cesspool!"

Jeffry squinted at me. I glared back at him, unmoving.

"Get us a whiskey!" shouted another man, slapping his open palm onto the bar. Jeffry walked away, and I stormed out.

*****

I returned, empty-handed, to the station. Lamech's body was brought in later that night, while White examined the remains of the explosive. Over the next twenty-four hours, the bodies from the explosion were identified. Further aid from other divisions of Scotland Yard stepped in to handle the workload. An Inspector Lestrade was put in place to interview survivors and speak with those who had lost loved ones, in the hopes of acquiring any leads.

*****

I dozed at my desk. A rattle at my door shook me awake. "Come in," I called, wiping the sleep from my eyes and seeing the morning sun pour through the windows.

"You look like hell, Reid," said White. "You've got a beautiful wife, go sleep with her rather than at your desk."

"I'd rather you not speak of me and my wife's sleeping arrangements," I said. "Tell me, what have you learnt?" White waved, and I followed him.

In his private working chamber, Lamech's body lay on a table. White had done the autopsy during the night. On a counter lay the remains of the explosive, along with some glass dishes filled with coloured powder, some magnifying instruments, and a few Bunsen burners boiling with strange liquids.

"Well, you were right. Lamech was poisoned," said White, looking over the dead body. "But not by any poison I'm familiar with. This purple colouring of the skin appears to be a side effect of the poison."

"A foreign poison," I said, walking over and looking down at the corpse. "How did it get into his body?"

"It wasn't injected into his system. There are no signs of a struggle or even so much as a needle prick on him. It was done orally, through food or drink." White walked over to a scope. I followed. "Have a look." I put my eyes to the scope and looked at the microorganisms. "His gut and intestines were full of the stuff. I can only imagine that this poison is tasteless and has no aroma, or at least was masked by another taste. He gobbled his food and drink, and by the time he got home, the poison had taken effect, and he died." I raised my eyes from the scope and looked at White. "So, there you have it."

"It was done through his food," I said. "The only place he went, or at least the only place his family told me he went, was the public house. I paid them a visit. They were, of course, no help at all. It would seem they have something to hide."

"Think you ought to pay them another visit. Perhaps a nice little raid is in order?"

"What of the explosive?" I questioned.

"It's definitely one of Lamech's designs. I knew that from the beginning," said White, as he ran his hand through his hair. "It's the chemicals he uses; they leave those colour marks which were left. The device used an unknown chemical compound that Lamech and his group have never used."

"What are you suggesting?"

"It's obvious. Where does an anarchist get a new chemical?"

"From someone like you."

"Exactly," White returned with a grin. "You need to find the chemist Lamech was working with."

"Our best lead is back at the public house. Burst down the doors and chase out the whores until we get answers."

Kipling burst into the room. "We've got a problem, sir!" He handed me The Weekly Dispatch. The headline read: JEWISH ANARCHIST RESPONSIBLE FOR WHITECHAPEL & MILE END BOMBING!

"Story by Eustace Brown? Damn, that reporter!" I shouted, throwing the paper aside. "Bring him in!"

"Another thing, Inspector Reid, Detective Chief Inspector Johnstone is here."

*****

"What the hell, Reid?" shouted DCI Johnstone as I stepped into my office. He was sitting atop my desk. "This is sloppy, very sloppy!"

"The reporter sneaked in, heard whispers, and crafted a story. There is no truth to his words!"

"It doesn't matter. We now have a newspaper all over the city claiming that a Jewish anarchist is blowing up rail stations. Not only will this affect people travelling on the Underground, but it's also going to cause unwanted hostilities between the Gentiles and the Hebrews!

Johnstone stood and walked around my desk, looking at the map of London that hung on the wall.

"I'll make him print a retraction, sir," said I.

"What are you doing about this anarchist?"

"He's dead. He was at the pub the night before the explosion, came home ill, and died sometime after the explosion. His body lies here. Mr White…"

"White is here?" he snapped.

"He is, sir."

"That man is no doctor, he's no proper scientist. He should not be getting his hands on police business."

"He's a good man, and he's a hell of a lot better than some of these police surgeons we've got wasting time on our payroll." I composed myself. "Now, I have a dead anarchist, a wrecked rail station, and a journalist I need to deal with. So, if you'll excuse me, I have work to do."

"See that all this is sorted, Reid. Don't let this be another Ripper." Johnstone walked out. I went around my desk and fell into my chair.

Chapter 5
Doctor Watson
A Visit to Mr Daniels

Autumn 1890

"Watson, would you visit Lestrade and see what information they might have on this Goblin Man, and the incident regarding Mr Daniels?" Holmes asked.

"I'll leave straight away," said I. "What are you doing?"

"I will follow another avenue. Meet me at Lancaster Gate at nine o'clock, and from there we'll go see Daniels."

I left Holmes and made my way to Scotland Yard. I did not find Lestrade at the Yard upon my arrival, and I waited some time before he appeared.

"Hello, Doctor." Lestrade greeted me with a handshake. I followed him into his small office. "What can I do for you?"

"I need to learn what you know about the Goblin Man and his connection to David Daniels," said I.

Lestrade leaned back in his chair and let out a sigh.

"The Goblin Man," Lestrade began. "He is a man who dresses up and scares people, but he is slippery as a fish, I tell you. We can't seem to catch him. His activity quietened down over the past few years. I know some people thought he might have been the Ripper because his attacks stopped about six months before the Whitechapel horrors started. Now the Goblin is back, or so we're meant to believe, and tormenting this man Daniels." Lestrade leaned forward, placing his elbows on his desk. "We've got nothing. Nothing other than Daniels' statements. Any piece of evidence or any claims, they've all been circumstantial." Lestrade shook his head. "We've had more patrols around Daniels' house, but this Goblin somehow slips through all our nets. He's just a man, but a bloody sly one, that's for sure."

"What about the bullets?" I asked.

"What bullets?" Lestrade questioned.

"The ones Daniels says the Goblin somehow took from his revolver." Lestrade looked befuddled for a moment. "Surely he informed you of this?"

"I can't say that he did. What did he tell you?"

"He told Holmes and me that he took a revolver with him to the club; on his way home, the Goblin was waiting for him. When he tried to fire, he realised the gun was empty, and somehow the Goblin had the bullets and dropped them on the ground before him."

"Well, this is news to me!" Lestrade exclaimed. "I'm going to send someone over to his house right away!"

"Holmes and I are going there tonight," I said.

"Then find out what game this man is playing. He's wasted enough of our time. I'm sorry I can't give you any solid information on this Goblin; sometimes I'm not sure he exists."

*****

I met Holmes at Lancaster Gate at nine o'clock; together we walked towards James Street. I told him all that Lestrade had said and that Daniels never spoke of the bullets to the authorities.

"Why would he tell us and not them?" I asked.

"Time will tell, Watson," Holmes said sagely.

"Lestrade questioned the very existence of this Goblin Man. Do you think it's possible that Daniels is… well, maybe he isn't in his right mind?"

Holmes looked off into the distance for a moment. "Lestrade may have a point."

"Where have you been all day?" I asked.

"Watching Daniels," Holmes said.

"Did you see anything of interest?"

"I didn't, no. He's been holed up in his house all day. No one has been seen coming in or out."

We stopped when we reached the top of James Street. Holmes motioned to go down an alley. We passed by the back of Daniels' house but saw nothing of interest. As we walked around the corner, Holmes pulled me back.

"Someone's there," Holmes whispered, peering around the corner.

My heart pounded. "The Goblin?"

Holmes confirmed it was not with a slight shake of his head. "It's a woman."

I looked and saw a tall, slender woman standing on the porch of Daniels' house. The light from inside poured over her, but she was too far away to make out any clear features. Her distinguishing feature was her blazing red hair. The front door was open and she was speaking with someone, presumably Daniels.

She was handed a small box, after which she turned and left. Holmes and I hid in the shadows as she walked towards us. As she passed us, she paused and turned her head slightly in our direction. We both stood still in the darkness, hoping she would not see us. Finally, after a few moments, she continued on her way.

"Who is she?" I asked when she had gone.

"A curiosity. Come, Daniels will be waiting for us."

*****

Mr Daniels greeted us with a look of relief. "Oh, Mr Holmes, I am glad to see you!" He ushered us inside and quickly closed the door. "How has your day been?"

"Informative," Holmes returned. "Has anything of interest occurred since we last spoke?"

"No, no," Daniels answered quickly.

"No sign of the Goblin?" I pressed.

"Not tonight."

"Show us your room," said Holmes.

We followed Mr Daniels down a hall and up a staircase. We were shown into his room.

"Burn marks on the floor?" Holmes asked in surprise as we stepped through the door.

"Yes, that's right," said Daniels, looking at a charred bit of carpet and wood panelling.

"I thought you said when you dropped the lamp, it didn't catch fire," said I.

"Did I?" he said with a blank expression. "Uh, no, it caught fire a bit. I put the fire out when the Goblin had left."

"Where was the Goblin when you came into the room?" I asked, looking around the room.

"Right behind you on the…" Mr Daniels paused. "Uh, he was there behind the door, right behind you, Doctor."

"Can we get the bullets?" Holmes asked. "The ones taken from your revolver." Daniels took us down into the kitchen, where six bullets lay on the table. Without touching them directly, Holmes put them into a leather pouch and tucked them away in his coat pocket. "We need nothing more," said Holmes, patting his pocket. Daniels looked surprised.

"You don't care to see anything else?"

"No, we have all we need. Good day, Mr Daniels."

Chapter 6
Martin Hewitt
The Wrong Room

Autumn 1890

"What do you make of that woman?" Hewitt asked after Mrs Goodtree had stepped out. He carried on before I could answer. "These games of love, they always appear to lead to crime." He paused a moment. "Never mind. Let us try, and find Mr Daniels and hope that we can obtain the information we need."

"Are we to call upon him at home?" I asked.

"Perhaps he could join us for dinner at the Savoy?" Hewitt suggested. "I will send a message requesting his presence."

*****

A few hours after Hewitt had sent his message to Mr Daniels, we received a reply. Hewitt took it into his hands and puzzled over the words written. With a sigh, he read aloud:

Mr Hewitt,
I am a busy man—I have no time to meet you nor to discuss any matter relating to Mr Phillias Jackson.

Sincerely,
David Daniels.

"This is greatly unfortunate," said he, putting the note down in his lap.

"Surely there is someone else who may aid us, perhaps someone from his previous workplace?"

"Yes, Nine Elms. Mrs Goodtree said he managed the factory there. We might even gather some evidence from the hotels where they would rendezvous. It seems that we have several avenues to take, as we cannot obtain a friendly audience with Mr Daniels."

*****

Our initial line of enquiry was to visit the hotels. We first went to the Savoy. The staff were a little apprehensive towards us, but once we explained ourselves to the management, they eventually allowed us to see their list of guests. A short, thin man named Evans took us into a private room where we could look through the names. Hewitt asked which of the names were individuals who returned on a regular basis with a woman. The man pointed out a few names: one, Walter James; another, Bryan Potts; and a third, Phil Jacks.

"What do these men look like?" Hewitt asked.

"Mr James is a red-headed man. Thin and wire-like."

"Where does Mr James hail from?"

"Worcestershire, if I'm not mistaken. Has a large mansion there. Comes from a very wealthy family."

"The others?" Hewitt asked.

"Mr Potts is also thin, but taller. Dark hair. Moustachioed. A nice man. I've had many conversations with him, a very excitable fellow. From south London, Putney, I believe," Evans said.

"Putney, you say?" Hewitt enquired. "What brought him here so often?"

"He said he works nearby, never said where, though. But he likes city life and entertaining his lass."

"And what of this Phil Jacks?"

"He was a strange man. Didn't speak much, at least to me. He, too, was dark-haired. Always a bit unshaven. He arrived and left at strange hours. He seemed to me like someone who was always looking over his shoulder, if you get me."

"I think I do," Hewitt affirmed. "These men haven't been here in several weeks."

"Correct," Evans said with a nod. Hewitt stroked his chin a moment.

"It might be fruitless, but can you show me the rooms they last stayed in?"

Evans agreed and took the keys to the last three rooms the men had used. Hewitt was thorough in his examination of each room, opening anything that'd open and moving anything that'd move. Unfortunately, no useful clues had been left behind.

*****

Next, we travelled to the Langham. Hewitt had a confidant there who made entry and access to information much easier than at the Savoy. The man's name was Wilfred Barnaby, an elderly, rotund little man with thick sideburns, beady eyes, and fat wet lips. We three sat with him in a room, looking at the guest list. Mr Barnaby's chubby fingers scrolled the list while commenting on people he recalled. Most often, he commented on the women he remembered.

"Oh yes, Madam Crane. She was a lovely bird," Barnaby said with his snicker. "Oh! Mhm. Mrs Jessica Owens. Yes, she was a pretty little thing. All the lads fancied popping her corset off, haha."

"Barnaby, I am grateful for your service. Might you do us one more favour?" Hewitt asked.

"Anything you wish, Mr Hewitt!" Barnaby exclaimed.

"Fetch us a spot of tea, would you now?"

"Oh, of course!" With a smile and shuffle, he left us.

"An excitable fellow, isn't he?" I commented.

"He is, Brett, he is," Hewitt said with an eye roll. "He has a one-track mind."

Hewitt's attention was fixed on the list of names. I found myself in need of a stretch, so I stepped outside for a breath of fresh air. The sun had gone in, and a gentle drizzle fell from the sky. Under the illumination of the street lamps, cabs clattered as fashionable and not-so-fashionable individuals hustled from one place to another on this chilly and wet night. I smoked a cigarette, then returned inside, only to find Hewitt pulling on his coat and ready to leave.

"What is it, man?" I demanded.

His eyes were ablaze. "Come now, let us go to St. Pancras!"

The light mist had become heavy rain by the time we arrived at St. Pancras. Hewitt and I emerged from our cab with no umbrella and fumbled our way through a crowd of people into the hotel. The doorman looked upon us with displeasure at our wet state. Hewitt patted the man on the shoulder and told him sardonically not to worry as we proceeded to the front desk.

"How may I help you... gentlemen?" a young-faced woman asked, eyeing us dubiously. Hewitt explained our situation and asked to double-check their records.

Her hesitation was minimal, but we did have to explain ourselves to the manager, Mr Hodder, who had some recollection of my friend, before we were allowed access to the information. Luckily for us, Hewitt had made a name for himself in London; while his fame was limited, he was nevertheless known by people that needed to know of him. Had it not been for the manager reading about his affair with the Red Circle, I'm not sure how successful we would have been.

Hewitt excitedly perused the records before us. The manager hung behind, watching his every action. I detected a glimmer of excitement in his eyes as he watched my friend work. There was a brief interruption when a messenger boy delivered a note to us. Hewitt eagerly read it.

"The field is narrowed!" he shouted, leaning back in his chair with tremendous force. The hotel manager and I looked at Hewitt with interest. "The ginger man from Worcester, Walter James, is none other than that which he says he is: Walter James." Confusion befell me a moment. "Phil Jacks and Bryan Potts!" Hewitt said, pointing to the ledger excitedly.

"Ah! So these two men are likely to be Phillias?" I asked.

"They are."

"It seems obvious that Phil Jacks would be Phillias Jackson, making a deviation of his Christian name to appear as if he's another man altogether."

"My good man," Hewitt said, turning to look at Mr Hodder, "tell us what Phil Jacks looks like."

"I can do better than that," said he. "Mr Jacks is in the hotel this very night. If he is a villain in some crime, I should like him to be caught sooner rather than later!"

We followed the man to the desk, where he picked up a key and then darted up a flight of stairs. We came to the room of Phil Jacks, and the manager pounded upon it heavily, calling out the man's name. We then heard a woman's squeal. Terror pulsed through me.

"My God," the manager whispered, and rapped on the door.

"Where is the key, man?" Hewitt demanded. We heard a crashing sound. "There is no time!"

The manager looked at us in fright. He forced the key into the slot and swung the door open. He dashed inside, with Hewitt and me following behind, only to find Phil Jacks and a maid in the act of coitus. There was a moment of severe embarrassment for all of us.

Mr Jacks shouted obscenities as he and the maid covered themselves up with blankets. Turning away, we quickly left the room. After a ruckus and further abuse, Mr Jacks opened the door. His face was red with anger, and the woman was nowhere to be seen.

"What in the hell is going on here?" Mr Jacks roared.

"I do apologise, Mr Jacks. This is Mr Hewitt, a private detective…" the manager began in a panicked tone.

"I don't care who this man is! Tell me why you barged into my rooms?" He looked angrily between the three of us. Then I realised something unique. The man was clean-shaven, had no scar upon his index finger, nor a mole on the left side of his face. Phil Jacks, this man might be, but Phillias Jackson he was not.

"It is our mistake. We took you for a criminal," admitted Hewitt. "We were being shown to your rooms in order to apprehend you, but unfortunately, you are not the man we seek."

"Forgive the mistake, Mr Jacks. I shall make it up to you," said the manager nervously.

"Indeed, you shall! The rest of my stay will be on your tab!" Jack turned and slammed the door shut, the force of which rustled our hair.

"Let's discuss this downstairs," Hewitt whispered. We were taken into a small office where the three of us sat down.

"This is not good. No, not good at all," murmured the manager.

"What can you tell me of Bryan Potts?" Hewitt asked.

"Potts?" Mr Hodder said. "My mind is too caught up in what just happened. I could very well lose my position here!"

"You will be fine, Mr Hodder. Now, I need you to tell me what you know about Bryan Potts!" Hewitt spoke sternly.

The manager pulled his nerves together at Hewitt's request. "He is an odd fellow, very loud and presumptuous. He's stayed here a few times…"

"Four times between March and September, going by your books," Hewitt added.

"Quite right," Hodder nodded. "It was rumoured that he was bringing a married woman back to his rooms. But you know how staff gossip, nor was it any of my business what the man does."

"Tell us of his appearance," Hewitt pressed.

"He was tall with dark hair. A bit of grey. He often appeared unshaven on his cheeks, not a beard, no, just untidy. He had a thick moustache. He always wore a bowler hat with a playing card tucked into the flap. I assume that he's a bit of a gambler."

I passed a glance at Hewitt, but he remained fixated upon the manager.

"Your recollection of the man is quite remarkable," Hewitt admitted.

"I possess no remarkable powers of observation or deduction," affirmed Hodder. "The final time Potts was here, he was most unruly, and I banned him from ever returning. The excitement over Jacks caused me to forget about the incident with Potts."

"What transpired?"

"He stumbled into the foyer about seven o'clock in the evening. He was incredibly angry and ranting about some indiscretion with his lady friend. He held a cloth to his face. It appeared to be blood-stained. I asked him to calm down and not to make a scene. He became aggressive and shoved me. I fell to the floor. I could see, even in his craze, that he regretted it. I told him he was to leave at once, and the belongings in his room would be sent to him, we'd call the police. He gave me his address, and that was the last I saw or heard of him."

"Did you retain his address?"

"I did." Hodder searched through his desk and withdrew a book. "The address he gave us, and the one that we sent his belongings to, was Davenport House, Wood Road, Putney."

Chapter 7
D.I. Edmund Reid
A Silver Lining

August 1890

I departed for *The Weekly Dispatch* with a couple of officers to accompany me. The day had turned grey and dismal, and a light mist waved through the air as we went through the city. Anger burned inside me. Eustace Brown was a foolish journalist. Ever since the Ripper events, journalists had become thirsty for blood to stain their papers, eager to rip at the flesh of a story and display its innards in black and white for the masses to see.

We passed through the doors of the newspaper headquarters. The officers and I walked through, calling out for assistance. No one came; everything was quiet. We looked through open doors into untidy offices, but not a single person was there.

"Inspector Reid!" one of the officers called. I stepped out of an office and into the hallway to see him coming towards me. "We found a body."

I followed him into another room. There was a man with his head pinned to the desk with a large blade. It was Eustace Brown. The blood that stained his desk was dried and brown. I could see a mark on the back of his neck from where the killer had held him down before ramming the knife through his skull.

I examined the paperwork on his desk: Brown had been in the middle of writing another report regarding the events of the Whitechapel Underground attack, and the effect they would have on London's growing Jewish population and the anarchists at large. There was an interview with Lord Myers, a Member of Parliament who made his negative position quite clear on the matter of Jewish immigrants. It seems he, too, was crying out for Jewish blood in light of the Whitechapel explosion.

"This is a mess!" I said as I walked over to the door. I leaned against the frame and looked into the room. Nothing appeared out of place. "What happened here?" I asked myself.

I looked over to the left and pictured the scene: when Brown walked in, someone could have concealed themselves behind the door, waiting for him. I looked behind the open door. When Brown sat down, the perpetrator could have revealed themselves, but whatever he did, Brown did not raise an alarm. The desk was a mess of papers, but nothing seemed out of the ordinary for a writer. The two might have engaged in conversation as the perpetrator walked behind Brown. I followed the trail and stood behind the dead body.

The indentations on the floor, from where Brown habitually scooted his chair, were old, not fresh, which meant he didn't try to thrust his chair back. He just sat there. The perpetrator grabbed him by the back of the neck, shoved him down, and killed him. He then, presumably, left by the front door. No, he wouldn't do that. Anyone who saw him would know he killed Brown.

"Gentlemen, find an open window!" I commanded.

We searched the rooms rapidly. There was nothing on the main floor. I ran up the stairs to the next level. There was a small room with cabinets and papers. At the far end, facing a back alley, was an open window. I looked outside. The drop would result in injury. As I started to pull my head back inside, I looked to the right and noticed something interesting.

A copper pipe was within arm's reach. It was dented, and at the top the guttering was bent and broken. The roof above was flat; it would make for a quick and invisible getaway. I reached for the copper pipe. I slipped. My heart suddenly raced. I was able to grab the inside of the window frame, stopping myself from falling out. I pulled myself back inside. I suspect the man who pulled this off had the aid of a rope and used the pipe and gutter for extra balance.

Around back, there was a metal stair that led to the roof. I left one officer in the room and told the other to look around outside on the ground. I raced up the stairs and made my way to the roof. The wind was cold and strong, and the rain was coming down harder. I looked at the area where the villain had climbed onto the roof. I heard a slam and looked to the adjacent building. A door was swinging open and shut with the wind.

I walked over and observed the gap between the buildings. There was a scuff mark and a broken brick on the ledge. The gap was no more than five feet. Someone with the right speed could have jumped it. I walked back over to the bent gutter. A rattling caught my attention. I looked down and caught a silver ring hanging from a piece of bent metal. I took it into my hand and noticed a Star of David embedded in the band. Where had I seen this before? It struck me like a brick. The tall man at Lamech's. He had worn this very ring.

*****

I made haste towards Lamech's lodgings. I tried the door. It was open. I went inside slowly and withdrew my revolver. The rooms were amok. Tables and chairs were overturned, shattered glass scattered everywhere, and torn pieces of cloth lay about. Burgled? No, someone left here in a hurry. I went up to the room where Lamech had died. It, too, had been turned to shambles. No one was there. The entire anarchist group had vanished.

We cleaned up the mess at The Weekly Dispatch, and my men scoured Lamech's old rooms for any clues that might be of use. Nothing turned up. It was as if the entire group had vanished into thin air. It was eleven o'clock at night, and the rain had turned the roads to mush. I sat in my office, the glow of an oil lamp keeping me company as I filed paperwork. I was eager for an update regarding the efforts made to speak with survivors of the explosion and loved ones of those who had lost someone to find any clue as to who planted that explosive.

Who poisoned Lamech, and why did his followers vanish? I reached into my pocket, and withdrew the silver ring with the Star of David on it. The tall man was my lead suspect in Brown's murder, but where was he?

*****

"All the bodies have been identified," said Inspector Lestrade, leaning back comfortably in the chair in front of my desk. "I've spoken to some of the families, and I can't see any connection to this Lamech. No one on that train posed any kind of threat to him or his organisation."

I buried my face in my palms for a moment. "They may not have posed a threat to him. Was there anyone of interest?"

"Nothing out of the ordinary that I saw. Men and women on their way to work, running errands. It seems a random attack. There's no motive from Lamech's end. Other groups in question have been accounted for that night as well."

"This can't be purely random, Lestrade," I pressed.

"I've got the list of the dead here, and the statements." He slid some papers my way. "Maybe you can find something I missed." Lestrade rose. "I heard the anarchists have disappeared."

"It's too convenient. I still have a couple of other angles I need to check first."

"Good luck." Lestrade turned and walked out.

After I read through the statements left by Lestrade, I found Mr White in his chamber at the station. Lamech's body had been moved to a morgue. White was hard at work trying to figure out the composition of the chemicals used to ignite the explosive.

"Any luck?" said I, standing behind him while he mixed solutions.

"None," he replied. "Maybe you shouldn't stand that close while I'm doing this."

I took a few steps back. "Is there no way to trace the chemicals?" I asked.

"I've been trying. I've got nothing. Whoever did this is a chemical genius."

"I need you to find me some answers!"

White put his work down and spun around in his chair to look at me. He removed the protective frames from his face and slid them upon his head. "I know you want answers. I assure you, I'm doing whatever I can to find them. Find out where the train terminates at night. That would be the best place to attach the bomb. Wouldn't have happened in between stops."

"Say again?"

"Do I really need to?"

"Explain your logic," said I.

"Well, the bomb wasn't inside the carriage, was it? It was underneath," White said. "Doesn't seem likely that a bomb would be attached while passengers were boarding. No, it would have been put in place sometime in the night when the train was not in use."

"And so whoever did it must have had an informant to know which train to put the bomb on. That is, unless they stole that information." I paused, captured in thought. The Yard was writing this attack off too quickly. I needed to find the motive.

"You got it."

Chapter 8
Doctor Watson
A Swift Drop and Sudden Stop

Autumn 1890

Back at 221B Baker Street, Sherlock Holmes was attempting to gain any clues he could from the bullets Daniels had given him. His attention was so fixated upon his task that he ignored several of my summons for food. For hours, my friend studied each bullet point. Then, with a bang, he smacked his hand down upon his worktable. I, sitting reading in my chair, jolted and turned to look at him. He sat slouched, with a look of agitation upon his face, rubbing his forehead and quietly mumbling to himself.

"Whatever is the matter, Holmes?" I asked.

"There are no other fingerprints upon these bullets," he snapped.

"But there are some?"

"Yes, but only Daniels'."

"The hour is late," said I. "Start afresh tomorrow, perhaps?"

"Off you go, Watson. I shall remain here a while longer."

*****

I was awoken by a pounding on my door. The sun had not yet risen.

"Watson, wake up. We must go back to Daniels immediately!"

"Good Lord, Holmes. What time is it?" I called back. He opened my door and poked his head in.

"The time is of no importance. We are summoned at once. There was an incident in the night."

"I'm not sure night-time has passed," I mumbled, tossing my sheets away.

"Hurry, Watson!" said Holmes before dashing away.

I quickly readied myself and found Holmes at the bottom of the stairs. The street lamps were still lit and the sun had yet to rise as we jumped into a cab. Holmes told me that Lestrade had sent an urgent message saying that Mr Daniels had hanged himself, and our assistance was needed.

We arrived to find a couple of officers standing near a police Mariah at the front of Daniels' house. The morning air was cold, and the newly risen sun revealed a thin layer of frost on the ground. Holmes and I were ushered in and greeted by Lestrade.

"Good of you to come so quickly, Mr Holmes," said Lestrade.

"Tell me what happened," Holmes said.

"My men saw you leave the house, and they kept a close watch. Everything seemed quiet and normal. About three-thirty this morning, they heard a commotion. Daniels was shouting at someone. My officers swear on their lives that no one had entered the house, nor did they witness anyone leave. They heard the breaking of glass and rushed in to find Daniels hanging by the neck."

"It was self-inflicted; this much I can tell," said Holmes, looking at Daniels. "Take him down." I looked around the room: there was a shattered glass bowl upon the floor, which looked as though Daniels must have kicked it when he took the fatal plunge. As the body was being taken down, Holmes began quietly examining the room, then left us as they laid the body on a table.

While Holmes looked around, I examined the corpse of Mr Daniels. I noticed an odd smell upon him, and a strange purple colouring on the flesh around his eyes.

"What do you reckon?" Lestrade asked.

"I'm not sure entirely," said I, "but it does look like an effect from substance abuse."

Just then Holmes returned, glanced at the body, leaned over and deeply inhaled before returning to his full height. "We have all we need. Lestrade, we will be in touch."

*****

In the cab, Holmes turned to me.

"What did you make of the body, Doctor?" he asked.

"The smell and discolouration? If memory serves me right, he was poisoned by a rare flower found in Afghanistan…"

"Yes, the fire flowers are known to cause such effects. I've some knowledge of it."

"It's a rare poison, Holmes. If I remember correctly, the petals appear to perspire under certain temperatures. The liquid created can be toxic if absorbed into the system. It will cause one to be slowly driven mad until death takes them. It leaves behind a terrible smell and the purple colouration around the eyes. During my war days, I treated a few men who suffered from this poison."

"How long does the poison take to kill its victim?"

"A small dose will take upwards of a month."

"Remind me of the symptoms?"

"Paranoia was common in all of them. It started slowly, then manifested into some kind of physical fear. One soldier attacked a captain whom he had thought disliked him, making the claim that the captain was planning to kill him. They also saw things that weren't there. Some would swear a spider or snake was on them when nothing was there at all. It manifests differently, but it's always a fear come to life."

"So, who poisoned Daniels, and why?" Holmes asked rhetorically.

"Maybe the Goblin isn't real?" I questioned.

"There is no such creature; but there is a man."

"How do you know?"

"Mud, Watson. A trace of it in the hallway from a large boot. Neither the police nor anyone else who was frequent at Daniels'. I found it near a window in the next room while you were looking over the body. Daniels, certainly, was not alone; he was shouting at someone."

51

"What do you plan to do next?"

"You can return to Baker Street. I need to go to the docks."

Chapter 9
Martin Hewitt
The Mystery at Davenport House

Autumn 1890

Taking the manager's information, we made our way back to our lodgings. The rain had lightened, but the hour was late, and Hewitt and I agreed we would continue the investigation after a hearty dinner and a good night's sleep.

Early the following morning, Hewitt and I procured a hansom to take us to Putney, to Phillias Jackson's lodging: Davenport House. The autumn air had become bitterly cold through the night, but by the time we reached Davenport House, the sun was high in the morning sky, and some warmth had returned to the air.

Mr Jackson's home was a large three-floor house. Hanging outside the house was a sign saying: Room for Let. His lodgings were shared, not his own.

"A further touch of the bizarre, Brett," remarked Hewitt, pointing to the sign.

"Not the kind of accommodation I expected from Mr Jackson," said I with a nod.

"My thought precisely." Hewitt raised his large fist and banged on the front door. A bespectacled man with bushy sideburns and slicked-back hair answered.

"May I help you?" he asked us.

"My name is Martin Hewitt. I'm an investigator. I'm looking into the disappearance of Phillias Jackson."

"Has he disappeared?" the man asked.

"A concerned party believes him to be missing. What, pray, can you tell us?"

"Do you have any credentials on you?" the man asked suspiciously. "For all I know you could be anyone."

"Anyone can be anyone, sir," said Hewitt, as he took out his identification with slight annoyance. The man took it into his hands and examined it thoroughly.

"Very well. I am satisfied," he responded, handing Hewitt's property back.

"Tell us what you know of Mr Jackson while you lead us to his rooms," Hewitt requested.

The man turned, and we followed him inside.

"Mr Jackson was a businessman—not a very good one, though. He was never too much of a bother to anyone. But he did keep some unruly hours, which made some feel uncomfortable."

"What do you mean by unruly?" I asked as we followed our guide up a narrow staircase.

"Unruly; quite self-explanatory, is it not? Well, that is to say that his work kept him in and out at all hours. In order not to disturb the other lodgers, he, for a small fee, did some of his experiments out in the shed."

"What experiments was he doing in the shed?" Hewitt asked.

"Not entirely sure—tinkering of some kind." The man paused. "Mr Jackson said he'd be away some time, so I'm finding it most strange that you are here looking for him."

The man stopped in front of a door and withdrew a set of keys. Selecting one, he slid it into the lock. The door opened, and we stepped into Mr Jackson's living quarters. The room was average in size. There was one single window that faced the back of the house, through which one could see the shed. A small bed with a trunk at the end of it; a few stacks of books; a desk, cluttered with papers, a pen, and a jar of ink. There was a cabinet with some clothes, and a small washroom as well. Hewitt spent some time wandering around while our guide and I watched.

"When did you last see Mr Jackson?" Hewitt asked.

"Oh, he's been away a short while. He said something about going to the continent for business."

"How long ago was that?"

"I suppose two months, maybe three?"

"So you haven't seen him in all that time?" I questioned.

The man shook his head. "But he paid his rent, so I'm not worried as long as he is up to date."

"Did he ever have any visitors here?" Hewitt asked.

The man paused and thought a moment. "A woman," he said in a low voice. "She'd come around several times a week. I could often hear him speaking to her in his room, but it sounded like they were speaking in foreign gibberish. Is she the one who is worried about him?"

"What can you tell me about her?"

"Oh, not much. I only saw glimpses of her." He lowered his voice. "But she did stay over with him quite a lot. There's only one kind of woman who will stay with a man without hesitation or care for decency."

"So she was a lady of the night?" I asked.

"I'm not one to judge," said the man. "I did tell Mr Jackson he needed to think about his actions, as this was meant to be a respectable lodging. He assured me that he meant no harm, but did tell me that he and this lass had big plans together."

"Did he ever tell you what these plans were?"

"Afraid not, no."

"Might you take us to the shed where you said he did other work—tinkering, as you say?"

We followed the man down the stairs and out into the back garden. The shed was a decent size, ten feet by five feet. The man opened the door, and a few gardening tools fell out.

"Will you allow us some privacy while I look around?" Hewitt asked. The man looked somewhat disappointed to be discharged so abruptly, but agreed and returned home.

"What do you make of it, Brett?" he asked me while he perused the interior of the shed.

"Well, it seems that this Mrs Edwards—I mean Goodtree—is perhaps unrealistically worried. If his landlord isn't worried about the length of time he's been gone, why is she?"

"Perhaps she has some information that she's not passed over to us. Are you not wondering which woman the landlord saw Jackson with?"

"Ah! So she must know about this other woman? She's worried he's run off with her," said I. "But why didn't she tell us this?"

"Quite right, why indeed," mumbled Hewitt. He ran his finger along a table and sniffed it. He knelt down and dabbed something on the floor. Then, with a heave, he withdrew a chest from underneath the table and opened the top. "Hmm, see what we have here, Brett."

I walked over and looked inside. "These are…"

"Explosives," said a voice from behind us.

Hewitt and I turned to see two figures standing in the doorway.

"How can you know that?" Hewitt asked, standing up.

"Elementary," said one of the men, taking a couple of sniffs.

"There is an aroma," said a moustachioed man who sniffed the air. "Yes, this place has certainly been a storage room for explosive powders."

"Who are you?" I demanded.

Chapter 10
D.I. Edmund Reid
The Thames Stand Off

August 1890

I looked at my clock. It was nine thirty, and the night air was crisp. The sky was cloudless, and the stars shone down like piercing white diamonds. I wished the peace of the heavens would descend upon us here and now.

"Tonight we go to the White Stag," I said to my group of officers. "We're going to raid and impound anyone we find with the whores. I care not who they are or what their rank is."

"Why are we singling out this whorehouse?" an officer asked.

"One by one, I'll see all these places closed. This particular one is connected to the Underground explosion a few days ago. A Jewish anarchist, Lamech, was there the night before the explosion." I pointed to Mr White, who was standing at the back. "Mr White helped to identify the explosive, which was attributed to Lamech. Now he is dead, poisoned by the food and drink that he had at the White Stag. The bartender, Mr Jeffry, was warned what would happen without his cooperation. Tonight we return and take his business away."

My small army of three Mariah rattled and rushed towards the White Stag. Hooves and wheels battered the cobbled roads, creating a sound akin to a warlike charge that reverberated between the buildings.

Two of the Mariah broke off to surround different exits, while mine continued towards the front. My men had arrived, and a few were standing watch outside the back doors while the rest and I stormed the front door. The others rushed up the stairs to the rooms immediately. Men shouted abuse as their whoring was interrupted. The women were screaming as they, and their clients, were apprehended.

"Where's the bartender?" I demanded of one of the staff. The men in the parlour were taken aback by our entrance. Some stared in shock while others jumped and ran towards various exits. I took a man by the collar. "Where is he?"

"He's out back!" said the man. "Ran like a headless chick—"

I darted behind the bar and pushed through the swinging door into the kitchen area. As I came through, I was greeted with an ear-piercing boom. I ducked at the sound; I was being fired upon. I withdrew my revolver and hid behind a couple of barrels.

"Jeffry!" I shouted. "Stop this now. You knew this was coming." I peered over the barrel. Another shot was fired. An officer burst through the door, and Jeffry fired again. As if everything had slowed down, I saw the bullet shoot through the air, hitting my man in the chest. I fired two more shots, but I missed him.

"Go on, get out'a here!" I heard Jeffry yell.

I looked, and to my surprise, it was the tall man from Lamech's. His clothes were undone, and he was struggling to reach the back door and escape. Jeffry fired a couple more shots; I took cover. I fired a shot and hit Jeffry in the arm. He cried out in pain as he fell over, nursing his wound. As I ran towards Jeffry, Lamech's associate darted from his hiding place and through the back door. Quickly, I grabbed a pair of cuffs and secured Jeffry to a pipe before making chase.

I ran out the door, following the tall man. It was unmanned! My blood boiled with anger; had my men kept a post at this door, he'd be in custody, and I'd not be chasing him. I heard shouting down an alley and followed. I could see him struggling to put on a shoe.

"Halt!" I cried.

He turned, panicked, and ran. He sprinted away from me and I charged onwards with full strength. He turned a corner, and I heard a crash. I was moving too fast; I stumbled and fell over several wooden crates that he had knocked over. When I hit the ground, a sharp pain surged through my shoulder; I rolled and quickly picked myself up and continued the pursuit.

He was not far ahead of me when he leapt into a four-wheeler and threw out the driver. He smacked the horses, and the carriage charged away down the narrow street. I turned and saw a hansom not five yards away. I ordered the driver to make haste and follow.

We charged down the poorly lit streets, causing chaos. Yelps and hollers whizzed past as people dove out of our way. We were not far from the Thames. My heart raced. I could see the river ahead now, and a small dock. I was not prepared for a water pursuit. I saw him pull his carriage to a fierce stop and leap out. I was jolted when my driver hit a severe hole in the road. A wheel broke and fell off, and the cab tipped over. The compartment was dragged some distance before the horse tripped and collapsed. I stumbled out; my driver was pulling himself up. The tall man was fiddling inside a small boat. I raced towards him, revolver ready, and yelled at him to stop. He was in the process of untying a small vessel, and I fired a shot into the air. He looked at me and stood upright.

"Step out of the boat!" I ordered.

"You can do nothing, Reid," he said.

"You are under arrest for the murder of Eustace Brown—"

"Me! I did what had to be done. He smeared my family's name in that paper."

"Dead or alive, you're coming with me." He smiled back. I could see his white teeth under the pale moonlight. "Step out of the boat." He began to laugh, and with a quick move, he pulled out a revolver and held it to his head.

"I tell you now, Reid, these are dark times." He tightened the grip on his revolver. "What will be will be. We fight the good fight." His hand was shaking. "I did what I did, and I won't go down for it. Not in an English court!"

"Put the revolver down, and we'll talk," I said softly. The man started to laugh.

"If only you knew… if only you really knew what was coming, Mr Reid. This is a dead end for you, but it's only a beginning for me. God welcomes me home."

"Where has your clan gone?" I asked.

"On the path of redemption," he returned. He pulled the trigger, and the bullet shot through his head. He fell to the side and into the murky water. I raced over to try to retrieve him, but it was too late. His body was gone. Eventually, it would break shore, but by then it'd be of no use to me.

*****

I returned to the station, where it was abuzz with the shouts of whores and angry clients. Jeffry was waiting for me in my office, being watched over by Kipling. I took a seat at my desk and looked at him. His arm had been bandaged, but he still held his arms like a pouting child.

"I told you, Jeffry," I began, "you cooperate or we end your whore business. This is what happens when one does not heed my warning."

"You're busy busting those who make money off whores rather than finding the man who guts them like pigs!" Jeffry shouted. My face flashed with heat as my blood boiled at his remark.

"Speak not of what you do not know," I said sternly. "Now, Lamech was at your establishment the night before the explosion, was he not?"

"He was, yes," Jeffry reluctantly admitted.

"What did he eat?"

"Can't remember," Jeffry shrugged.

"But he ate."

"Well, yeah. He and that other chap," Jeffry confirmed.

"What other chap?" I pressed.

"A whiskered man with a cut on his face."

"Who is he?"

"I don't rightly know. Never seen him before."

"Never? What did he look like? Did he engage with any other people?"

"He wore a flat cap that was pulled down low, I remember. So I never got a good look at his face," said Jeffry.

"What was his and Lamech's demeanour?" I asked.

"They were quiet, sitting at a table in the corner away from people. Both sat with their backs to the wall. I supposed they wanted to see what people were doing."

"Did they leave together?"

"No, the other man left first."

"How did the two depart? Peaceful or agitated?"

"I don't know. It was a busy night. I didn't just watch them!" Jeffry was flushed.

"Why were you helping Lamech's associate escape?"

"What do you mean?"

"We caught him, Jeffry. Don't treat me as the fool."

"What did he tell you?" Jeffry squirmed in his chair.

"Who poisoned the food Lamech ate?"

"Poisoned? I don't know what you're talking 'bout." His eyes shifted and he held his arm a little tighter.

"He told us everything. You'll do well to tell me the truth."

"I don't know what he told you about poison, but we—or I—had nothing to do with that! That wasn't our plan!"

"What was your plan then?"

"Err, we… we didn't have a plan."

"Don't play games!" I shouted, smacking my fist on the desk.

"I know nothing!" he yelled back.

"Well, you'd better clear your story, then." Jeffry hung his head. "You're going away, forever. I'll make sure you never feel fresh air upon your face again. I'll make sure you are buried so low that sunlight will be nothing but a fairy tale to you."

"I didn't poison him! I just helped Jacob, Lamech's dead, lanky associate, get his family out of the city." I took the name down and looked back at Jeffry. "Why was Jacob at your inn?"

"He was seeing things through. Making sure everyone was gone and there was no trace. If he knew anything about the poisoning, he didn't tell me. He simply paid me a good sum of money to help get the anarchists out before people like Myers came storming at them."

"Take him away," I instructed, exhausted.

Kipling grabbed Jeffry and stood him up. I leaned back in my chair and gazed at the ceiling, puffing my cheeks out.

*****

Kipling and White entered my office an hour later. White took a seat while Kipling remained standing. I leaned forward, resting my elbows on my desk.

"What can we do now, Reid?" White asked, crossing his legs and stroking his chin.

"We can only hope some clue crops up where the train was stationed the night before."

"Otherwise?" Kipling asked.

"Otherwise, we're dead in the water!" I snapped. I paused a moment. Kipling was shocked at my outburst. I allowed myself to calm before I said, "There are no other options. With the tall man, Jacob, dead, and the anarchists vanished, there is little we can now follow."

"Don't suppose there's more the bartender isn't telling you?" White asked.

"He's a buffoon. We'll keep him within arm's reach for the time, but I cannot say with conviction that he is of aid to us," I returned.

"I'm sorry I can't be of more help myself," admitted White. "The compounds in the explosive and the poison—I wouldn't

62

even know where to begin looking for them in this city, or any city for that matter."

"There must be another thread to this mystery… there must be," I whispered. "Gentlemen, let's follow the rail tracks."

*****

It was with great disappointment that we returned from our investigation empty-handed. We learnt nothing from where the train had been kept overnight. Not a single person had seen anything or was willing to tell us if they had. The whole thing became one of many open investigations that would remain dead in the water.

Over the next few months, Jeffry was locked away in Pentonville. Before his hanging, we attempted to obtain more information from him regarding Jacob, but it proved useless. His public house was searched repeatedly, and it, too, yielded no results. We looked far and wide for any sign of the anarchists, but Lamech's entire tribe had all vanished.

Whoever killed Lamech had got away with it. Whoever planted the explosive had also escaped our grasp. DCI Johnstone's temper burned red when he came to see me on the matter. He showed no mercy on my department and threatened my job on several occasions.

I looked for hope, for an answer to the solution that would help us solve this problem, but I had nowhere to turn.

Chapter 11
Doctor Watson
Discovery at Nine Elms

Autumn 1890

"Watson!" echoed Holmes' voice. I heard the sound of his feet racing up the stairs. I rose from my seat as he burst into the study. "Come, Watson. We're off to Putney."

"Are you going to tell me why or where in Putney we are going?"

"Davenport House! Now come, Watson."

Once we were in a cab, I demanded Holmes tell me what he had learnt.

"First, I know how Daniels was being poisoned." My interest was piqued. "The mud found in Daniels' house was telling. We know he hadn't been anywhere suspicious since we met him. We also know the state of his house upon our visit. There was no mud. Yet I found some there. Daniels was certainly not alone. He was yelling at someone. I could tell from the mud that it came from a factory by the river; I have narrowed down the mixture of mud and sand to somewhere near Nine Elms. As it happens, Daniels has a small factory just there. So someone from around his factory had come into his house, and mud had fallen from their shoes."

"That doesn't explain how he was being poisoned."

"I ventured into the factory, where I was stopped by a warden.

"'What are you doing, sniffing around here?' he yelled.

"'I am looking into the death of Mr Daniels, your employer.'

"The man froze stiff. 'Dead, you say? What happened?'

"'Hanged himself,' I returned. 'It is most important that I have a look through his offices.'

"'Now, sir, I can't let you do that.'

"'I assure you, you can.' I introduced myself to him, but he was not impressed.

"'I don't care who you are, private detective or not. This here is my factory, and I can't let people go sniffing around.'

"'Every man has his price.'

"He paused a moment, and I handed what would have been to him a considerable amount of money. His eyes lit up, and I knew I had him. 'What can you tell me of your employer, Mr Daniels?'

"He slipped the money into his dirty charcoal jacket and said, 'He was a decent bloke, as far as I could tell. He was always careful about who he put his trust in, and if you ever broke it, you'd be gone.'

"'What do you mean by "be gone"?'

"'Well, if you ever got on his bad side or were just inept, he'd cut you loose. Send you packing. That sort of thing.'

"'When did you see him last?'

"'I haven't seen him in some months. He's only telegrammed. After Thomas was killed in the explosion at Whitechapel Station, he stopped coming into the factory.'

"'How long have you held this position?'

"'Oh, only a few months.'

"'Who was in the role before you?'

"'A man named Phillias Jackson. Of course he wasn't here very long.'

"'Why was that?'

"'Not quite sure. I remember him coming in with Mr Daniels and Mr Thomas and being shown around, then about two weeks later he was made warden and we were informed of some new business that we'd be doing.'

"'What kind of business?'

"'Thomas opened up some trade with India and Afghanistan.'

"'What kind of trade?'

"'Nothing important. Some of it was animals, some was fabrics, and some was spices. That sort.'

"'Back on point, then. Why did Mr Jackson step down from being warden?'

"'Well, not sure. I remember hearing them, Thomas and Daniels, that is, arguing about Jackson. It seemed like Thomas didn't trust him all that much. Think he wanted too much money for his job. At least that's the way Daniels put it to me when he gave me the job. See, Jackson was let go, but no one really knew why, and all I was told was that financially he didn't agree with them.'

"'And how long did Jackson work here?'

"'Probably six months or so.'

"'You've been quite helpful. Now, if you can give me access to the offices, I shouldn't be long.'

"He quickly showed me to them. I asked for some privacy, which he reluctantly gave. I went through papers and shipment logs. There was nothing much of note. In the office was a safe. I enquired with the warden as to the whereabouts of the key. He said only Daniels had it. I had no time to travel back to Daniels' and find it, so I managed to pick the lock. Inside, I came across some very telling things. A contract drafted by Phillias Jackson that made him an equal partner in the company. Deep lines of ink were scratched through it. When the warden thought money was the issue, he was wrong. It wasn't Jackson's wage at the factory; it was the fact he wanted to be a partner." Holmes reached into his jacket pocket. "I also found these letters between Goodtree and Daniels.

David,
We must remove Jackson.

Goodtree

Thomas,
I agree, but he's put us in a peculiar situation. This will take a lot of legal action and probably a hefty sum of money to get rid of him.

Daniels.

David,
Whatever the cost, he needs to be removed from our employ and our lives. We need to rid ourselves of his cunning.

Goodtree.

Thomas,
Meet with me tomorrow, at the club. We can discuss things there.

Daniels.

Thomas,
It's been done. At what cost, I cannot say. But he has been removed. We can only hope he leaves us in peace.

Daniels."

"These men sounded suspicious of Jackson, as if he had something on them." Holmes looked at me inquisitively but uttered no response as he trailed off into his thoughts.

"So you think Phillias is behind the poisoning?" I asked.

"During my search, there were unmarked shipments labelled private. Some of the shipments were from Burkum and Lynn."

"The weapons manufacturer?"

"The very one. It was mostly explosive powder, but it vanished after it arrived at the factory. The other shipments were vegetative in nature from Afghanistan. This is where we were lucky— someone had scribbled down 'flowers'. It seems no harm to speculate that these flowers were the fire flowers. However, where these shipments went after arriving is a mystery."

"How does this help us?" I asked.

"It's quite obvious," said Holmes with a grin. "All of these shipments stopped once Jackson was fired. Daniels cancelled all shipments post-Jackson."

"So Jackson used the trade with Afghanistan to bring in the poisonous flowers while he also acquired powder from Burkum and Lynn. He surely is responsible for poisoning Daniels!" I declared.

"Unfortunately, he's dead."

"Dead!" I cried.

"I went to see Inspector Lestrade. I found him sitting in his office, going over paperwork. I asked him if they questioned Jackson or anyone in Daniels' and Thomas' employ after Thomas' death.

"'Why would we do that?' Lestrade asked me. My irritation was no secret. 'Don't hang your head like a disappointed parent, Holmes!' he snapped.

"'It is not your fault,' I comforted the Inspector. 'It is reasons like these the Yard comes to me for aid. I have reason to believe he is behind the murder of Daniels and Thomas.'

"'We've no proof that Daniels was murdered,' Lestrade stammered. 'He clearly hanged himself, and that Thomas fellow was just on the wrong train at the wrong time. The explosion was caused by a Jewish anarchist. D.I. Reid has been on the case. I'm sure he'll hunt them down.'

"'Don't you see, Lestrade? It's all there in the shipments.' I told him of the fire flower and missing powder shipments. 'Get me a report; the powder from the explosion will be from Burkum and Lynn.'

"'You'll have to see Reid about that, Mr Holmes. I know he's got a man working on the explosion, and they've come up with nothing. You're just offering a stab in the dark here. Now, I'm knee-deep with this Daniels case. I'll follow up with our surgeon, see if he thinks Daniels was poisoned. But I'm not sure Jackson is your man.'

"'Why is this?'

"'His body washed up near the Tower of London this morning. His face was severely mutilated, but the mole confirmed it was him, on the right side of his face.'

"'Where did he live?'

"Lestrade gave me the address, and I came to collect you before going out there."

"Could there be a fourth man?" I asked.

"I believe there may be. Daniels, it seems, isn't a wholly honest man."

"What else do you know, Holmes?"

He did not respond to my question and remained quiet for the rest of our journey to Davenport House.

Chapter 12
Doctor Watson
The Detective and the Investigator

Autumn 1890

Holmes and I stepped into the small shed where the landlord had informed us another group of detectives were investigating. Holmes and I were both curious about who was following a similar trail to ours and why. We opened the door to see two men, both fairly tall, one thin, the other slightly older and rounder.

"Who are you?" the thin man pressed.

"My name is Sherlock Holmes, and this is my friend and colleague, Doctor Watson." Holmes turned and smiled at the round man. "Mr Hewitt, I should thank you for looking after things while I was in America some time ago."

"It was my pleasure," said Hewitt, walking over and shaking Holmes's hand. "But you really must explain what you are doing here. Did Mrs Goodtree come and see you as well?"

"Our role in this narrative began when a Mr David Daniels came to see me about a strange haunting by the 'Goblin Man'," said Holmes.

"I thought that goblin fiend had left the city?" Hewitt asked.

"It seems he did not—or someone was posing as the Goblin."

Holmes relayed our entire investigation. Holmes and Hewitt became deeply invested in discussing the poisonous flower used on Daniels. Hewitt's interest was piqued by Holmes's accusation of Jackson, the shipped powder, and the Whitechapel explosion. Both Hewitt and his associate, Brett, were taken aback when Holmes informed them of the baffling news that Mr Jackson was dead.

"How can he be dead?" Hewitt asked. Looking back up at Holmes, he asked, "Did you have a chance to examine the body?"

"I have not," Holmes acknowledged.

"Let us not forget we saw an unknown woman approach Daniels' door, hand him something, and dash off into the night," said I.

"An unknown woman?" the thin man questioned. "Any chance it was Mrs Goodtree?"

"You've mentioned this name before. Who is she?" Holmes asked.

"As it happens, we are working for Mrs Goodtree, the former wife of Mr Thomas Goodtree, Daniels' business partner." Holmes's eyes lit up with realisation. "She and Jackson were having relations. She is with child, and wishes us to find Jackson. If you say he is dead, then we should have a look at the body and have her identify him for us," said Hewitt. Holmes began looking around the shed, scraping powders and putting them into envelopes while Hewitt carried on. "However, I believe Mrs Goodtree to be withholding something from us. She told us that she did not know where Jackson lived, but the landlord here informed us earlier that Jackson was prone to having a lady visitor."

"You suspect Mrs Goodtree is covering something up?" I asked.

"It's likely, but what I cannot say. The landlord has no suspicion of Jackson, and informed us that Jackson was off to the Continent."

"The Continent?" I asked. "Why would he go there?"

"This might be of interest," said Holmes. The three of us turned to look at him. He had opened a box that contained a most interesting assortment of grotesque objects: a strange yellow rubber mask with light-green, bulbous lenses in the eye sockets, two gloves with sharp black fingernails on the tips, some torn-up clothes, and a battered top hat. It dawned on me what I was seeing.

"My word, Holmes!" said I. "This is surely the Goblin's outfit!" Hewitt walked over, and the detective and investigator examined the findings.

71

"Could all this be a blind?" Brett asked. "Might Mrs Goodtree know about all of this and be trying to help Jackson flee the city?"

"You're jumping ahead, Brett," said Hewitt. "You forget the corpse."

"Yes, the corpse," murmured Holmes as he rifled through the box. Something appeared to catch his attention, and with a sudden jolt he stood up. "These are the facts we know. A: we have a suit that resembles that worn by the Goblin Man. B: we have what appear to be traces of powder and explosive materials. C: we have cause for his death—with Jackson being fired and sleeping with Mrs Goodtree. What we don't have yet is proof he was behind any such explosion, or that he was the one in the Goblin suit."

"Our next course of action," Hewitt said, "Brett, would you fetch Mrs Goodtree and bring her to Scotland Yard, where we can have Inspector Lestrade show us the body."

"Watson, Hewitt and I shall go straight to Lestrade. Would you take this envelope and speak with Detective Inspector Reid? Ask him about the findings at Whitechapel. This powder will likely be the same as that in the explosion. If he can spare the time, bring him to us."

We departed quickly; Holmes and Hewitt took one cab while Brett and I shared the other.

Chapter 13
Doctor Watson
Whitechapel

Autumn 1890

For the sake of speed, Brett and I abandoned the cab at a nearby station and took a train into the city. We came into Victoria Station, where we parted company. I took the District Railway east from Victoria. The train shot through the tunnels like a bullet. The roar of the train was in some way soothing: the clicking of the wheels as they clapped over the tracks, the gentle sway of the cabin, and the creaking of the wooden doors. The train stopped at Whitechapel Station, where I disembarked. I looked at my fob watch upon stepping out into the stale East End air. The time was six o'clock, and the sun had vanished. Within sight stood Saint Paul's Cathedral. Its towering steeples were erect like sentinels, and atop its dome rested a golden cross—a hopeful reminder to this destitute area of justice and judgment.

I quickly made my way to Leman Street and H Division. Having been to Scotland Yard many times and been around the ruffians there, H Division has a unique sense of chaos that other divisions lack. The station was alive with the shouting and wailing of inmates and drunkards. A couple of officers were attempting to clap irons on a drunk man who had lunged at a man nearby. A couple of prostitutes were arguing over a fare. One of them spat in the other's face, and two young officers tried to keep them at bay.

An exhausted-looking officer stood behind a desk, writing in a book.

"My name is Doctor John Watson. I'm here on an urgent matter. Is D.I. Reid around?" I enquired.

The man looked up.

In a raspy voice, he replied: "He ought to be in his office, sir."
He pointed in the right direction. I nodded and hurried down the
corridor till I came upon his office. The door was shut. I knocked.
I heard rustling, and the door was flung open. A tall man stood
before me with dark bags under his bloodshot eyes, a wild beard,
and dishevelled clothes. He looked worn and exhausted, a man
who had not touched a decent plate of food in several weeks.

"May I help you?" he asked groggily.

"I am Doctor John Watson. Are you D.I. Reid?" I asked. The
man nodded. "I am here to speak with you about the explosion at
the station a few months back. We might be honing in on the one
responsible."

Reid's eyes ignited as if he was a prisoner of war, trapped in a
dark pit and the light of freedom had fallen upon his face. He
motioned me to enter.

*****

He asked me to remain in the office while he went to fetch someone. The echoes from the chaos came down the hall as I waited. A
few moments later, Reid returned with a bespectacled ginger man.

"This is Doctor Vigo White," Reid said, taking a seat across
from me. "This is Doctor John Watson. He wishes to speak about
the explosion. I thought it best if you joined us."

"I work alongside Mr Sherlock Holmes."

"The bohemian detective of Baker Street?" White asked.

"The very one," I returned.

"Aha! So you're that John Watson!" A grin lit up White's face.

"I am he."

"Continue, Doctor," said Reid.

"A man named David Daniels came to us and told us about a
haunting which had befallen him. As Holmes and I looked into
the case, Daniels became more panicked, and we eventually found
him dead, hanged by his own hand. However, I noticed a purple

discolouring upon his skin and, upon closer examination, I discovered that he had been poisoned. Inspector Lestrade is conducting his own examination to be sure, but I know this to be true."

"A purple discolouring, you say?" White asked.

"Yes. The poison came from a flower found in Afghanistan. We discovered that a man named Phillias Jackson had worked for Mr Daniels and his partner, Thomas Goodtree, at their shipping and imports factory on Nine Elms. It was further discovered by Investigator Martin Hewitt that Jackson was having an affair with Mrs Goodtree, who is now with Jackson's child. Before Daniels' and Goodtree's deaths, they fired Jackson from his position over a disagreement in his work contract, so far as we know. Now it seems that Jackson had been importing this deadly flower, along with accumulating a large amount of explosive powder from a company called Burkum and Lynn. Inspector Lestrade has informed Mr Holmes that Jackson's body washed up by the Tower of London this morning. He and Mr Hewitt are at the Yard now, looking over the body. Holmes believes Jackson is responsible for the explosion. We have a sample of the powder that was found at Jackson's lodgings. We need to cross-check it against whatever you have."

"Can I see the sample?" Mr White asked. I nodded and withdrew the envelope Holmes had given me.

"Mr White, test its value at once," Reid ordered. White left the room in a rush, and Reid turned to me. "Doctor. Tell me more of this man, Jackson. What does he look like?"

"From what Hewitt was told, he is a tall, dark, whiskered man, who is often seen wearing a bowler hat," said I.

"Many men are seen wearing such hats. I have one behind you on the peg, and I have dark whiskers too. You see the problem?"

"Yes, I do. However, your bowler hat does not have a playing card pinned to it. Jackson's does."

"A card pinned to it, you say?" Reid sat back in his chair and stroked his beard. "I know this description. This man was seen with a man called Lamech the night before the Whitechapel explosion. However, the sole difference is that the man was said to have a severe scar on his face. My man, White, recognised the explosives' maker, or at least part of it, which led us to Lamech, a Jewish anarchist. This man, Lamech, as you may have seen in the papers some time ago, was killed. He was poisoned. White did the autopsy, and Lamech's symptoms were similar to Daniels': a discolouring of the skin, the appearance of mental illness." Reid lifted his eyes as Mr White came back through the door.

"No doubt. The powder is the same," confirmed White. "Could be a coincidence—Burkum and Lynn are very well known."

"It's no coincidence," said Reid.

"A Jewish anarchist who builds bombs dies by the same poison that Daniels dies from. Goodtree dies in an explosion caused by an explosive connected to this anarchist. Connecting all three of these men is this Phillias Jackson, who had gone missing and is now dead on a slab at Scotland Yard," said I.

"And this anarchist was seen in the company of a dark, whiskered man in a bowler hat with a card pinned to it the night before he died, which was also the night before the station explosion," said Reid. He rubbed the sides of his head in annoyance. "Jackson is dead, which means we have another killer and another loose end to this case."

"Could it be the anarchists?" I asked.

"It's possible, but they have been out of sight since just after the explosion. They fled the city and haven't been seen or heard of since."

"Who else would want to see Jackson dead, if he is the one who killed this man, Lamech?"

"True, but what was Jackson's motive, though?" Reid questioned. "Why did he kill Daniels and Goodtree? I understand he impregnated Goodtree's wife, so perhaps he wanted to have her to himself. But why get rid of Daniels, other than payback for firing him?"

"Mr Holmes has asked that you come and see him right away at the Yard. You can see the body there. There could be a lead," said I.

"No more time shall be wasted here, then," said Reid. White nodded.

Reid and Mr White gathered themselves, putting on their coats and hats. Reid stuffed a few papers into a case, White had a Gladstone bag in hand, and we hastily took a Mariah to the Yard.

Chapter 14
Mr Brett
The Unexpected State of Mrs Goodtree

Autumn 1890

I departed from Doctor Watson at Victoria Station. I grabbed another cab from outside and told him to waste no time. The hour was getting late, and I could hear the chime of Big Ben ringing as the clock struck a quarter to six. I made my way past Trafalgar Square and towards Oxford Street, turning up Baker Street and then towards Regent's Park. Following the Outer Circle, we came to Primrose Hill and quickly to Elsworth Road. We stopped outside Chester House, and I dashed out.

I rapped upon the door impatiently, but no answer came. I pulled out my watch and glanced at the time. Thirty minutes had passed since I left Victoria. With every tick of the watch, I grew impatient. I beat upon the door once more. There was no response. Could she have gone out? I speculated. I gave the door a final pounding.

"Mrs Goodtree?" I shouted as I leaned closer to the door. "It is I, Mr Brett. Investigator Hewitt sent me."

I pushed the door, but it didn't budge. I motioned to the cabbie to wait. Four houses up, there was an alley. I walked around and counted the houses back in order to find Mrs Goodtree's. A brick wall rose six feet, topped with jagged stones. Climbing was not an option, unless I wished to seriously injure myself. There were, however, wooden doors leading into the back gardens.

I tried the Goodtrees'; it was locked. I raised my leg and thrust it through the door. A shooting pain went straight up my left leg. I bent over in pain, clutching my knee. Despite having a pile of crime and adventure novels at home, I had not realised how painful some of the antics were until I tried them myself. When the pain subsided, I realised that my actions had been a success. The door was swinging open. I limped through the garden to the back door. As assumed, it too was locked. There was a window that led into a sitting room of sorts. I put my fingers at the base of the window and lifted. To my relief, the window rose with ease. I painfully climbed in and landed clumsily on the floor.

I walked through the house, looking for any sign of Mrs Goodtree. The kitchen was in a terrible state of disorganisation and untidiness. There were dishes layered in mould, rotting bread, and fruit with swarms of flies. I noticed a thick layer of dust upon the counters and furniture in the other rooms. This was no state for a pregnant woman, or indeed anyone, to be living in.

Upstairs, I stepped into a study. I assumed it was Mr Goodtree's. The room was in a sorry state. Shelves, which I had pictured could have been filled with books, were now empty. The floor had become the new resting place of dozens of books. A sitting chair had been knocked over, and the curtains that hung in the window were ripped and hanging loosely. A small table by one of the windows held a few bottles.

A crystal bottle had been smashed against the wall, and the aroma of stale alcohol lingered in the air. A desk in the room appeared to have been rifled through. There was a stack of legal papers which, upon examining, I realised pertained to Goodtree and Daniels' business. I could not be sure what the cause of this mess was. Foul play was certainly an option, or someone on a rampage. I noticed a card for the Peckham Liberal Club. Despite having a fair knowledge of London societies, I could not recall having heard of such a club. Next to the desk was a waste bin filled with papers. A letterhead featured the same design as that on the Liberal Club's card. I picked the letter out of the bin and read:

"Mr Goodtree," it began. "The actions of your associate, Mr Jackson, are beyond repentance. It was our good nature that allowed him into the club. He has in every way disrespected us and betrayed you. Thus, we demand his immediate removal from the club. He has brought insult upon us all. You have one day to respond, informing Mr Brown of Jackson's demise."

The letter was signed "Osgen".

I was startled when I heard a rattling. I tucked the letter into my pocket and stepped out into the hall. To my surprise, I saw Mrs Goodtree standing in a doorway. She was dressed in a dark blue sleeping gown; her hair was dishevelled and untidy, and there were dark bags under her eyes. One of her sleeves was rolled up, and I noticed red spots on her arm; cocaine. She leaned against the frame with half-open eyes.

"I lost it..." she said in a sober tone, her gaze adrift.

"What have you lost?" I asked her in bewilderment.

"It! I lost it!" she violently yelled back.

She began to sway, and I ran over to her. She collapsed into my arms. She was shaking. How could this be the same woman who had sat in Mr Hewitt's chambers just a short time ago? Consciousness was lost to her, so I carried her back into the room. Her body was burning with fever. I picked up a long coat, which had been tossed onto the floor, and wrapped it around her. Her house was in no state for her to remain there. Doctor Watson, I thought, would be the best man to look her over. I carried her down to the cabbie, who looked at me with a mixture of surprise and horror.

"This is not my doing, you fool," I sneered at him, putting her inside. He scowled.

"I'm not having no part of whatever business yer up to," he said, stepping down from his seat to make a statement.

I could feel Mrs Goodtree shaking.

"I said, don't be a fool! I need you to take us to Scotland Yard at once!"

"To the Yard?"

"I suppose you do not wish to take me there?" I returned. "She needs aid, and the one whom I need is there!"

The cabbie looked at me a moment and stroked his beard.

"Very well." He took his seat again.

I situated Mrs Goodtree in the cab and knocked on the roof, telling the driver to go. Mrs Goodtree rested in my arms. Her forehead was dripping with sweat. She began to moan as we raced down the streets. She suddenly woke, screaming in a panic. She swung her arms in a fit. I tried to grab them and hold her down, but took several blows from the hysterical woman.

"All will be well, Mrs Goodtree, it will be." I tried to assure her, but she was not responsive. She squirmed and struggled before calming down. She was pressed against the other side of the cab. Her chest violently moved up and down as she tried to catch her breath.

"What… what am I doing here?" she mumbled in her delirium. Her eyes were rolling in her head.

"I'm taking you to a doctor, Mrs Goodtree," I informed her.

"A doctor… they can't save me… I lost it. I already lost it," she mumbled. Her head began to bob back and forth. "Oh dear…" Her eyes rolled back as she fainted and fell towards me. I put her back in her seat. The fever had overcome her.

"What are you two doing back there?" the cabbie yelled.

"The woman had a moment of hysteria. Press on to the Yard, make haste!" I shouted back.

Chapter 15
Doctor Watson
The Body of Phillias Jackson

Autumn 1890

"They are in here," said the officer as he escorted Reid, White, and me into an examination room. Inside stood Inspector Lestrade, Holmes, and Hewitt. On a table lay a corpse. Holmes leaned against a counter, smoking a pipe. Hewitt was bending over the body, examining it. Lestrade stood at the foot of the examination table. We were greeted as we entered.

"Ah, Mr Reid, good of you to come," Lestrade said, walking over and shaking his hand. "And who is this?" he asked, referring to the red-headed scientist.

"I am Vigo White, associate of Mr Reid."

"I asked him to join," Reid said.

"It seems we all have our associates here, apart from yours, Mr Hewitt," commented Holmes.

"Brett shouldn't be long, I suspect," said Hewitt. He pulled his fob watch from his waistcoat and looked at it intensely.

"Mr Holmes, Mr Hewitt," Reid said with a nod at the other men, "it's good to make your acquaintance."

"I take it that Doctor Watson filled you in on all our happenings?" Holmes asked.

"He has, indeed," Reid affirmed.

"Care to examine the body, Doctor?" Inspector Lestrade asked.

"I would, yes." I walked over and looked upon the body of Phillias Jackson.

"Mind if I take a look too?" White asked.

"Very well," said Lestrade, leery.

"Mr Reid, would you tell us your part in this tale?" Hewitt asked.

While I looked over the corpse, Reid recounted his tale from the day of the explosion through to its climactic dead end, when one of Lamech's men committed suicide on the Thames.

"The other murders seemed to feature that poison you spoke of, from the fire-flower. I'm not seeing any similar signs here," White said as we looked over the body.

"Neither do I, no," I returned. "But most of the signs are revealed upon the face. This has been quite badly mutilated, as if some beast had had its way with him."

"A hound perhaps?" said White. "I've seen mutilations like this before, and I'd say a large dog did this."

"It's possible, yes," I returned with a nod.

"Looks like someone took a blunt instrument to the left side of his head," said White, pointing. "There is quite a severe indentation here. So after the dogs, someone bashed him over the head and threw him in the Thames," White finished his speculation.

I looked at the wound. His head had certainly taken a tremendous blow.

"But look here," said I, "these bruises on his shoulders; handprints. And here, these bruises look like fingerprints at the top of his forehead, just barely visible on his hairline. It suggests he was forcibly drowned. Open the man up, and his lungs will likely reveal that outcome. Why crack someone over the head after drowning them? Or why feed them to a dog?"

"The water has, unfortunately, washed away any evidence," said Sherlock Holmes, "and one should never theorise without facts." He, Hewitt, and Reid approached the body.

White withdrew a magnifying glass and examined Jackson's forehead.

"There are indentations around the fingerprint markings. Sharp fingernails peeled the skin here."

"From the body's current state, he must have been in the water for four hours," said Hewitt.

"Where is the autopsy report, Lestrade?" Reid asked.

"We've not done it yet," he admitted. "Our surgeon has been away on another case."

"The dazzling ineptitude of Scotland Yard," tutted Holmes. "Unfortunately, Mr Hewitt, I see another story. I'll need to be left alone as I gather more data from our cadaver."

"Holmes, you know I can't let you do that," said Lestrade. "This isn't Bart's, where you can just walk in and take your pick of dead specimens and inflict your own unique scientific experimentation."

"Then I'll stay," said I. "You've used my consultations in the past."

Lestrade rolled his eyes.

"There's little to be gained from arguing with you."

The door suddenly burst open.

"I need your help, Doctor Watson!" It was Brett. He was panting. "I've got Mrs Goodtree, but she's in a bad state. Burning with fever and bursting out in fits of hysteria!"

"Carry on, Watson," said Holmes.

"What about this?" I asked.

"I can help, if the Doctor wishes to stay?" offered White.

"I'd rather a proper doctor," Brett said with a sharp tone.

"Help Holmes, I'll go," said I, looking at White. He nodded back at me, and Brett hurried me out of the room.

*****

I could hear Lestrade instructing Holmes and White to be careful and to remember on whose behalf they were working as we ran down the hall.

"Mrs Goodtree is greatly disturbed," Brett said. "Her house was in utter shambles, and her husband's study a wreck. She kept saying that she 'lost it'. I think she went mad and destroyed the study. I was taken aback by her appearance and crazed actions."

Mrs Goodtree lay on a cot in an empty room. Her forehead was burning, and her body trembled. Her pulse was racing. Brett showed me the marks on her arm. I confirmed them to be from the use of cocaine. I called for some cool water and a towel. Her nightgown was drenched with sweat. I removed it and covered the woman with a coarse grey blanket. Hanging on a chain around her neck was a silver pendant, which I also removed. An officer came in with cool water and a rag, and I laid the soaked rag upon Mrs Goodtree's head. I left the room to gather some equipment from the police surgeon's chambers, then returned and continued my examination.

"What can you tell me about this woman?" I asked Brett.

"I know little of her," he replied.

"She told you nothing of importance when she was with you and Hewitt?" I asked sharply.

Brett's eyes lit with realisation, but it was too late. I had worked it out already.

"She was…" he began.

"With child," I finished.

Brett nodded, his face grimaced.

"Has she…"

"Lost it? Yes, she has," I confirmed. Brett lifted the blanket and we looked at her discoloured stomach. "She's bleeding from within. She won't last much longer."

Lestrade and Reid walked in in time to hear the news. Lestrade put his face in his hands and sighed. Pulling his hands away from his face, a look of intrigue fell upon Reid's face. He walked over to the dying woman and gazed upon her.

"This woman, Mrs Goodtree, I know her," he said thoughtfully.

"Of course you do. She was in the papers when her husband died. He was a well-known chap," said Lestrade. "And, as you remember, I questioned her."

"I knew her name, but I never saw her face, Lestrade," said Reid. "No, I knew her from somewhere else. Somewhere else…" Reid looked at the woman's clothing. "This was on her?" he asked, picking up the pendant and opening it.

"It was, yes," I confirmed.

"Aha! See? A picture of a crown. I thought it most odd when I first saw it. She was one of the many I helped out of the Whitechapel & Mile End station," said Reid. "This woman embraced me when I led her out and this very pendant fell from her neck."

"That's impossible, Reid!" said Lestrade. "I questioned the woman myself. She was at home during the explosion!"

"The man is correct," came the faint voice of Mrs Goodtree.

"Dear woman, rest," said I. "Lestrade, take this ruckus elsewhere!"

"No, I need to… I need to speak," said the dying woman. "I don't wish to go to hell." The woman looked upon me with horror.

"Which of us is correct?" Lestrade asked.

"He is," she returned, looking at Reid. She groaned, her face twitching with pain. "I was there. Jack… Jackson… he promised a better life after it was… over."

"Was Jackson responsible for the explosion? Can you confirm it was he who planted the bomb?" Reid demanded.

"Thomas and David, they were… vile. We were… we were doing the world a service by being… being rid of them."

"Who is 'we'?" Lestrade demanded.

"Mrs Goodtree," said Brett softly. He walked over and knelt down by her. "What sin is it that you seek repentance for?" She looked at him. Her eyes began to drift shut. "Mrs Goodtree. You came to Hewitt and me to find Phillias Jackson, and we have found him." Her eyes opened, and a glimpse of life returned to her. "What is your sin?"

"Where is Jackson?" she asked. "I am his… his queen, you know."

"You are now a queen without a king. Jackson is dead," Brett informed her.

Tears welled in her eyes. "Dead?" she asked painfully.

"Tell us, Mrs Goodtree, what is your sin?"

"Murder…" She trailed off. Her eyes closed, and her head slumped to one side. I checked her pulse, but it had gone. Mrs Goodtree had died.

Hewitt came into the room and saw the grim scene.

"Oh dear, what a terrible shame," he said, looking at the lifeless body.

"It is as if the universe is orchestrating against us with this case. A door opens then shuts as we approach!" said Reid bitterly.

"We know all we need to know," said Lestrade.

Reid looked at him with disdain. He rushed upon the Inspector, who backed up against the wall.

"You above all should see your tremendous blunder, Lestrade!" shouted Reid. "It was you who questioned Mrs Goodtree! The rat was in your cage and you let it go!"

"Are you telling me that there was no way someone who was in that explosion could have slipped out? We gathered as many names as we could. We cross-referenced and interrogated dozens and dozens of people! She had a solid story. There was no reason, no link, that connected her presence at the explosion!"

"Apart from yours, Mr Reid," said Brett. Reid turned an angry eye towards Brett.

"At the end of the day," came the voice of Hewitt. The investigator stepped into the room. "We could pass blame until we are blue in the face. We must now decide what our next action will be."

"What of Holmes and White?" I asked.

"They continue their work on the unknown body," said Hewitt.

"Unknown?" questioned Lestrade.

"Yes, correct, that man on that slab is not Phillias Jackson."

Chapter 16
Doctor Watson
The Problem with the Body

Autumn 1890

"Explain yourself, Mr Hewitt!" Lestrade demanded.

"It's quite simple, really. I looked over the body and determined that it was, in fact, not the body of Phillias Jackson."

"Yes, but how?" Reid asked.

"When our poor woman here came to enquire about our services in locating Mr Jackson, she informed us that he had a mole on the right side of his face…"

"Which we saw! After a mutilation like that, we were lucky to find that clue," said Lestrade.

"You found a man with dark hair, whiskers, and a mole. What you didn't find was a man with dark hair, whiskers, a mole, and a scar upon the index finger of his right hand."

"A scar?" Lestrade questioned.

"Indeed. Mrs Goodtree told us of his scar. That body does not have one; ergo, it is not our man. He still runs free."

"Then he made it to the Continent?" I questioned. "If that is the case, then he is utterly lost to us. By this time, he could be deep in hiding."

"All might not be lost," said Brett. "I found this in Mr Goodtree's study." He withdrew a letter and a card.

"The Liberal Club? What's this?" Reid questioned.

"I've not heard of it at all," said Brett.

"Fortunately, I have," said Holmes. He and White entered the room.

"What is it?" I asked.

"I'm not entirely sure," Holmes admitted.

"I thought you knew about it?" Lestrade questioned.

"Did I say I did? I said I've heard of it. They are a tight-lipped club, and membership is nigh impossible to obtain."

"Have a look at this," Reid said, handing Holmes the letter.

"So Daniels, Goodtree, and Jackson were all there. Two of these three are dead, and Jackson is missing," said Holmes. "What happened to Mrs Goodtree?"

"Miscarriage, Holmes. Bled to death from the inside," said I. "She did confess to a sin, and not that of infidelity. She confessed to murder. She also said her husband and Daniels were vile and she was doing the world a service by ridding us of them." A look of distress came over Holmes' face.

"Inspector Lestrade?" said an officer. "We have a lawyer here with regard to Daniels, his will, and the business. He said he must speak with you at once."

"Very well. I'll be there in a moment." The officer nodded and departed. "You work out the next move while I see to this."

"May I accompany you?" Reid asked. Lestrade looked unsure. "I beg you, forgive my words earlier. We are working together, not against each other."

"Come then," said Lestrade, and the two men departed.

*****

Holmes led the five of us into an empty cell. Hewitt took a seat on the stone bench, White leaned through the bars looking in, Brett and I stood with our backs to the wall facing White, and Holmes stood opposite Hewitt.

"In some way or another, little things have slipped by during the course of this investigation," began Holmes. "Whether that be Reid and Lestrade's blunder with regard to Mrs Goodtree, or perhaps your mistake at Jackson's lodging in Putney, Mr Hewitt—"

"My mistake?" Hewitt cried.

Holmes withdrew a card from his pocket and handed it to him.

"Jackson has departed for the Continent. This was left in his rooms. There is only one explanation." Hewitt looked at the card, his eyebrow arched. A look of realisation befell him. "You understand?" Holmes confirmed.

"I do."

"Mind sharing this understanding with the class?" White asked, pulling his glasses off and biting the arm.

"In time, we shall," Hewitt said. White rolled his eyes.

"According to Jackson's landlord, he's been out of the country for about three months," said Holmes.

"Mrs Goodtree also gave us a similar timeframe."

"That means the last time Jackson was seen was the night before the explosion at the Whitechapel Underground station with Lamech," said White.

"He arranged the explosion, and left for the Continent to avoid suspicion, or perhaps lay blame on Mrs Goodtree?" I asked.

"I think not, Watson," said Holmes. "Had he wanted her to be the scapegoat, she would have been snared long ago. Another game is afoot."

"But the Goblin outfit that was found among his possessions. It was he who tormented Daniels, poisoned and killed him," said Brett.

Holmes took an envelope from another pocket.

"While you were talking back in the shed, I found several long strands of hair in the goblin mask." Holmes withdrew them and held them near a light. "These hairs do not correlate with Mrs Goodtree. One can't be sure that they are female. But it does imply someone with long hair had worn the mask recently."

"Jackson had an accomplice," said White.

"And what of the body?" I asked.

"Someone wanted us to think Jackson was dead," said Hewitt.

"The body here wasn't drowned in the Thames. As you noticed, Watson, the bruises on the shoulders and the marks on the forehead indicate he was forcibly drowned. Then he was mutilated to disguise his face. The markings, as White observed, indicate that it was done by an animal. It is here our trail ends, with a murder confession from Mrs Goodtree on her deathbed," finished Holmes.

"What's next?" Brett asked.

"Two, possibly three, things must be investigated at once. The Peckham Liberal Club and Mr Goodtree's study," said Hewitt.

"What's the third?" I asked.

"That will be left with me," said Hewitt. "I must depart at once. I shan't be gone longer than one week."

"A week!" Brett exclaimed. "Where are you going?"

"The less you know the better," he returned. "I want you to stay here and accompany Mr Holmes and Reid. They'll need you more than I at this stage." Brett looked confused and irritated by the lack of information. His partnership with Hewitt was different to that of Holmes and me. I, however, was used to Holmes and his vague responses.

"There is no time to lose," said Holmes. Hewitt rose at once and quickly left the cell. "Brett, if you and White will remain here and await Reid, Watson and I will be off at once to the Goodtree residence. I need to have a look around. My instruction to you is to look into the Liberal Club. See what you can find, and try to shed some light upon that letter."

Chapter 17
Doctor Watson
The House of Mr Goodtree

Autumn 1890

It was drawing near midnight when Holmes and I arrived at Mr Goodtree's residence just near Primrose Hill. Brett had informed us of the open window around the back, which we used to gain entrance.

Holmes lit a lamp, and I followed him through the dark house. Brett's report was accurate; the house was in a terrible state. We crept up the stairs and found the study in shambles. Holmes examined the room. He looked over the desk where liquor bottles were toppled and smashed.

"I'll look around a bit more," I told Holmes, but he did not respond.

I ventured forward towards the room, which I assumed had been where Brett retrieved Mrs Goodtree. I held a light over her bed and pulled the covers off. To my horror, there was a large spot of dried blood on the sheets and a metallic smell in the air. The blood trailed off the bed and onto the floor. On one side of the bed was evidence of cocaine use, the other a bundle of stiff, bloody rags which had turned brown. I followed the blood through another door and down a back stair. The trail led into a toilet where the evidence of Mrs Goodtree's miscarriage remained. My heart hung heavy with what was before me.

"Watson?" called Holmes.

"I'm down here," I called back.

"Your assistance, if you please," he answered. I made my way back to the study where Holmes stood. "What do you make of this room?"

"It's a mess. After what Brett had said about Mrs Goodtree's actions, it is possible that she did this to the room in a fit of rage."

"There is something yet more telling," said Holmes.

"What is that?"

"Dust!" he exclaimed. "Dust is elegant! The room is covered in it, and it tells me a story."

"That being?" I questioned, feeling somewhat impatient as my mind thought upon the macabre scene downstairs.

"No one has been in this room for some time, nearly three months, I would hazard. The desk itself is in a state of disorganisation, but not like the rest of the room. Papers have been arranged to re-order them, so the desk was more important than the books and other clutter. Brett found that letter in the bin here, and the card upon the desk. Now, why was the letter tossed aside? Unlike the other papers in the bin, this is the only one which remained unwrinkled. Here, on the desk." Holmes picked something up. "An empty envelope." He showed me excitedly, "Which was postmarked 18th of July. That is roughly three months ago, just a few days before the Whitechapel explosion, and not long after Jackson was fired and his mysterious departure for the Continent."

"Where are you going with this, Holmes?"

"Somewhere quite important, I assure you," said he. "See there, on the door frame, a brown smudge?"

"I do, yes."

"How high would you place it?"

"Around six feet," I returned.

"Now, I noticed these broken shards of glass, and kicked under the sofa, here, was this one," Holmes pointed to a large shard which lay upon a table. A residue had dried upon it. There was no mistaking it; dried blood.

"Jackson is said to be around six feet," said I. A moment of realisation befell me. "Aha! He and Goodtree got into a brawl and tore up the room. Goodtree then cut Jackson's face quite severely. So Jackson is the scarred man that was seen with Lamech the night before he died and the Whitechapel explosion!"

"Well done, Watson!" said Holmes cheerfully.

"But what was Jackson doing here? And why hadn't Mrs Goodtree spoken of this incident? She told Hewitt there was no tension at all," said I.

"Think it through, Watson. You make great strides in your deductions only to hurl yourself backwards," scolded Holmes. "Mrs Goodtree wanted Jackson safely returned to her so they could live out their dreams. Had she spoken of ill feelings, it would have aroused suspicion."

I nodded in agreement with my friend.

"Still, why was he here?" I asked.

"That, I shouldn't wonder, has something to do with that letter from the Liberal Club."

"We can only hope Brett and the others have made positive headway in that regard."

"Let us return to the Yard and await their return," said Holmes.

"What about Baker Street? We could do with a bit of rest."

"We will rest at the Yard."

*****

The night air was cold. The moon hung in the middle of the sky; a thin cloud cover danced before it in swirls. Its silver illumination shone down upon the city as we rattled back to the Yard. Holmes sat in quiet contemplation.

"Where is Hewitt going?" I asked hesitantly, breaking my companion's concentration.

"He is looking into a matter for us. Something I've speculated since we first arrived at Jackson's lodgings, but until Hewitt returns with solid data, I don't want to entertain the theory."

"Why are you keeping me in the dark?" said I in a raised tone.

"We have a larger team working with us, Watson. Each step we take must be made with caution rather than throwing around every speculation. Do not take it personally. It is for everyone's protection," Holmes assured.

Agitated by my friend's response, I turned the other way and crossed my arms. We sat in silence, my grand gift to my companion, for the remainder of our trip to the Yard.

Chapter 18
D.I. Edmund Reid
The Lawyer & the Liberal Club

Autumn 1890

With Holmes, Watson, and Hewitt following other threads, I, along with Mr White and Brett, needed to begin our hunt for information regarding the Liberal Club. We waited for Lestrade, who was in his office speaking with Daniels' lawyer.

A short, round man with a large top hat emerged from Lestrade's office. A leather folder was in his hands. I looked in on Lestrade. His face was planted in his hands.

"A word?" I asked.

"Come in, take a seat," he said. I sat across from him, White took a seat along the wall, and Brett remained standing.

"Anything important from the lawyer?" I asked.

"No, nothing really. There is something in Daniels will that entrusts the company to another. He needed to discuss it," he returned.

"Have you any information regarding the Liberal Club in Peckham?" I asked.

Lestrade leaned back and stroked his chin. "Can't say I've heard of it."

Brett proceeded to tell him what he had found in Mrs Goodtree's home regarding the club, and Holmes's command to investigate further while he and Hewitt saw to other matters. When Brett had finished, Lestrade let out a deep sigh.

"I have a certain revulsion for these London clubs," said Lestrade. "They cause more drama than they're worth. There always seems to be some chap who has done something to upset the order, but of course, the order responds with a lashing against anyone who upsets them."

"I agree," said White. "I've been kicked out of most clubs in London." He smirked.

"Can't imagine why," Brett muttered sarcastically.

"Son, if I had to tell you that, I would likely be slapped in irons and locked behind bars."

Lestrade gave him a perturbed look.

"Maybe you should be," Brett sneered.

"Ignore my man, Lestrade," said I, moving the conversation on. This was no time for a petty quibble, and whatever was between Brett and White could wait.

"Do you know anything about this club?" he asked.

"I don't; never heard of it before," White returned.

"Hmm. So you need to find the Liberal Club, then, right?" Lestrade asked.

"We do, yes," I said.

"How do we find this place that no one knows anything about?" Brett asked.

"We will send a message to M Division. They might be able to aid us," said Lestrade.

"Aha!" shouted White, clapping his hands together. "I might know someone." The three of us looked at him, bemused.

"You know someone?" Brett questioned.

"Care to be more specific?" Lestrade asked.

"Actually, no, I don't care to be," was White's response.

"This isn't a time for secrets!" said Lestrade angrily, his face turning red.

"Just as you have Holmes and tolerate his quirks, I, too, have my man, and you will tolerate his," said I sternly. "For all his oddities, White produces results for me."

Lestrade calmed, his face returning to its natural colour.

"Gentlemen, this is not the time or place to be getting angry with each other. We are, apparently, working on the same side," said Brett, though the look upon his face showed me he was trying to swallow his pride and get on with the work.

Lestrade gave a nod, as did I.

"It might take me a while," said White. "I'll send you a message with my findings. But be ready when I do." White stood and moved his glasses further back on his nose before running his hand through his ginger hair and darting out of the office.

*****

Whilst White was away and we waited for a response from M Division, Brett and I looked through the files at the Yard to see if there was any mention of the club. Our search turned up nothing.

"What do you make of all this, Reid? Do you think White will be able to find something?" Brett asked.

"He's a savvy man," I returned.

"He isn't conventional, though, is he?"

"What's convention?" I asked.

Brett shrugged. "A sense of propriety, perhaps, or honesty?"

I put down a folder which I had been perusing and looked over at Brett.

"These are strong words from a man who knows little of whom my associate is," I said.

"I do know him," said Brett. "I'm a journalist."

"What do you mean?"

"White has a dark past that he's tried to outrun. But it's one I'll never forget."

The door swung open before I could question Brett further. Lestrade stood in the entry, holding his arm in the air. Pinned between his forefinger and thumb was a slip of paper.

"We've got an address," the Inspector confirmed.

*****

White had found the club and instructed that we meet him at a local public house on Peckham High Street. Jumping into a Mariah, Brett and I made our way towards Peckham. We passed the Houses of Parliament; the clock tower shone like a beacon. We crossed over Westminster Bridge and continued towards South London.

When we arrived, White was standing outside the entry, smoking a cigarette. He gave a nod and pointed for us to leave the Mariah down an alley. He walked around the corner, tossing his cigarette on the ground.

"Good of you to make it so quickly," said White sardonically.

"We got here as quickly as possible," said Brett with a sharp bite in his tone. "Tell us what you know."

"Leave it to the journalist to be the bigger ass than the police," White remarked. Brett tensed. I put my hand up to break the tension.

"Tell us what you know," said I.

"A hundred yards up the road on the right, you'll see Elm Grove; the Liberal Club is up there across from the side entrance to the station. It's a two-storey building with a square, columned entrance and a blue door. Wooden shades block out the windows. I noticed a few men in fine dress knock on the door in the same pattern. I hear there is a large hall inside, a bar, and that's it," concluded White.

"Who is your source?" Brett asked.

"Does it matter?" White returned.

"To me, yes."

"It matters not, Mr Brett," I interjected. "We know the location; now we need to get inside."

"I was told not to go in flashing your badge, Reid," White informed. "They don't take kindly to that. We need to be diplomatic with them. They need to believe us to be prospective joiners from out of town. Our story: we're from Brighton, and the club was a recommendation by Daniels and Goodtree when we had them ship cargo to South Africa."

"Very well," I returned. Brett nodded.

*****

We walked up to the blue door. A light hung outside, illuminating the entrance. There was a bell, which Brett pressed. We waited a few moments before White pressed the bell for a second time. Just as my patience was about to break, the door creaked open.

A short woman of around five-and-twenty years answered. Her hair was styled up. She wore a loose gown which hung by a single strap across her left shoulder, exposing a large portion of her right breast. Her gown ended at the top of her thigh, revealing striped lace stockings and high-heeled shoes. Her face was paint-ed, and her lips were red.

"'Ello, fellas. What can I do you for?" she asked.

"The club came recommended to us, so we've come to look around," said White.

"Who told ya about the club?" she asked, making a pouty face, which she finished off with a smile.

"Business associates of ours, Daniels and Goodtree, God rest their souls," said I.

The woman squinted her dark eyes and bit her red lips.

"Why are ya here?" she whispered.

"We told you, woman, we're here upon the recommendation of our associates! Are you going to play games or let us in?" Brett snapped.

She stepped back and put a hand on her chest as she gasped. "Well, you've got some fight, I like that," she said as she moved close to Brett and put her hands upon his chest. I looked over at White, who had a smirk upon his face.

"Our friend has had a rough couple of weeks. He needs a bit of relief, my sweet," said White to the woman. Brett gave him a fierce look of disapproval. "My friend found his wife with another man—it's not been good for him," White continued.

"Well, I'm sure we can help with that," she said, taking Brett's hand and tugging him inside. We followed. Brett turned back and gave White an angry look.

Directly inside was a corridor. Immediately to our left and right were two closed rooms. At the end was a stair which led both up and down. She led us down the stairs and into a large hall. The room was filled with well-dressed and prestigious-looking men. Dotted about the room were more women dressed similarly to the one who led us. She led us to a table and asked for our drink order before leaving.

I watched as the perky woman scampered away. Several men called out to her and reached for her as she darted past them. By the look on her face, she enjoyed the teasing and taunting. As I observed the room, the men had all drunk themselves stupid; it was the women who were in control. The combination of bare flesh and alcohol shot them up as dominators within this tiny kingdom. How long this power could last before one of the drunkards used their brute force to get what they wanted, time would tell.

"What the hell were you doing?" snapped Brett at White.

"Calm yourself, man. You don't want to draw attention. All that matters is that we got in. You don't have to do anything with the bird. Besides, you probably couldn't afford it," White retorted. He pulled his glasses off and rested them upon his head.

"What do you make of this place?" Brett asked, looking at me.

I glanced over the room again.

"It has the air of a prestigious brothel; chambers for rich bigots to go and indulge themselves in intoxication and sexual encounters. This entire establishment reeks of destitution and filth," said I.

A hand rested upon my shoulder.

"I would hope that a prospective member would have more positive things to say about my establishment. Clearly, this place is not your forté."

A tall woman with fiery red hair gently squeezed my shoulder before she walked around to face us. She wore a green velvet scarf draped around her neck and arms. Her upper half was pressed tight by the aid of a corset, exposing her breasts seductively, as most Whitechapel women would. The lower half of her dress was covered in a pattern made up of red roses. She wore lace gloves which cut off at her knuckles.

"Who might you be?" I asked.

"Not nearly as interesting as who you are," she returned softly. A maid followed her with a tray of drinks, which were placed onto the table. "Please, gentlemen, drink and tell me about yourselves."

"I'm Mr White, this is Mr Brett, and the gentleman with a coloured outlook on your establishment is Mr Reid. We're in the shipping business. An associate recommended this club to us, so we came to see for ourselves."

"And where do you hail from?" she asked.

"Brighton," said Brett.

"I suppose all that sea air keeps you boys fresh. How are you doing with this dense London air?"

"Clogs the mind a bit," said I.

"Well, maybe we can unclog it?" she returned with a coy flutter and bite of her lower lip.

"My flower, are you going to grace us with your name?" White asked, extending his hand.

She placed her gloved hand into his. He pulled it to his lips and kissed it. I noticed that she wore a ring of a unique design. It was silver with a dazzling red gem at its centre. Wrapped around the gem was a silver snake, the serpent's teeth holding the jewel in place.

"My name is Miss Osgen. Some people here call me Mother," she replied.

"Well, Miss Osgen, who might be in charge of this establishment?" Brett asked.

"Isn't it obvious?" she returned.

"Is there a Mr Osgen or a, err, father?"

"Dear man, you are quite funny and naive," Osgen returned. "Fathers, men—they think they are on top both in terms of domination and sex. They are fools. It is women, the all-mother, who rule this world. Take women away, and men would starve, their fat bellies would shrink, their organs would fail, their lusts and desires would evaporate like a cloud. Men are our puppets, and we rule the world through them. The hierarchy does not go father, mother—nay, it goes mother and her children."

"So you are in charge?" I asked.

"Correct, Mr Reid."

"Clarify something for me, darling. You run this parade, you say you control the men, but your girls give the men what they want," remarked White.

"I give the men what they think they want. They are like pups; I give them a bone to play with, then put them in a cage. Please, you haven't touched your drinks. I'm offended!" Osgen said. White and Brett shot theirs down. I sipped mine slowly.

"We don't want to lose our faculties just yet," said I. She smiled a charming smile my way. "What is membership like? How does one get in?"

"Initiation, as always," she said, resting her hand on my shoulder and squeezing gently.

"Which is what?" Brett asked. She removed her hand from me and looked towards Brett.

"You'll see and experience it soon enough, my boys—if we think you're the right material for our club."

"Do people ever get kicked out of the club?" I asked.

"You want to know the limits, eh?" Osgen returned.

"Always good to know how far things can be pushed," said White, taking another sip of his drink.

"Have you ever heard of a man named Phillias Jackson, Miss Osgen?" I asked.

Her face turned briefly sour when I mentioned the name.

"I believe he was one of our children, but I thought he sadly passed from this world into the next?"

"Has he now? What a shame," said I. "He was partners with our friends. I had hoped to meet him. Do you know what happened?"

"This isn't really the place to speak of the dead, Mr Reid. If you'll come with me, I'll take you into my chamber, and we can discuss this further," she offered.

"I shan't leave my friends," said I.

"Don't be daft, Mr Reid. Look at them; they will be fine."

"Go on, Reid," said White. "We'll have another drink and marvel some more."

"Come, Mr Reid. I'll take care of you." She extended her hand. I took it and departed from my colleagues.

She took me back up the stairs and then to the first floor. We entered a warm and well-furnished room. She lit a few candles and opened the wooden shades. Below was Elm Grove; the soft glow of the gas lights illuminated the empty street. Osgen took a seat upon a sofa. She motioned for me to come over and sit next to her.

"Please, sit. I won't bite." Hesitantly, I walked over and sat next to the woman. "Tell me, then, what do you want to know about Jackson?"

"Tell me why you wrote to Mr Goodtree about Jackson's removal from the club."

Her face grimaced. "He was a bad boy. He needed to be punished."

"And did you… punish him?"

"I didn't need to," she replied.

"Oh yes, because he's already dead?"

She nodded. "He is."

"How did you hear of his death?" I asked.

"People talk."

"Except a body was only recovered today."

She raised her eyebrow at my response. "Shall we get a drink?" She stood without waiting for me to respond and walked over to a table.

"So why was Jackson being removed?" I pressed. She poured two glasses of brandy, eyeing me thoughtfully.

"Who are you, Mr Reid?" she asked as she walked back over with the brandy. "You're not an associate of Daniels or Goodtree." She handed me the drink. She put her red lips to the glass and sipped. She nodded for me to join her. I did.

"I'm just curious, that's all," I returned, setting the brandy to one side. I then felt a surge of heat through my body.

"You feel the room spinning? You must by now."

My head felt heavy. "What did you do?"

"I put a drug in your drink. Now, you didn't take much, but your friends—well, I've got them safely put away for now. Until you and I finish our conversation." With a jolt, she whipped a knife from her ankle and pressed it to my neck. The cold metal pressed firmly against my flesh. "You might as well talk, or this will be the last conversation you ever have."

Chapter 19
Mr Brett
In the Lion's Den

Autumn 1890

Inspector Reid left with Osgen. The bounce of her dress caught the attention of every eye. Reid attracted many dirty looks as he left the room with his arm through hers. I looked over at White, who had his index finger and thumb pressed on either side of his nose. In his other hand, he held his spectacles. He looked up, put his spectacles on the table, and ruffled his ginger hair furiously for a few seconds before looking over at me wide-eyed.

"What's the matter?" I asked.

"Genuine concern? Or just worried you'll be left on your own?" White returned.

"I can handle myself."

"Why are you so short with me?" White asked.

"Can I offer you a drink?" asked a waitress with two glasses of brandy on her tray. "It's on the house. Compliments of Mother." The girl's painted lips lit up with a smile. White returned it with a smile, grinning like an idiot from ear to ear.

"Let's have it, then," said White, winking at her. White took his before she could rest it on the table, and held her hand. "Thank you, love." She winked at him and blew him a kiss before walking away.

"Despicable," said I.

"What? Mind yourself, Brett."

"I don't trust you," I said. "You found this place all too easily. What are your connections?"

"I have no connections to this case," White replied.

"But you do have connections; ones of a less than savoury nature."

"What do you know?" White smacked his fists on the table.

107

I took a swig of my drink. "Does Isabelle Taylorson mean anything to you?"

White paused a moment, squinting his eyes. He picked up his glasses and slid them back on his nose.

"That was a long time ago," he murmured.

"Tell that to the lost souls."

"Shut up, Brett!" he shouted. He leaned back, agitated.

Suddenly I felt my head beginning to spin. The room suddenly felt like it was pounding; as if with every beat of my racing heart, the room was pulled in and pushed out.

"Shit, Brett... there was something in our drinks," said White, his face flushed.

"What is this?" I asked him, attempting to shake off whatever had befallen me.

"I... I..."

"Gentlemen," said the waitress from moments earlier. "We've prepared a private room for you. Follow me, or your friend whom Mother took away will die." The girl took White by the arm and led him away. Another girl took mine, and we followed them.

We were taken to the back of the hall and through a door on the left-hand side. My head was still throbbing, but the girls told me it was simply the drink. "You must be a lightweight, Mr Brett," they chuckled. White laughed with them. We were led down a long, cold corridor. I turned and saw that the door to the hall had been shut. Behind me, the corridor was badly lit with oil lamps spaced five or six feet apart. We were suddenly thrust into a dark room. My head was spinning furiously. I could feel the girls running their hands over my body, but I had no control and could not stop them. My jacket was taken off, something cold was secured to my wrists, and suddenly all I knew was darkness.

*****

"Brett!" a voice shouted.

108

I opened my eyes. I was in a field. Off in the distance, I could see Westminster Palace and the City of London. I was on Primrose Hill.

"Brett!" the voice shouted again.

I looked and saw a woman. She was waving to me. I knew her, somehow. Her auburn hair danced in the breeze, and a beautiful smile graced her angelic face. "Come on, Brett!" she called with a laugh.

I ran towards her, but as I did, she too ran. Who was she?

"You're not going to get me, silly man!" she cried, giggling.

I knew that voice. I knew it well. How could it be? We raced through the park and down residential streets. She ducked down an alleyway and was lost to my sight. I ran in search of her. My heart raced, and I felt a panic fall over me. I turned a corner and, to my horror, I saw her. She was lying on the ground, covered in blood. Standing over her body was a fiend, a creature of some kind. Its big, green eyes gazed menacingly at me. Its yellowish, lumpy skin hung morbidly off the bones.

"Brett!"

I looked at the body. Despite the monstrous Goblin-like creature holding her innards, she was still screaming my name.

"Brett! Wake up, you damn fool!"

My eyes rolled and I shot up. I had been lying on the floor. Across from me stood White. His hands were cuffed behind his back, with a chain binding him to the wall. My head rolled on my shoulders while my senses returned to me. I, too, was bound like White.

"Come on, man. Get on your feet."

The room was dimly lit by a couple of oil lamps. White's shadow was thrown into dramatic relief by one of the small oil lamps, which rested on an unstable-looking wooden table not far from me.

"What happened?" I asked groggily.

"They drugged us."

"Why?"

"No clue, but I'd rather not wait around to find out. You?"

"Do you have a key?"

"No, but we have that oil lamp." I looked at it, and then back at White. "I need you to get it. Slide the table near you, get the lamp, and slide it over."

"What are you going to do?"

"This." White tugged his left arm, and with a sharp pop it came out of its socket. He bit his lip, trying to hide the pain. He sat down on the ground and managed to pull his hands down and under his feet so that his hands were in front of him.

"Come on! Get the lamp!"

I pulled the chain connected to my cuff as far as I could. I knelt down and extended my leg. My left leg just clipped the table. The table wobbled, and the lamp shook.

"Don't knock it over!" scolded White. I slowly began tugging the table leg and slid it near me. "Blow it out."

"I know what I'm doing!" I snapped. I blew the flame out and turned my back, trying to grab it. I touched the lamp and felt a sharp burning on my palm.

"Grab it from the bottom."

I did just that, and slowly lowered myself down onto my knees.

"Roll it over quickly—I don't want to lose too much oil."

I tilted it and rolled the lamp towards White. He reached out and grabbed it with his right hand, groaning as the pull on his left sent pain through his body. He picked the lamp up and poured some of the oil over his left hand as he began tugging on the cuff. He moaned as he scraped it over his hand, tearing the skin in the process. With a loud moan and a grunt, White slid the cuff off his hand. He paused for a moment to catch his breath.

"Are you alright?" I asked. He nodded. He then took his left arm to his right. With a twist and snap, he put his arm back into its socket.

"Blimey, that hurt!"

"My God, man!"

"Time for the other hand…" White poured the remaining oil over his other hand and painfully removed the cuff. When he was free of his bonds, he walked over to the door. He turned the handle, and it swung open. He looked back at me, grinned, and walked out into the hall.

"Where are you going?" I called out. "Are you just going to leave me here?"

No response.

I stood there alone in the darkened room, not knowing how I'd escape. I leaned against the wall and looked up at the ceiling. I heard a rustle out in the corridor and expected to see one of the girls walk through the door, but to my surprise, it was White. In his hand, he held a key.

"Where did you get that?" I demanded.

"The key was hanging on a hook outside," he smirked. He walked over and began to unlock my cuffs. "You passed out from the drugs. I kept my wits and watched the waitresses. Heard them hang it outside." He tossed the cuffs to the ground, and we went to the door. The corridor was empty. "Go left."

"We came from the right!"

"Yes, and if we go out that way, we'll go right back into the halls. I'm not so sure we will be able to slip past the crowds." He snickered.

I glared at him.

We continued down the corridor, which seemed peculiarly long. I looked behind, and judging from the distance we had travelled, we were no longer inside the Liberal Club. A few doors presented themselves to our right and left. We listened for any sign of life inside; all was quiet. I opened a door, and inside was a chamber with a large bed, sofa, and table with drinks. The walls were panelled with wood and hung with large mirrors.

"How peculiar," said White.

"You don't know what's going on here?" I asked sarcastically. "You still don't trust me?"

"I am not going to put any faith in you. You might have fooled Reid and his colleagues, and Holmes and Hewitt may know nothing of you, but with what I know, let's just say I'm keeping a close eye on you," said I as we looked around the room.

White sighed.

There was a fireplace in the room. It was filled with logs, but there was no indication that it had been lit. It was, in fact, the cleanest fireplace I had ever seen. There were scattered items on the mantel, above which hung one of the large mirrors. There was a tiny wooden box with a floral design on its lid. Inside, I found snuff. There were two large golden candelabra with seven candles on either side of the mantel. Oddly, the middle candle in both had been unlit while the others were considerably depleted.

"Who is Antonia?" White asked while he rummaged through a chest of drawers.

I felt my heartbeat quicken.

"How do you know that name?" I asked.

"You were saying her name when you were recovering from the drugs, when I was shouting at you."

"She's... forget you ever heard it."

"I just assumed since you knew about Isabella Taylorson, then I should know about this."

"Keep your mouth shut. Never utter her name again!"

Silence fell.

"Hold on, do you see that?" White said.

"See what?"

"There are candles all over the room, but why are those two candles not lit? Actually, why is there a fireplace in here?" He walked over and tapped on the wall. "Oh my, oh my."

"What?"

"Hold the centre candle, Brett."

I reached for it, but it wouldn't come out.

"It's not wax. It's hard rubber made to look wax-like!" White grabbed the other candle. "When I say so, push it down."

He counted from three, and we pushed the candlesticks down. There was a loud click, and a door opened in the panelling. We stepped through. Light shone in from the room through the mirrors, and we saw a narrow hall that outlined the entire room.

"The mirrors," said I, "they are transparent."

"Here's why," said White. He held up a piece of photographic equipment.

"What is this place?"

"Blackmail," said White. "Those women bring men in here and capture them on camera doing their nasty deeds. The woman, Osgen, I reckon she funds her entire operation off blackmail money."

We walked around the outlining hall.

"There's a door here!" I said, opening it slowly.

A dim light lingered inside. Hanging on a string were photographs. White and I examined them. They were vile. They were not just images of sexual encounters between men and women. There were images of orgies, men performing unspeakable acts upon each other, as well as women, both old and young. Individuals are being strangled, bleeding, beaten. The presence of narcotics was overly evident in the images. What I saw turned my stomach. Even White appeared appalled at the evidence we had uncovered.

"We need to take some of these with us. We will need evidence," said White. "Some of the people in these photographs are mere children!" He and I gathered a few photographs and stuffed them into our pockets.

"We should leave now," said I.

We continued down the corridor until it came to an end. A stair presented itself, and we proceeded up. White pushed the door at the top and opened it gently. Inside was a large, well-lit room. A roaring fire popped under the mantel. There were comfortable places for sitting: a sofa, armchairs, and a large cherry-wood desk.

"Must be in someone's house," said White as we looked around curiously.

I peeked through a window. It faced an empty garden.

A work desk was covered in sheets—engineering designs. I noted that the initials R.L. were inscribed upon the papers.

"What do you know of Isabella Taylorson?" White asked hesitantly. I looked at him. For the first time, he wasn't smirking, nor did he have any look of mischief upon his face.

"It was an inn, up north in Manchester. I would frequent it back then when I was writing for a paper, the *Manchester Gazette*. I wasn't the only one to call this inn my local. Many of the college students did so, and so did a bespectacled ginger doctor-in-training. He would come in and regale us all with tall tales of adventures. One day this ginger boy comes in speaking about a lady he fancies, only she's not a free lady. You picked a married woman, soiled her, ruined her marriage, and killed the husband."

White gazed upon me, holding papers in his hand. His eyes were glazed, as if I had witnessed some sort of odd transformation in his person.

"What has you so sure it was I who did the murdering?" he said in a calm and rather queer tone.

"I was at the hearing—I reported on it. The letters between you and her, which discussed, vaguely, a way of being rid of her husband. You manipulated her. The destruction of that woman and her family and future were all upon you and your inability to keep your hands to yourself."

White lowered his head. "My alibi," he said.

"I care not!" said I. "You very well might have had nothing to do with his suicide, but you were the reason she put a pistol in her mouth and blew her skull open in the city's centre."

"I was young, Brett," White began. "The incident ruined my potential career."

"Hardly the justice you deserved," I returned sharply.

With no warning, the door burst open. White and I stood in disbelief. I felt the blood pulsing through me. White dropped the papers he had in his hand. To our great horror, standing in the doorway, with green bulging eyes, a reddish froth around the mouth, bulbous yellow skin, and growling deeply, was none other than the terrible Goblin Man. In one hand he held a large blade. His grip upon the handle was tight and his grin was menacing. He charged towards us….

Chapter 20
D.I. Edmund Reid
The Conversation Between Reid & Osgen

Autumn 1890

The blade was pressing into my skin, and I knew that with any swift movement, I could be choking on my own blood. Osgen's manic eyes looked upon me, her teeth grinding together.

"Tell me who you are," she commanded.

"Tell me your connection to Jackson," I returned.

She frowned at me. "I told you, he died."

"Who told you he died?"

"What does it matter?" I felt the knife pressing as she spoke.

"There's no way you can know this," I told her. "His body was only retrieved today. His death has not yet reached the papers. So how do you know?"

A look of confusion passed across her face, then a grin.

"You fail to realise my clientele." She moved the blade up my neck and pressed it under my jaw. "I have fingers in many pies. Information comes to me, and I to it."

"Then your information is flawed."

"How so?"

"Because the body isn't Jackson's."

She stared. "It… isn't Jackson?"

"No. He lives, yet."

"Oh dear." She removed the knife from my neck and rose. She walked over to a desk and leaned upon it, her hand stroking the edges.

"I need you to tell me what you know of Jackson, and why he was being forced out of this club by Goodtree."

"How do you know this?" she asked with an eerie calm.

"I've seen the letter of instruction."

"Jackson got into an argument with Goodtree and Daniels."

"Over what?"

"Over rights. The argument that is nearly as old as time. We fulfil a person's desire here. Some people, like Goodtree and Daniels, like to indulge in forbidden fruit—ethnic fetishes, and so on."

"Jackson was outraged when he learnt of their fetish?" I pressed.

Osgen hopped up onto the desk and crossed her legs. She fondled the knife in her hands.

"To engage in the act of pleasure, to embrace carnal nature and give in to that inner beast which longs to break free from our oppressed society is what we do."

I looked at her, bewildered.

"You don't understand, do you, Mr Reid?"

"I believe I do."

"I believe you do not." She stepped down from the desk, leaving the knife behind, and walked over to me.

"A moment ago, I wanted to kill you. Cut your throat and spill your blood right here on the sofa. I wanted to watch you gag as you lost the ability to breathe. Why hide these carnal impulses?"

She put her hands on either side of my face and leaned in. With her body pressed against mine, she kissed my lips.

"You know you want to give in," she whispered into my ear.

"Stand back, woman!" I said, putting space between us.

A look of thrill and surprise came upon her. Her eyes were on fire, and she twitched her fingers with excitement.

"Now, Mr Reid," she said, approaching me again. "You are in a safe place. What you do here stays here."

She reached behind and stripped off the skirt of her dress. She stood bare-legged in her corset as she ran her hands down my chest.

"Are you telling me that deep inside that shell of yours, you aren't bursting to just give in and take me? To forget this gentlemanly façade that so many try to hold up when all they really want is to be an animal?"

"I assure you, I am not." I remained placid.

She smiled and, despite my words, brought her face closer to mine.

"I suppose Jackson wouldn't give in either, and you had him removed?"

"Oh! Jackson this, Jackson that! Hell, Reid! You have a woman ready to pounce and purr, and all you can think about is the damn work! I can't be having this. It looks like I will have to kill you now. Which is a shame."

She pushed herself away and walked over to the desk.

"And how, pray, are you going to do so?" I approached her slowly.

She held the knife up.

"I can defend myself against a knife."

She looked at it and acted as if she was going to throw it at me. I ducked. She laughed.

"This is a fun game, Mr Reid." A smile graced her face. Then she slammed the knife into the top of the desk. "But now it's time to end."

She withdrew a concealed revolver. I dived as the gun went off, darting towards the back of the sofa as each bullet came closer and closer to striking me. I crouched behind it and could hear the clicking of the empty gun. Osgen began to chuckle.

"Come out, Mr Reid!"

I could hear her opening drawers. I reached for my revolver and slowly peeked around the corner of the sofa. When she caught me, she fired a shot from another gun and burst into laughter. I reached around and fired a shot.

"Oh! That was close!" she cried in glee. She fired again, and the bullet tore through the back of the sofa and struck me in the arm. I held back my cry of pain as best I could.

"Did I get you? Did I?"

I quickly rose and fired a shot at her. She screamed as my bullet pierced her arm. She growled like a wild animal, and I could hear her shoving things off the desk in a fit of rage, throwing whatever she could get her hands on.

"I need you to calm down!" I called out while I nursed my wound.

Suddenly, the noise stopped.

I looked around to see what she was doing, but she was not at the desk.

"Here I am," she smiled at me and cackled.

I turned. A shot was fired, and my revolver was blown away. With cat-like agility, she had crept up on me from behind. Her left arm was a red mess, blood covering her corset and streaking down her white legs. In her right hand, she held her revolver aimed directly at my head.

"I don't wish to kill you, madam."

"You're not in a position to kill me."

"Tell me who killed Jackson."

Her eyes blazed. "Stop bloody asking about Jackson!"

"If you're going to kill me, grant me that, Mother Osgen."

Her eyes cooled. Her scowl softened.

"It pains a mother to have to punish a child. Men will never know what it was like when God had to punish her children with the curse of death, and continuing that punishment will never be easy."

"Then you contradict yourself. You said you give in to carnal impulses—like Cain killing Abel. But now you wish to kill me, yet it pains you. Thus, your carnal instinct isn't to kill, but to live."

"Mr Reid, don't try and make this philosophical. You must die."

"So you'll kill me to protect the person who attempted to kill Jackson."

"Yes." She stretched out her arm. I looked down the barrel and awaited the bullet.

"Goodnight, Mr—"

Her words were cut off by the bang of a gunshot.

I jolted back, my eyes closed and my heart beating furiously. I opened them and saw Osgen standing before me, wavering. The gun dropped from her hand and crashed onto the floor. She fell to her knees. I could see a tear in her left eye. Then she fell over, dead.

Her body lay collapsed to the right, and in her fiery red hair I could see a cold crimson thread of blood.

I looked at the doorway, and there stood Doctor Watson, his revolver still smoking.

Chapter 21
Doctor Watson
The Hunt for Brett and White

Autumn 1890

Inspector Reid looked at me with utter shock and bewilderment. The red-headed woman lay dead on the floor. The room was in complete disarray, and bullet holes speckled the walls. I ran over to Reid once I saw his arm had been wounded. I took my cravat and wrapped it firmly around the wound.

"I thought I was dead," panted Reid.

"A moment later, and you may have been," I returned.

"Where is Holmes?"

"Downstairs."

"We need to find White and Brett. Their drinks were poisoned, and I have no idea what these women have done with our colleagues or what they will do to them." I helped Reid up, and we made our way towards the stairs. "How did you get in, by the way?" I asked as we descended.

"We heard the shots from the cab outside, and Holmes and I kicked the door in. I came up here while he looked elsewhere," I informed him.

When we came downstairs, no one seemed to be aware of either the gunfire upstairs or our entrance. Down in the hall, the members were still drinking while scantily dressed maids served them.

"Her, that maid over there. I remember her. She served us initially. She might be able to tell us where the others are."

"Ah, there you two are," said Holmes, approaching from behind. He evaluated Reid. "Is she dead? The red-headed woman?"

"This is no time for amazement at your powers, Mr Holmes, but how can you know it was a red-headed woman?"

"By your sleeve. Red hairs wrapped around the button on your cuff. The hair is too long to belong to Mr White. The logical conclusion is that you were in a battle with a woman with long red hair."

"What you observe is truth. She is dead."

"Shame."

"She was going to kill him, Holmes!" I cried.

"Can I help you, gentlemen?" a maid asked.

"Yes, girl," said Reid. "You may recall me from earlier. I was speaking with Mother, er, Osgen. Where has she taken my colleagues?"

"I don't know."

"Pupils dilated, pulse increased, aversion to looking any of us in the eye," said Holmes.

"What?" she replied.

"You're lying," said he.

"You're making me nervous, is all," she stammered.

"Girl, your Mother is dead, there is no salvation for you. You will tell us where our colleagues are, or I will arrest you for aiding in a kidnapping," said Reid.

She stepped back a moment. "Follow me."

She took us to the back of the hall and through a door that matched the wooden panelling of the walls. The hall we went through was dark, with little light to help us see. She opened a door and gasped. The room was empty. Holmes darted inside and looked around. He found a shattered oil lamp.

"A nice trick," said Holmes.

"What?" demanded Reid.

"Oil," Holmes pointed out. "One of the two used it to free their hands before escaping." As Holmes stood, he looked at the mirrors around the room. "Hmm, false mirrors. Interesting."

"There's a key in this cuff," said I.

"And the oil is still warm," Reid said.

"Tell us, miss, where did they go?" Holmes asked.

"I don't know, honest, I don't!" she replied nervously.

"Is there another way out?" I pressed.

"I don't know! I don't, I'm not allowed to go beyond this room."

"It's likely they went deeper in rather than risk being caught going back through the hall," said Reid.

"Agreed." Holmes nodded.

"Girl, you have to come with us," said Reid. I took her by the arm and put her in front of us as we continued down the hall.

As we walked, we heard a blood-curdling scream. Holmes and Reid ran ahead while I followed behind with the girl. A light led me up a flight of stairs.

The sight inside was one of utter horror. Brett lay by the window. He held his side, groaning in pain. Holmes stood over White, who lay on the floor by an open door. Reid was nowhere to be seen. The girl screamed at the grotesque scene; I covered her mouth, telling her to quiet herself. Her breathing calmed after a moment, and I removed my grip. She curled in a ball in a corner, tears running down her face.

I raced over to Brett. "Don't worry, Brett. You'll be fine," said I, examining his wound. He was covered in blood, but his wounds were manageable. He had a few gashes in his abdomen, a deep wound in his left leg, and a broken hand.

I turned to Holmes. He looked at me and shook his head. I looked down at White. He lay in a thick pool of blood. His throat had been slashed and someone had ripped his belly open and yanked his intestines out. Holmes glanced at Brett.

"Is he… is he… dead?" Brett asked with tears in his eyes. "Is White dead?" I held Brett's face in my hands a moment, and his panicked eyes looked at me.

"He is, Brett. He's gone." The journalist burst into a shower of tears. "I tried, Doctor. I tried to help! White, he… he… I was wrong about him."

"Tell us what happened," I asked.

"We already know," said Holmes.

"What?" I turned to look at Holmes, who was shifting through the desk and looking at some kind of mechanical blueprints.

"It was the Goblin Man," Holmes said coolly.

"The Goblin Man?" I questioned.

"A hideous creature," gasped Brett. "It came in like a devil. No, no, I can't speak of it. I won't."

"Calm yourself," I assured him.

"Reid chased him out. He was ripping at White when we came in," said Holmes.

"I thought Jackson was the Goblin? We found that attire at his lodging in Putney."

"So we did, Watson. Someone else has taken on his mantle." Holmes began looking through the disrupted papers on the floor and in the desk.

"But why?" I asked.

"I don't know yet…" Holmes trailed off. "What is this?"

"Tell us."

"A letter to Mother Osgen from Daniels. He's agreeing to the passing over of his company to an unknown benefactor."

"Why would he do that?"

"It is curious, Watson."

"His pocket," said Brett.

"Pardon?" I asked.

"White's pocket, there are photographs. Get them."

Holmes found them and looked upon them with disgust. I approached and saw the reason for his revulsion. Grotesque images of filth.

"I've seen images like these before," said Holmes.

"Where?" I demanded, scandalised.

He reached into his inner coat pocket and withdrew a photograph. I took it into my hand. It was an image of Mr Daniels and

Mrs Goodtree in the midst of an explicit sexual encounter with several young Jewish women.

"I found this the day I searched Daniels' office. It was in his safe. Its connection remained unknown until now. But clearly Daniels didn't believe it had any connection to the Goblin Man, otherwise he would have said."

"You think he would have divulged something like this?"

"Most probably." Holmes put the photographs into his pocket.

"Holmes!" I exclaimed. "The woman, do you remember? The one we saw outside Daniels' house. He said she was nobody."

"Yes, it would appear to be this Osgen woman. She must have been delivering those papers. Daniels was losing his company to her, and she was blackmailing him with these images."

Perspiring and panting, Reid stood in the doorway. He walked over and knelt down by his fallen friend and colleague. He clenched his fist and struck the floor. Holmes, though rarely one for sentiment, reached over and put his hand on Reid's shoulder.

"He was a good man, a smart man. A bit misguided but good." Reid wiped his face and stood up. "Still, we have work to do."

Holmes nodded, then showed the pictures from White's pocket, and then the picture of Daniels and Mrs Goodtree.

"It's likely others were being blackmailed by this woman. Which means it would be important to get a list of the clientele and smoke out the rest of the rats here," said Holmes.

"I agree," nodded Reid.

"Reid. Remind me, what was the name of Lamech's wife?" Holmes asked.

"Ruth, why?"

"Curious."

We turned when we heard the rustling in the corner. The maid had tried to slip out the door.

"Girl, come here," Reid ordered. The maid stopped and returned upon command, her face streamed with makeup. "Whose house are we in?"

"It's the missus' house," she responded.

"Is that why you were not allowed to go beyond the rooms in the passage?"

"I suppose so. Well, we weren't given any real explanation for it. But it was known where the tunnel led," she whispered.

"You will have to come with us."

"I don't want to go to jail!" She began to shake and cry.

"If you help us, we can help you," Reid assured her.

*****

The local authorities were called in, along with Lestrade, to clear out the Liberal Club. We saw that Brett was looked after and received medical attention for his wounds. His leg was badly injured, and he would need to keep off it for some time. White's body was removed, as was Miss Osgen's. The young maid proved useful in giving us important information about the clientele, which aided in making many high-profile arrests over the next week as the club was washed out. Holmes kept himself busy but spoke little over those few days about his whereabouts.

*****

"We are still no closer to Jackson!" exclaimed Reid, as he stood in the window of 221B Baker Street. "I don't know why you called me here to look down dead ends!" He turned towards Holmes and me, who were sitting in our usual places. The glaring sunlight silhouetted the Inspector's back.

Holmes, who was surrounded by a hoard of papers, reached for his pipe and Persian slipper, in which he stored his tobacco. Slowly, he began packing the bowl of his cherrywood pipe.

"Not all is as dark as you believe," said Holmes, igniting his pipe and taking a few puffs before rising. He reached into the pocket of his mouse-coloured dressing gown and withdrew a card, handing it to Reid.

"What's this?"

"A card, a doctor's card." There was a buzz at the door. "Aha! Good, he's right on time." Reid looked to me for an explanation, but I could offer none.

The door swung open, and the large figure of Investigator Hewitt stood before us. "After racing here from Victoria, those seventeen steps were something of a final trek up the mountain's peak," he said.

"Pray, take a seat and tell us what you know," said Holmes.

"First, where is Brett?" he asked.

"Mr Brett," Reid began, "was injured. He's alive, but his leg was badly wounded by a knife. He won't return to us for some time."

Hewitt's face dropped. "What happened?" he pressed.

We informed Hewitt of all that had happened at the Liberal Club and of the arrests that had resulted from our investigation. He was disgusted with the inner workings of the club, and further revolted by Daniels' and Goodtree's darker secrets. Lastly Holmes mentioned the will of Daniels and the new owner.

"Now, Holmes," said I. "You and Mr Hewitt have kept us in the dark with this mysterious trip to the Continent."

"I will reveal all," said Hewitt. "It is connected with that card you hold, Mr Reid." Reid glanced at it again. "Doctor Jean-Christopher Jonqueres, a Paris-based physician, is at the forefront of medical science. He is widely known for skin grafts, helping disfigured individuals reconstruct their appearance in a more nat-ural-looking way. His first patient was a young African boy who had been bitten by a poisonous spider and lost a large chunk of his face. Doctor Jonqueres performed a series of grafts to cover the wound, returning the boy's face almost back to normal. As the science has progressed, the questions, both in the realms of possibility and of morality, of changing one's face to look radically different have been raised."

"Might someone change their appearance to hide their identity?" Reid questioned.

"Precisely," said Holmes.

"To what end?" I asked.

"Any," Hewitt returned. "An attempt to start a new life, running from something, anything—it may even come to a point where natural beauty will be replaced with falsities. The possibilities could be endless."

"Why did you look this man up?" Reid asked.

"Mr Holmes was fortunate to pick up something that I missed, that card. It was in Jackson's lodgings. We were told he took an unexpected trip to the Continent, but then his body mysteriously turned up on the Thames bank. Now, with this false body of his in place, the rumour that he was off to the Continent, in correlation with the card we now possess, is quite suggestive."

"It's circumstantial," I protested.

"Or is it?" Holmes returned. "It's the little things that count. The mud from the Goblin's shoe led us to Daniels' factory, which led us to Jackson."

"Well," Hewitt continued, "Holmes showed me the card at Scotland Yard. One of us needed to speak with this doctor. I gathered what I could and made my way to Paris. I would say for all the legwork I did I don't feel much lighter; the cheese and wine were much too tempting. Anyway, I did my own investigation to find Doctor Jonqueres. He was out of town, staying in his country home some miles outside of Paris. I continued my journey to find him. I would hardly call his lodging a country home; a mansion would have been a more apt description. It rose three stories high, made out of solid grey limestone, with large arched windows, wide doors, and towering peaks. I pounded on the door and was greeted by a beautiful French maid. She was a lovely creature. She showed me into a room where I waited for the good doctor. When he arrived, he greeted me warmly.

"'Hello, Monsieur Hewitt,' said he. 'It is my pleasure to make your acquaintance.'

"'As it is for me as well,' I returned.

"'What is it that I can do for you?' he asked.

"I proceeded to tell him of our investigation and our hunt for the man, Jackson, whom we believed might have come and had surgery performed on him some time ago. The doctor sat bewildered for some time.

"'How is it so that I have been pulled into this English drama?' he inquired, smiling. Though, realising the seriousness of the situation, he quickly sobered. 'No, no—forgive my jest. I take photographs of all my patients, before and after. I do not remember a man by the name Jackson, but the description reminds me of a man named Edward Wilder. An English businessman who came to see me some months back. We had corresponded for a while regarding some reconstruction surgery. I found him most odd, but he was eager to undergo the experiment. When he arrived, he had a terrible gash on his face, no more than a day or two old. This made the surgery slightly more difficult, but he did not want to wait. So I performed the surgery. When it was completed, he looked like a new man. However, there was a scar from the gash on his face. He was not bothered, though.'

"'Can I see the pictures of him?' I asked the physician.

"'But of course, Monsieur Hewitt,' he exclaimed, and jumped from his seat. 'Now I must tell you the truth. Mr Wilder did not want any photographs before or after, but I could not resist capturing my work while he was still unconscious.'

"He went into a drawer and withdrew a couple of photographs." Hewitt reached into his pocket and laid the photographs on the table. We saw the face, before and after, of Phillias Jackson. His brow had been changed, his lips, ears, and nose too. It was a confusing set of images to gaze upon as, for a moment, the faces looked similar yet oddly different.

"I suspect he will change his hair colour as well," said Reid.

"Well, as it happens," said Holmes, "Daniels' lawyer came to see Lestrade. His company is being passed over to another person." Holmes picked up a newspaper and laid it down onto the photographs. He pointed to a small article. "A Mr Edward Wilder will be hosting a ball in celebration of his new shipping business and revealing some kind of forefronted technology that will aid Britain as threats and rumours of wars continue to heighten."

"Jackson is Wilder," said I. "He must have been working with Osgen in order to blackmail Goodtree and Daniels. But what I do not understand is the Goblin mystery now. We thought it was Jackson."

"It was not Jackson himself, but it was his associate," confirmed Holmes.

"Who is this person?" Reid asked.

"Ruth Lamech," confirmed Holmes.

"But she was… how is that possible?" Reid asked.

"On the blueprints at the Liberal Club were the initials R.L., and the writing on the prints was distinctly feminine. While Lestrade and the rest were looking into the clientele of the Liberal Club, I decided to try and find Reid's missing Jews. It was confirmed to me by a trustworthy source, a connection my brother Mycroft forbids me from disclosing, that Ruth was a mechanical genius and was the one responsible for designing the explosives used by Lamech and the anarchists. Second, in the Goblin Man outfit we found in Jackson's shed, I discovered two markers: some long, dark hair strands inside the mask and a fingerprint. I was able to match her print to one in Lamech's former East End lodgings. She is our Goblin, and she, I believe, enhanced her explosives design for Jackson to use on Goodtree, but could not do so until he ordered in the equipment: the powders from Burk and Lynn."

"So we have it then!" exclaimed Reid. "Jackson used these players to acquire Daniels' and Goodtree's business. Though Mrs Goodtree thought he was the unlucky but brilliant businessman, it was Ruth who aided him."

"Haven't you realised how the poison got into Lamech on the same day Jackson was seen with him at the public house?" Holmes asked.

Reid's eyes lit up. "It was her. She got the poison into his food? She betrayed her husband with Jackson!"

"With the promise of a new and better future as a wealthy businesswoman," said Hewitt.

"Rather than the wife of an anarchist living in a slum," said I.

Holmes sighed. "So Ruth was posing as the Goblin while Jackson was away. Osgen and Ruth would have put things in place while he reconstructed his face, but something even more concerning is this." Holmes laid out the blueprints with R.L. initialled on them. "Do you know what this might be? Take a look at the guests due to attend the event tomorrow." We looked at the paper and saw that Lord Myers was to attend. He had, in the past, been the target of many anarchist attacks. "The scarlet thread of murder, which has run through this case, has led to this: Jackson's assuming a new identity and running the Daniels and Goodtree business, with Ruth Lamech being his engineer. There is only one more personal matter to see to, Lord Myers. He is to be at the demonstration, but he is not meant to leave alive. Jackson has what he wanted; now Ruth wants Myers' death. All it takes is one mistake in a demonstration, a sudden bit of chaos, and he could be killed. Now we set the final trap for our little mouse."

Chapter 22
Doctor Watson
The Final Trap

Autumn 1890

Edward Wilder's grand event was to be hosted at the Royal Geographical Society opposite Hyde Park. It was by invitation only, but Holmes and Hewitt managed to acquire a set. The previous night, we had formulated a plan. Jackson, or now Wilder, would be easy to catch, but we needed his final accomplice. If Holmes's information was right, we needed Ruth. Holmes explained that the blueprint designs were for something quite grand and terrible. As Hewitt looked over the information, he explained that the Whitechapel explosion was but a demonstration on a smaller scale. The design had been enlarged and perfected, which would explain the whereabouts of all the powders purchased from Burke and Lynn. Though Reid's concerns were greater, he speculated that the explosive might be laced with the fire-flower poison as well, meaning that anyone not killed by the blast might still be affected by deadly toxins. Without capturing Ruth, White's death and Brett's injuries would never be fully avenged.

The following day, Inspector Reid, Martin Hewitt, Sherlock Holmes, and myself took a cab from Baker Street. Hewitt updated us with Brett's recovery. He was speedily on the mend, but not fit enough to join us for the last leg of our adventure. Hewitt informed me that Brett was curious if I would write about this particular investigation.

"Brett had taken his time to write up his side of the investigation thus far, and he asked me to share it with you," said Hewitt. Reid informed me that he, too, had kept a journal of the events and would also be happy to share once it was completed.

We arrived at the R.G.S. and were warmly welcomed into the event. We were shown into a grand ballroom with elegant maps of the world reaching from the floor to the ceiling. One wall was glass, and led out into an immaculate garden lit with the soft glow of lamps. Outside was a tent where members of the party were gathering, feasting, and smoking. Inside, women in glorious ball-room dresses glided about across the marble floor with glasses of wine and champagne in their hands. Waiters and maids were catering to everyone's needs; the room seemed jolly. At the far end of the room stood a podium, and before it were a few rows of chairs. Behind the podium was something round and shrouded in white cloth.

"Do you notice anything, Watson?" Holmes asked me. I took another look around the room. I saw it.

"The flowers," I acknowledged. He nodded. The room was covered in the fire flowers, but to add to the danger, the guests were each wearing one. "So they aren't in the explosive?"

"Of course not," he said. "Keep an eye out for Lord Myers."

Reid was standing at the back of the room, watching the guests come and go. He held a glass of brandy but did not so much as sip it. Hewitt was wading through the crowd towards the door leading out into the garden. I saw him go through.

It was not long before Lord Myers arrived. A maid ran up to him and presented him with a flower. He graciously accepted. After taking a quick whiff of the petals, he put it into his front pocket and picked up a drink.

"Keep a keen eye on him, Watson," ordered Holmes. "I'll return later." I nodded and watched as Holmes vanished into the crowd. Moments later, an announcement was made that Mr Wilder would be coming in shortly to give a speech. The guests outside began to make their way inside.

"Have you ever met this Wilder fellow?" someone asked me.

"Afraid not."

"A bit queer. He seems to have just come out of nowhere. Apparently, he's amassed a fortune in the Americas but wanted to come back to a civilised land."

"When did you make this acquaintance?" I asked.

The man twisted his blonde moustache as he pondered. "Well, I've not actually met him either. I became aware of him about a month ago. Members of the R.G.S. were invited to meet this exuberant businessman. Naturally, his travels are what drew us to him."

"Everyone here is a member, then?" I questioned.

"As far as I know. Aren't you?"

"Of course I am," I lied. "I thought I recognised most members, but some faces are unfamiliar to me."

"There are a few new faces, but this is a members-only club. Wilder must have done something very sweet to get Lord Myers to come. Maybe a few pennies for his campaign." The man nudged me with his elbow and smirked. Then Mr Edward Wilder entered the room.

With an abundantly charming disposition, he began greeting everyone, shaking the men warmly by the hand and kissing the women on the tops of their gloved hands. I could see the scar on the side of his cheek from where Goodtree had sliced him and Doctor Jonqueres had struggled to repair it.

Seeing Jackson as Wilder was a most unusual sight. He had, as guessed, changed his hair colour from dark peppered black to a blonde, almost white, colour. His attire was most fashionable. He wore shiny leather shoes with white tops, a green and blue checked suit, and reddish-brown gloves. Under his jacket was a dark waistcoat and around his neck a red cravat. He wore spectacles with a bluish tint to the lenses. Everything about this man was completely the opposite of Jackson. Jackson, while bold and aggressive, was not showy. This version was. Perhaps it was the man he always wanted to be. He walked towards me and greeted me with a firm handshake.

"Hello there, sir, so glad you made it tonight," he said to me.

"I'm happy to be here," I returned.

"Good man, good man!" he returned with a bright smile before carrying on greeting the others.

I glanced towards Reid, who stood still as a statue, watching the room and keeping an eye fixed on Wilder. Lord Myers was near the door leading towards the gardens. When Wilder greeted him, he motioned for the two to go outside. They started for the door, but then Hewitt made a grand entrance, expressing his delight to see both Wilder and Lord Myers. Hewitt's interruption resulted in Wilder proceeding without the nobleman as Hewitt struck up a conversation with him instead.

A short time later, the guests had taken their seats as Wilder had found his place in front of the podium. Holmes was nowhere to be seen while Reid and Hewitt hung towards the back of the room.

"Ladies and gentlemen, from the depths of my heart, I thank you for coming tonight. It is an honour and a privilege to share this evening with you. As some of you know, I have spent most of my time in the Americas. I left our fair green country for that great American outback—rolling deserts, Indians, cowboys. The Americans, for all their faults, have crafted a wondrous land. Business is booming, but now it's time to come back home and serve our Queen.

"Through some mutual acquaintances, I came into knowledge that was widely secret, that Mr Daniels and Goodtree were looking to sell their company over to pursue other avenues. I happened to be in a position to purchase it, which I did. Sadly, the two men were victims of fate. God rest their treasured souls." Wilder carried on for some time, praising the two men whom he had killed before his ignorant audience. "Many of you know that travelling the Atlantic is no small feat, nor is making your way down to Australia or to India. There's a bounty of wealth and trade that criss-crosses the globe. What I propose is a faster, more efficient way of doing business, but creating a more streamlined trade is not our only mission.

"As I said, I've come back to serve our holy monarch, Queen Victoria. War is nibbling at our toes, not just from outside our borders but from within, as Lord Myers can testify to with the Jewish problem. One of the best weapons manufacturing companies in the country, Burke and Lynn, has partnered with me to take Britain to the next level of warmongering. Our lands will be safe from intruders, our borders will be tight, thanks to my brilliant engineers." The room lit up in a roar of applause.

I found myself taken aback by their praise for this man. It was no secret that trouble lurked on our doors, but to suggest our streets were riddled with a pest such as the Jews was despicable. I turned towards Hewitt, but he had vanished. I looked back at Reid, and he nodded towards the door. Hewitt had left. I felt a stab of surprise; this wasn't part of the plan.

"It's time for a demonstration!" cried Wilder. He pulled the shroud off the contraption. "A new form of explosive with enough power to peel the skin off a rhino sixty feet away."

He opened the container up and began explaining how the components worked. The bomb was meant to be planted in the ground, like a mine. Wilder claimed it could take out charging cavalry. He offered people the chance to look inside the deadly machine. Groups of three or four began walking up and looking inside while Wilder dazzled them with details. My heart began to race as Lord Myers got closer to the piece.

Reid approached me. "This doesn't feel right," he said. "Look at the way they are all freely tinkering with the inside. If that was to be the killing machine…"

"Unless he's going to kill them all?"

Something seemed to catch Reid's attention. A man leaning against the wall was pulling on his collar. As he did so, his wrist was exposed.

"My God," said Reid.

"What is it?" I asked.

"The missing anarchists."

"Explain!"

"That man, his wrist, the marking on it is the same marking found on the anarchists."

"I noticed the marking myself," said Hewitt, approaching. "I snooped around; there are a fair number of people with the anarchist markings. All were personally invited by Wilder and are not members of the club," Hewitt informed us.

"Who are they?" Reid asked.

Hewitt pointed out six individuals he had spotted with the marking, all of whom were hanging around Myers.

"One man said something to me earlier," said I. "He mentioned Wilder must have dropped him some money for his coming campaign."

"It makes sense. This is what Jacob meant! Lamech's man, right before he shot himself. He mentioned a bigger game. The anarchists have got their greatest enemy into a room and will kill him," said Reid.

"It's not going to be a straightforward killing!" said I.

"We're running out of time. We need to get Lord Myers out of here," said Hewitt.

"The flowers?" Reid asked.

"Everyone is wearing them; is that their method of murder?" returned Hewitt.

"Poisoned food or drink?" I offered.

"Where is Holmes?" Reid asked.

"I don't know," I said. "I thought he would have come back by now."

"Doctor, I think you should keep an eye on Lord Myers before he gets up to that machine," said Hewitt.

I nodded and made my way towards the Lord. He looked at me oddly. He fingered the glass in his hand before setting it down and walking over to me. Crowds of people still gathered around Wilder's machine.

"I know your face," said Myers. "You're that doctor chap who partners with that sleuth, aren't you?"

"Come again?" I asked.

"Yes, you helped one of my colleagues out some time ago, I remember. Reginald Donovan, the little incident with the missing gem. He said the sleuth could tell the thief was left-handed and had recently spilt vinegar on their hands. Turns out it was the cook who took the gem. And it was all done by examining the box from which it was taken!"

"Yes, that is me," I returned. "My name is Doctor Watson."

"Of course, Doctor Watson… where is your friend, the sleuth?"

"Mr Sherlock Holmes? He's not here presently."

"Is he on another case?" the Lord asked.

"He is, in fact. If you'll step out into the hall, I'll tell you all about it." He gave me an odd look.

"Why can't you tell me here?"

I said nothing. His expression went from excitement to fear.

"My life isn't in danger, is it?"

I drew near the Lord and whispered into his ear: "Though I strongly disagree with your beliefs and prejudices, my Lord, I do not wish to see you come to harm, which you will should you remain here."

He gave me a piercing stare. He walked towards the door and I followed behind.

I saw Reid in conversation with an old woman. He looked perturbed. As we left the room, I noticed someone following us; one of the anarchists must have seen us leave. A few of the guests were outside, blocking a secret exit. I told Lord Myers to follow me. We went in the opposite direction, and then down the first corridor we came upon.

I told Myers to stop a moment. I could hear footsteps. I looked back down the hall and could see a long shadow approaching. I started trying door handles. They were locked. We turned down another hall just as the figure came into view at the other end. I pulled on a handle, but the door was locked. Lord Myers grabbed my arm. I looked at him and saw his gaze was ahead. I turned and saw, to my horror, the tall, lanky figure of the Goblin Man. I could hear the footsteps getting closer. We were trapped.

The Goblin Man slowly crept towards us. His dead eyes pierced me. He held a blood-stained blade. In the other hand was a cricket bat with a number of nails sticking out of the top. Lord Myers turned to run back down the hall. He was out of my sight, but I would not take my eye off this goblin. I heard a gasp. Lord Myers was escorted back around the corner with a revolver to his head by the man who had followed us out.

"Come with usss," came the voice of the Goblin Man.

We were taken through a series of corridors and out through a side door. The Goblin ordered us to get into the cab. Lord Myers was put into the cab first. The Goblin stood back while the man with the gun pressed it into my back, pushing me forward. I turned to sit in the cab. As I did, the man holding the gun lowered his hand. I quickly grabbed his hand and, twisting it, loosened the gun from his grip. The Goblin charged at me. I snatched the gun and fired a shot. He stepped back and growled. I was struck from behind and fell to the ground.

The gun fell out of my grip, but before I could get it I was surrounded by the other man and the Goblin. The goblin picked up the gun and handed it to his partner before standing over me and putting his foot upon my chest. He rolled the blade over my face and chuckled. With the point down, he stepped off and ran the blade down my torso. I waited for any moment when he would drive the blade into my stomach, and I would watch in horror as my insides were torn out, just like White. With a shout, the two turned as Lord Myers leapt from the cab at them. The three rolled on the ground. I heard a blood-curdling scream as I witnessed the Goblin leap upon the Lord and pierce his right shoulder with the blade. The Goblin picked him up and held the blade to his neck. The Goblin's partner aimed the gun at my head. We were pushed inside. The Goblin yelled for the driver to carry on.

*****

Silence hung heavy in the cab as it rattled through the darkened London streets. The windows were covered with thick curtains, which prevented us from seeing out or anyone from seeing in. Lord Myers held his wound; the blood was seeping through his clothes and running down his hand. The Goblin sat next to the dignitary with one foot on the seat, his arm resting on his knee, with the stained blade in his hand, ready to lunge forward. His partner sat next to me with his gun at the ready.

We were in the cab for some time; how long I could not tell. By the time we stopped, Lord Myers had lost a fair amount of blood. As we stepped out into the night, with the moonlight falling upon us, I could see that he was sickly pale. The Goblin grabbed him and jerked him around. It took me a moment to get my bearings; we were on a bridge with the Thames rushing beneath us. With a revolver in my back, I watched in terror as the Goblin cuffed the lord and attached a long chain to the cuffs before forcing him onto the ledge.

"Do you know the story of Moses and the Pharaoh?" the Goblin asked.

"Wha… what?" returned Myers, whimpering.

"Yes, you see the Pharaoh had oppressed the Jews, turned them into slaves, beat them, killed them, raped the women; all the while he lived high up in his castle."

Lord Myers wobbled on the ledge while the Goblin paced behind him. I could see Myers trying to keep an eye on him as he anticipated the inevitable fall.

"What have I ever done to you?" Lord Myers cried.

"What haven't you done?" the Goblin yelled.

He jerked Myers back, causing him to scream. Suddenly I felt the revolver move from my back and heard a strange grunt from behind. I turned to see my captor being held from behind by a mysterious figure. I looked at the Goblin, who was still yelling at his victim, unaware of what was happening. The man fell unconscious, and I looked up to see the face of Sherlock Holmes. He picked up the man's revolver and nodded at me.

"You, Lord Myers! You have oppressed the Jews of London, tried to smoke us out like rats, and acted as if we are a poison to your elitist society. My people have wanted your head for many years, and now, now it will be delivered to them; but more than that, the money, all that money, you gave to Wilder—he's a Jew. A Jew will be feeding Britain with a new array of weapons, ones that we will use to hunt scum like you down; and our God, he will crush you. Crush you in the water just as God did to Pharaoh's people as they charged after the freed Jews through the Red Sea."

Holmes fired a shot. The Goblin leapt back and looked over towards us. The bulbous eyes shone in the moonlight. He grabbed the Lord. "Take one more shot, and he will die."

"It's over, Goblin," said Holmes. "Wilder is already arrested. You were the final piece. The game is over, Ruth."

The Goblin Man stood there, motionless. "It might be over, but it doesn't mean our task has failed. The murder of this man will be righteous!"

He pushed the Lord, and we watched him fall. As he plummeted, he let out a terrified scream that echoed about us. The chain rattled as it ripped over the edge. Holmes and I charged after the Goblin, who ran away laughing.

"Get Myers!" yelled Holmes as he chased the Goblin.

I looked over the edge. Lord Myers was under the water. I pulled the chain as hard as I could. Slowly but surely, I lifted him from the water. My arms strained as I tugged the chain. It was then that I realised how cold the air was, as the metal chain felt like it was burning against my skin. I could hear Lord Myers panting and coughing as he emerged from the waters below.

I could feel my arms weakening. Give me the most strenuous task on the hottest day, and I shall not flinch, but ever since my Afghan campaign, the cold has not been something I could handle with ease.

I felt my arms begin to give. The chain nearly left my hand, but Holmes had returned and grabbed it. He and I pulled the Lord to safety. When we pulled him over the edge, he was shivering and going into hypothermia. We put him into the cab, and I tore the curtains off in order to keep him warm. Holmes left whilst I saw to the patient, but he came back a moment or two later. He threw the goblin mask into the back of the cab. I looked out and saw Holmes standing there with a woman lying on the ground. It was Ruth Lamech. Holmes had subdued the woman with chloroform.

Thus, the Goblin Man mystery, the disappearance of Phillias Jackson, and the Whitechapel Disaster came to a bitter end on a cold autumn night over the Thames.

*****

Meanwhile, back at the Royal Geographical Society, Reid had been approached by an elderly woman. He informed me later that it was none other than Lamech's mother. As I was escorting Lord Myers out, she saw and recognised Reid. She, feeling guilty, told him that Jackson was Lamech's step-brother and was heir to their anarchist throne. She claimed she was too old for any more fighting or revenge.

Wilder was arrested by Reid and tried before a court for his crimes. He admitted to the use of the fire flower and the poisoning of Daniels and Lamech with Ruth's help. He also admitted to planting the explosive on the Whitechapel train. Jackson had planned to frame Daniels and Goodtree in order to acquire their business and use it to fund his anarchist schemes. The top of the list was to murder Lord Myers. Doctor Jonqueres came from France, at the request of Mr Hewitt, to offer his testimony, along with that of Lamech's mother. Jackson's connections to Osgen, the leader of the Peckham Liberal Club, became quite clear. It came out that she, too, was a target of the anarchist group for forcing young Jewish girls into prostitution, and when she learnt who Jackson was she wanted him out of the club and threatened to expose his connection to Lamech. Part of Osgen's blackmail resulted in Lord Myers being removed from his place in Parliament, as photographs of the Lord involving young Jewish girls were found in the Liberal Club. Ruth was further tried for her involvement and for the murder of Mr White and the attempted murder of Lord Myers.

*****

The rooms at Baker Street were filled once more with rolling smoke from Holmes's cherrywood pipe. Mrs Hudson had served us warm meats, roast potatoes, gravy, and hot tea. A fire created a soft golden glow in the room. Mr Hewitt and Brett, Inspector Reid, Sherlock Holmes, and I sat smoking and feasting together on the 17th of December. A light snow shower had fallen that day, and the roads were white.

"It's all very peaceful in this study of yours, Holmes," said Hewitt.

"It serves as an epicentre for all things outré in this jungle," Holmes returned, taking a puff of his pipe.

"It seems, Mr Brett, that you are well on your way to a nice recovery," said I.

"I am indeed, Doctor. I am only sorry I could not see the case out to the very end."

"Worry not, my dear Brett," said Mr Hewitt. "We are glad to have you with us."

"Though Mr White, that fiery, ginger doctor, he will never be forgotten," Brett said thoughtfully.

"He shall not, indeed," said Reid. "He was, for all his faults, a good man."

"I knew him from a past long ago," said Brett. Reid looked curious. "While I was ill, I wrote up the short story about the events that led me to believe White was a terrible man. But after the events at the Liberal Club, which I haven't the heart to speak aloud yet, I know him to be an honest one."

We all raised a glass of brandy and toasted White's memory. After much chatter, feasting, and smoking, we wished each other the compliments of the season as our friends and colleagues departed. Before Brett left, he handed me a pile of papers and told me it was his side of the case. After what happened with White, he did not feel he could hold on to it, but wanted it in safe hands. I took it and held it with care.

*****

A few days later, while Holmes and I sat in the study smoking and reading, I received a package from Inspector Reid containing his notes from the case. The events had taken their emotional toll on both Brett and Reid.

"Are you going to compile them?" Holmes asked, setting the paper he was reading down. "With your story included?"

"Our story, Holmes," said I, flipping through the pages.

"Quite right," he said with a nod.

"I think I shall. But I won't rewrite any of it. I shall keep their stories intact and not interweave them until our stories become one."

"Well, Watson. We all share the same interwoven story; simply the characters change as they come and go."

"You are correct, old man."

Holmes put his pipe back to his lips, opened the paper, and continued reading.

Epilogue
An Article by Mr Brett

This article was written by my colleague, Mr Brett, regarding a truth about Mr Vigo White. I have included it as an end piece to our narrative, as I feel it brings about the final conclusion:

Vigo White of Whitechapel, a man of science with fiery red hair, died at the hands of a brutal murderer in autumn 1890.

Mr White was in no way a famous man or one held in high esteem, save by a few within H Division. He led a long and difficult life, which followed him to the end. What can be attested to, however, is his strength and courage. He was no white knight, but a dark rider. A man with questionable morals, but a good heart nevertheless. He first came to my acquaintance many years ago while he trained to be a doctor in the North of England. He was born in Oldham to a Mr John and Darcy White. His mother was half Italian, and they named their son after her grandfather, Vigo. It was a series of events in December of 18— that brought our paths together for what I thought would be the only time.

Many will remember the tragic story of Isabella Taylorson, wife to a Mr Archibald Taylorson of Salford. Archibald Taylorson was a wealthy man who built his name within the steam industry. It was December 24th, 18—, when his wife, Isabella, pressed through the busy crowds in Market Street, withdrew a revolver, and shot herself dead. Found on her person was a note from Mr Vigo White, pleading with her to leave her husband.

As a result of the court case, it was revealed that Vigo White and Mrs Taylorson had entered into a relationship. Mr Taylorson had forbidden the two to see each other, but Mr White repeatedly tried, time and time again, to coerce Mrs Taylorson to leave her husband. It was said that drugs were used on Mrs Taylorson which affected her mental stability and caused her to end her life in such a dramatic fashion. It was suggested that Mr White was responsible for the death, as he was using experimental medication on her. It was all conjecture, and no solid proof was ever unearthed to pin Mr White to Mrs Taylorson's suicide. As a result of the hearing, Mr White was expelled from his medical training, and withdrew from all social circles.

I was with Mr White before he was viciously killed. A series of strange events brought us together that I can now only see as an act of providence. A final opportunity to clear a man whom I thought was completely guilty of what were false accusations.

It is true that Mr White had entered into a relationship with Mrs Taylorson; it is true that he pleaded with her to run away. What was never revealed during the initial case was his complete motivation for his pleas. It was partly due to a forbidden love between the two, this much we knew, but also his desire to see her in safe hands. Further investigation revealed that Mrs Taylorson had a series of bruises on her body—Mr White was accused of this treatment. The truth is Mr White met Mrs Taylorson at a social gathering. He was a young man, and she was an elegant bride of a rich man. It was at this gathering that White noticed a coldness between Mr and Mrs Taylorson. As Mr White got closer to Mr Taylorson, he discovered a dark truth: Mr Taylorson regularly beat his wife, and subjected her to forced sexual encounters. She confided in Mr White and no one else. The two made plans to run away, but when Mr Taylorson caught them on a December afternoon, he made sure she was never to see Mr White again. While it was told that she never left the house due to fear of Mr White, the truth was that Mr Taylorson had locked her up in her rooms. Mr White continued to sneak letters to Mrs Taylorson, and they continued to make plans for her escape.

Mrs Taylorson was meant to creep out of the house and take a cab to the city centre of Manchester, where she was supposed to find Mr White waiting for her at a small inn. She managed her escape, found her way to the city, and without any warning, shot herself dead. After the case was over and Mr White was released of the charges and forced to stop his medical education, he was visited by Mr Taylorson. Mr Taylorson informed Mr White that he knew all along what was happening. He planned his wife's death around their 'escape'.

Mr White recalled what Mr Taylorson said to him: "I came up behind her, shot her in the head in front of everyone, and no one knew. That, Mr White, isn't luck or chance. That is power. Something you'll never have. If she wasn't going to be mine, she wasn't going to be yours."

It was March 18— when Mr Taylorson was found dead in his study. He had taken a fatal injection of cocaine. On his writing desk was a note which read: "I, Archibald Taylorson, am the destroyer of lives, including my own."

On April 18—, Mr White relocated himself to London. Despite being forced out of professional medical training, he continued to study medicine and became of great use to Scotland Yard's H Division for several years. If my younger self had the wisdom I do today, perhaps I could have seen through the cracks in the story when they transpired. Perhaps I could have aided Mr White rather than worked against him with every stroke of my pen. As I said, providence has given me this chance to right a wrong.

Before Mr White's passing, we were thrust together for one final adventure. My heart was, at first, cold towards him, as I regarded him as a fiend, a destroyer of things good, and a devil who slipped through the Law's grip. I regret, now, that I'll never get to know him better for who he really was—a good man, a brave man. Moments before a terrible attack befell us, he confided the story which I told above, and, while at first I was sceptical, he proved to be a good man by saving my life. He will be remembered.

A Scandal in America

The Letter

To Sherlock Holmes, she is always the Woman. It was, as I recall, late March of 1888 when a most peculiar case descended upon my friend. The King of Bohemia had sought the aid of Sherlock Holmes when a scandalous photograph of the King and the beautiful Irene Adler had surfaced. The King feared Miss Adler's intentions were to ruin him by exposing this photograph prior to his wedding to the daughter of the King of Scandinavia.

Holmes put his remarkable mental powers to work to locate and retrieve this photograph, thereby ending the ordeal for the Bohemian King. He was, however, outsmarted by the woman, Irene Adler. When he attempted to take the scandalous photograph, Holmes simply found a note from Irene Adler and a photograph of herself. The note stated that she had fled the country with her new husband, Godfrey Norton, a lawyer, and that they would not return. There was, however, no need to chase Irene Adler and Godfrey Norton. It was made clear that she had no intention of using the scandalous photograph, but held it solely for her own protection.

My friend had only the greatest respect for Miss Adler. It was common for him to keep small souvenirs from his cases, and in this case, he kept her photograph. There were very few women that Holmes and I encountered in our career together towards whom he showed any signs of 'attraction'. In fact, Miss Adler was the only woman he admired enough to possess a photograph of. Lastly, Irene Adler was the only woman for whom he would willingly set aside his pressing cases to answer her call when she was in great despair.

*****

It was, as I look through my notes, the summer of 1890. Between my marriage and practice, I hadn't seen Holmes in some time and found myself sitting with him in our old rooms of 221B Baker Street. Holmes, dressed in his mouse-coloured dressing gown, was slouched over in his chair, rummaging through papers, and I, sitting in my former chair, was quietly sipping a warm cup of tea while reading the morning newspaper. Since I had last seen Holmes, he had been engaged on the Katharine Dobbs case, which had recently concluded. With no warning, Holmes dramatically threw the papers which he had been looking through onto the floor and shot up from his chair, letting out an exhausted sigh as he stretched.

"Katharine Dobbs, Watson, was a vile woman!" he declared. "Are you aware of the matter yet?"

"I must say that I am not. You have yet to tell me the ins and outs of the case," I replied.

"She had become so disgusted with her father's new wife that she attempted to poison her stepmother, Annabelle, who was, in fact, a lovely woman. Had it not been for Katharine's sister Dorothy bringing her concerns to me, their stepmother would be dead this very moment!"

"Thank heavens this Dorothy came to you when she did," said I. "What has become of Katharine Dobbs?"

"She's dead," said Holmes coolly.

"Dead!" I cried. "Pray, tell me what happened?"

"When she discovered I was on her trail, primarily by the fact that stains on Katharine's fingernails revealed frequent use of arsenic, she attempted to hurry the matter up and prepared a lethal dose of poison for her stepmother. Her sister, Dorothy, caught her, per my instructions to keep a close eye on her, and Katharine fell victim to her own deadly chemical when the sisters engaged in a brawl."

"I should like to look over the notes from this case when there is time. I'm sorry that I could not accompany you," I admitted, envious of my friend's ongoing adventures without me.

As much as I enjoyed my medical career, there was nothing quite like the excitement of the chase, which was always the norm in my friend's life.

"I am sorry for that, too, Watson," said he. "The case has birthed an interesting train of thought. I should like to look deeper into the effects that one's personality may have on their physical appearance.

"Had this case never been brought to me and I happened to pass someone like Katharine Dobbs on the street, I would know at first glance that she possessed no good qualities whatsoever. If ever a morbid personality affected the way in which one was presented, she would have made a fine case study. She had the appearance of a vile witch found in any of the Grimm tales," concluded my friend.

"What is the next case which you plan to take up?" I asked.

"As you know, old boy, there are many ongoing cases that I am always toiling over. However, let us see what we have." He picked up a stack of letters from the mantel which had accumulated over the previous weeks. "Fionnula Goggin, Reverend Fitz-Lloyd, Royston Luckinbill, Bill Bramble, Rose Pickles, Wilber Plaskitt." Holmes smiled, reading out the names written upon the letters. "I say, Watson, what foreigner could read these names and believe the English to be a stiff and sombre-minded people?"

"Says the great Sherlock Holmes himself," I replied. "Names are a funny thing…" Our attention was arrested by a gentle tapping on the study door.

"Come in," said Holmes. The door opened, and there stood a young pageboy. He was somewhere near thirteen years of age, stood roughly five feet tall, was neatly dressed, and held a small square parcel, no bigger than my palm, under his arm. He rubbed his nose and looked at both Holmes, who was now standing, and me.

"Mr Holmes?" he asked.

"The one and only," he returned.

"I have a package for you," said the young lad as he walked towards Holmes, holding the parcel out.

"You have a curious look upon your face, my boy. What is on your mind?" asked Holmes.

"You see, sir, I mean no disrespect to you at all. I know of you, all right. I've heard lots of your cases and, well, I ain't never seen a picture of you and, that is, I thought you'd be stronger-looking, Mr Holmes," the boy reluctantly admitted.

I chuckled at the boy's comment. Holmes looked over at me; he, too, was amused by this, and a smile graced his face.

"Do you hear that, Dr. Watson?" Holmes said. "I'm not very strong-looking, it seems." He motioned for the boy to hold still, and raced over to a pile of old newspapers before withdrawing one and walking back over. "My boy," continued Holmes, "do not rely on outward appearance to determine strength. The strongest muscle one can exercise is the mind, but I must also defend my honour, as I do not wish for you to go back and tell all your friends that the great Sherlock Holmes is but a weak old man!" As he spoke, he handed the boy the newspaper. "Do you recognise that man in that picture?" he asked, pointing somewhere on the page.

"I do," acknowledged the boy. "That is Danny, the Steam Engine, Palmer. He's a champion boxer!"

"He was a champion boxer," corrected Holmes. "As you can see from this paper, he was arrested a few years back and sentenced to hang for his involvement in the Fleet Street murders. He acted as the gang's muscle, and was paid a hefty price for his service. The cherished minds of Scotland Yard were having trouble bringing the gang to justice, and sought my aid. As you see from this picture, Danny 'the Steam Engine' Palmer was found badly beaten upon his arrest. Who do you think did that?"

The boy looked up at Holmes, his eyes wide and his mouth open. "You?" he asked.

"Indeed!" exclaimed Holmes. "Though I value the constant stimulation and workout of the mind, I am also a very skilled fighter. I have trained both in baritsu and martial arts. However, you don't need to be weighed down with pounds of muscle to be an effective fighter."

"I never thought of it like that!"

"Now you have something to ponder for the day, my boy," said Holmes.

The boy smiled at Holmes and nodded. "Good day to you both!" he said, turning and darting out the door.

Holmes discarded the old newspaper, and reached for the parcel which he had laid down. Taking it into his hands and holding it high in the air, he began to examine it.

"Who is it from?" I pressed.

"No name," said he, taking a seat in his chair. Holmes tore the paper away, and revealed a small wooden box with a latch on the front. He popped the latch, and as he did so, his eyes widened. "My, my, Watson, this is most engaging," said he.

He lifted something out of the small parcel. I could hardly believe my eyes when his extended palm revealed the contents. It was a large emerald. Holmes held it up into the light pouring in through the window; it sparkled beautifully.

"My word, Holmes! Is that real? It must be worth a fortune!" I exclaimed.

Holmes stood up and went to his desk, pulling out a pair of jeweller's glasses, and then shot over to our bay window where the sun shone, and studied the emerald.

"It is real, and certainly worth a fortune," said Holmes after a lengthy examination.

"What are you to do with it?" I asked, standing up and walking towards him.

"Hand me the box it came in." Holmes took it from my hand and pulled out a small envelope. He opened it, and read the letter concealed inside.

Having seen Holmes read many unusual letters in our time together, none seemed to impact him as this one. This letter was from no ordinary client. His eyes were not lit with excitement from the strange; rather, he was deeply concerned. When finished reading, he held the letter at his side and uttered not a word. He walked past me to his chair, and seated himself once more.

"What is it?" I asked.

His face was turned from me, and he gazed into the fireplace.

"The woman," he returned.

"Irene Adler?"

"Correct."

"What does she want?"

"She wants us to come to America to investigate the death of her husband, Godfrey Norton," said he, slowly turning and looking at me.

"Norton is dead! Dear Lord, and she begs audience with you in America?" I questioned.

"Yes, Watson. That is where she and Godfrey relocated to after our incident with the Bohemian King. She took up operatic roles and has become well settled, from what I've read." He extended his hand and gave me the letter from Irene Adler, which read thus:

My Dear Mr Sherlock Holmes,

I need your assistance. Godfrey, my husband, has been killed. I found him shot dead in his office in Manhattan. It is a murder staged as a suicide. The police have bought into the charade, but I will not. How do I know it wasn't suicide? Three trifles that the police ignore.

First, the gun was on the left side of the floor; Godfrey is right-handed. Second, there was a unique ash left in the tray. Godfrey, though he occasionally smoked, kept his office clear of any such tobacco use. The ash was not his. Third, lying just by his face was a gold doubloon. Someone was threatening him, this much I am sure. His behaviour was erratic and very unlike himself the week leading up to his death. What secrets Godfrey had, I am not sure, but I am sure he was murdered. Mr Holmes, I can only do so much on my own. This is still a man's world; women are still awaiting their liberation. I trust this case only to you now.

I have sent this wire with instructions to first obtain the emerald you now hold. I left it in London in case I ever needed a bargaining chip to obtain your services. The selling of the emerald will pay for your and Dr. Watson's travel costs, and the remainder will be your payment for the case. If I am correct, you will receive this letter in the late morning five days from my writing it. You will have two hours at most to make arrangements and let Dr. Watson persuade his dear wife to let him accompany you before you make the journey to Southampton by the 2 p.m. train, where the steamship The Eagle will be departing at 6 p.m. to carry you both to New York.

Find me at home in Salem in Westchester, at Bell House. Mr Holmes, as you need Watson, so I need you. Please hurry.

Always,
Irene Adler

P.S. I hear you kept my picture.

"What are you to do?" I asked.
"She is not the kind of woman who would simply ask for aid. She is a bright woman, the most savvy of her sex," said Holmes contemplatively. "Nevertheless, Watson, I will answer her call!"
"You're going to America?"

155

"No," he replied, "we are going to America. She's called for us both. Now we've already wasted valuable time. Go speak with Mrs Watson and get her permission, and make the necessary arrangements for your practice. Meet me here in an hour's time!" Before I could utter a reply, Holmes threw off his dressing gown and ran out the door to some unknown destination.

*****

Taking a hansom, I made haste to my home, where I found Mary sitting in the lounge. I told her of the letter and Irene Adler's call for help in this investigation.

"John! This is so sudden!" my wife protested.

"I know it is," said I. "I would not ask this of you if it were not of great importance."

"What am I to do? How long will you be gone for?" she asked. I could tell by the look upon her face that she was deeply troubled by my wishing to go away. One of my wife's most admirable traits, however, was her ability to put up with my desire for adventure.

"I am not entirely sure. It would be an adequate assumption, at best, to say a month," said I reluctantly. "There is no telling how long or short a case will be, but considering the distance…" I took Mary into my arms and embraced her.

"John, I want you to be safe," she replied quietly. "I should not wish to keep you from an adventure, and I know how much excitement you have when you are off with Holmes. You two are like silly schoolboys exploring in the woods."

I looked into Mary's eyes, which were very bright as she smiled at me.

"Thank you, my dear," said I, and kissed her.

"Come, let me help you pack!" she said, and we darted into the bedroom where I pulled out my brown case.

By the time I had packed and found a local doctor who was willing to see to my patients in my absence, I realised I had but twenty minutes to return to Baker Street. I took my wife by one hand and my case in the other, and asked her to come with me to Baker Street and see us off from there.

*****

Mary and I found Holmes standing by the window, smoking a pipe while he waited for me in the study. "Ah, Mrs Watson," said Holmes, turning towards us as we walked inside.

"Hello, Mr Holmes. I see you are taking my husband away from me yet again," Mary said with a smile.

"I did send him to get your permission. I would not dare take him away without it," said Holmes.

"All I ask is that you both be careful. America is such a rugged land, and lacks the civility that we have obtained here in Britain."

"Fear not, my dear," said I, "Holmes and I will be safe and back soon enough."

"I swear to keep your husband safe, Mrs Watson, and perhaps bring him back a few pounds lighter. Your cooking has certainly wreaked its havoc."

"I take it you've made arrangements for any clients that come to you while we're away?" said I, diverting Holmes and Mary's conversation from my stomach.

"I have. There is an Investigator named Hewitt near the Strand. He will stand in for me in my absence."

"Very well," said I, "I think we should be off if we want to arrive in Southampton in time to board The Eagle."

"Correct, Watson."

Mary and I descended the stairs, and Holmes followed behind with his luggage. We loaded our cases into a cab, and I embraced Mary before taking my seat next to Holmes inside.

"My dear Mrs Watson," said Holmes, leaning over me and poking his head through the open door of the cab. "Do keep an eye on Mrs Hudson while we are away. She worries far too much, and your company would be most welcome."

"I will," Mary replied. She blew me a kiss, and with the crack of the driver's whip, we were on our way.

*****

The journey from London to Southampton was not thrilling in any sense; rushed for time, but nothing more. Holmes was captured in thought and spoke little. He held the letter from Irene Adler and skimmed over it repeatedly.

"She wrote this the day Godfrey died. Her handwriting is rushed. I suspect that the local authorities brushed off her case rather quickly," said Holmes towards the end of our train journey.

"Is there any chance Mrs Adler has let her emotions get the better of her?" I asked.

"I trust you have not forgotten our first encounter with her, Watson. She is quick and not one to be played as the fool," said Holmes. "A woman like her would not ask our aid if it was not needed."

"Do you suspect the police?" I asked. "If they brushed it off so quickly, are they hiding something?"

"I haven't the facts to back the theory, but that is not an outlandish assumption. Ah, we are pulling into the station. Let us hurry."

Holmes and I quickly made our way to the docklands, where we found The Eagle waiting. It was a large and remarkable piece of steamboat engineering. Holmes acquired our tickets while I stood with our luggage. Looking at the ship, I judged that the length of this vessel was close to six hundred feet. There were two massive cylinders which expelled a cloud of steam as they prepared to leave the dock.

Crowds of people were rushing by with their luggage and racing up onto the deck. I looked at my watch and saw the time was a quarter to six. If Holmes did not hurry, we would miss the boat. My worries were quickly settled when I saw Holmes push through the hordes of people with two tickets in his hand.

We made our way onto the deck, through a door, and down some stairs. We descended a couple of levels and squeezed through narrow corridors before we reached our shared room. There were two single beds, a table with two small chairs, a dresser, and a shower room.

"Come, Watson," said Holmes, "let us leave our luggage and watch the ship depart from the dock."

With not a moment to lose, Holmes and I made our way atop. It seemed that all the passengers had the same idea we did. We pressed through and stood against the railing, and looked down below as the flocks on the dock waved at us. The ship let out a great blast, and with a jerk and a tug, the great vessel pulled away.

Holmes and I stood there for some time, watching our island grow further and further away before he said: "Thank you for coming with me, dear Watson."

Arrival in New York City

The journey across the Atlantic was filled with peaceful relaxation. At times, during this venture, I forgot my true reason for even being on the ship. The sea air, the bright blue sky, the star-filled nights—it was all most refreshing to the mind and body.

Irene Adler's case was far from my thoughts. Holmes, however, spent a great deal of time locked away in the room. He would often come out in the morning for a bit of fresh air before going into the dining hall, which was adorned with a large glass ceiling, crystal chandeliers, bright gold trim, wonderfully crafted pillars with intricate patterns, firm oak tables with shining silver cutlery, and crystal glasses.

I found myself wandering the deck and leaning over the rails, watching the water splash as this mighty vessel ploughed onwards. On a few occasions, I witnessed dolphins leaping out and racing along with the ship, the creatures letting out cheerful chirps as they exploded out of the water.

I rose early on the day we arrived in New York City. The sun itself had but only begun to rise and sparkle off the glass-like water as I came out upon the deck. I could see land in the distance.

"Marvellous, is it not?" said Holmes as he walked towards me.

"It is," I returned.

We stood there together as The Eagle made its way from the open sea into the bay. With astonishment, we gazed upon the great copper Statue of Liberty, now starting to turn a teal-green from weathering, erected high with its torch raised into the heavens. We approached the island of Manhattan, which was cluttered with immense towering buildings, much taller than anyone would see in London.

"There is certainly a desire for grandiose designs, wouldn't you say, Watson?" Holmes chuckled.

"How right you are."

"Let us retrieve our luggage and be ready to vacate the ship as soon as possible. We will need to get a train as close as we can to the address Miss Adler gave us."

I accompanied Holmes to our room, and we gathered our belongings before returning to the deck. When The Eagle docked, we were among the first to alight. With a few directions, Holmes and I wandered into the jungle of Manhattan. Holmes often referred to London as a jungle, a reference I wholeheartedly understood, but if London was a jungle, New York was the wild Amazon. Though the atmosphere was not entirely foreign to us, the locals were an unusual breed. The chatter of men and women with harsh, bitter accents made some of the strongest Cockney or Irish accents seem almost poetic.

Holmes had no trouble blending in. He approached a young man who was sitting atop a barrel eating a banana, and asked, in a perfect American accent, mind you, where we could find a cab. Holmes thanked the man and shook his hand, then signalled for me to follow by a slight tilt of his head. We passed between two brown brick buildings and found ourselves on a busy street. Holmes whistled and hailed a cab to stop.

"Where'm I takin' ya?" asked the driver.

"To the nearest railway station by which we can travel to Westchester," Holmes replied.

"Very well, sir," said the driver. "If you don't mind, where's that accent from? Are you an Englishman?"

"Yes, we're English," I replied rather sternly.

"Well, boys, I hope you got the grit to last here in these United States of America! God's land, it be," he replied with a devilish grin, and let out a howling laugh. "Well, whatcha waitin' for? Get in!"

"As you wish," Holmes said. He looked at me with a humorous glance as we stepped inside the cab and pressed on with the next leg of our venture.

After a shaky journey through the streets of Manhattan, Holmes and I found ourselves at a train station, where we bought return tickets to Salem, where Irene Adler had told us to find her. We boarded the carriage, and from Manhattan to Salem Holmes took the time to read the letter aloud to me, and I postulated, further, the cause of Mr Norton's death.

"What of the Bohemian King?" I remarked. "Might he have gone to extreme measures to retrieve, or force the hand of Irene Adler, so as to get the scandalous photograph back?"

"Ha! Watson, my man, you really are quite remarkable and imaginative," said Holmes. "The Bohemian King has long since forgotten that once-royal scandal, preoccupied with his country and his own children and wife."

"Well, Miss Adler was prone to scandal. Perhaps her affections swooned for a local boy…" We continued discussing for some time as the green landscape, not unlike our very own English countryside, dashed past us.

When we arrived in Salem, we found that the station was a wobbly wooden platform, void of shelter or benches. Surrounding us was a deep green wood that I assumed, at one point, would have been home to many natives. Holmes and I walked up a long dirt road, kicking up dust with every step. As we continued, my thoughts turned to my wife and her well-being. She was strong; I had no reason for concern, but this was the first time that the two of us had been separated by such a great distance.

"Here we are," said Holmes, cutting off my train of thought.

We stood before a tall iron gate with brick pillars on either side, connected to a stone fence that surrounded the home. I pushed the gate; it was locked. Holmes withdrew his burglar's kit and, in a matter of moments, opened the lock, and the iron doors swung open with a loud creak. We followed a pebbled path up to the front door of the large two-storey colonial home, which was painted a dazzling white. I went to knock on the door, but Holmes abruptly stopped me, grabbing my arm.

"Holmes?"

"Something is wrong," he said in a quiet voice.

"What do you mean?"

"Here," he replied, and pointed to the door handle and the crevice where the lock would have bolted into the frame. "These markings. You see them, Watson?" Holmes pointed out very small indentations in the wooden frame.

"Yes, I see them."

"Someone has already been here and pried the lock. See here, flakes of paint by your shoes. This is recent."

I set my luggage down and quickly opened it up, pulling my service revolver out.

"We need to make sure Miss Adler is safe!"

Holmes nodded, and with a slight push of the door, it opened, creaking at the hinges. We slowly crept inside. Directly within was a staircase. To our left was a passage, which led into a conjoining lounge and dining hall. The air inside was stagnant and stale. I could hear Holmes repeatedly sniffing the distasteful odour that permeated the air.

"What do you suppose that smell is?" I asked.

"Not entirely sure," whispered Holmes, "but I wager it is a type of tobacco."

"A type of tobacco you can't recognise?" said I.

"Come now, Watson," said Holmes as we continued to search the rooms.

The house had been ransacked, as if someone had been hurriedly looking for something. We walked quietly up the stairs, doing our best not to creak the wooden steps. It did not take much time to poke inside each room and realise we were alone and void of immediate danger.

I found Holmes shuffling through some clothes inside a bedroom that I believed to be Irene Adler and Godfrey Norton's. On the wall, framed, were posters of various plays and operas she had performed in since our encounter with her in '88.

"What do you think, Holmes, was she taken by whoever dismantled the house?"

My friend did not respond at once, but walked about the room quietly. I stepped into the room and pulled the door to see what was behind it.

"Aha!" exclaimed Holmes.

"What is it?" I asked, turning towards him.

"Watson, look around. Tell me what you see!"

"I see a bed, which has been torn apart and cut at by a sharp object. I see a closet, which has been emptied of everything inside. I see a vanity with drawers hanging out, and cosmetics and powders over the floor, and," I paused to look behind me, "a dresser that has also been rifled through."

"Tell me more about the dresser, Watson."

"Is this the time for games?" I asked.

"Irene Adler is safe, fret not. We have time."

"Safe? How can you possibly know that?"

"The dresser," Holmes said.

I looked at it thoroughly for any clues, any signs that she might have left, but saw nothing but clothes and garments hanging out of the drawers.

"I see nothing," I admitted.

"On the contrary, you see everything I see, but you fail to pick up on one thing. In a house where everything is tousled, what stands out? Do not strain yourself, Watson, I'll tell you. A vase of flowers filled with fresh water that has not been knocked over." I then saw what Holmes had seen. Upon the dresser on the corner nearest the door was a glass vase of flowers. The water inside was indeed clear, and the flowers, too, were fresh.

"You think this is a message from Adler?"

"No, the message is underneath. From where you stand, the white card hidden under the vase is blocked by the stems, but from where I stand, I can see its reflection where the glass bends."

I picked up the vase, and sure enough, there was a small card under it. Handwritten upon the card was this message:

227 Lenox Ave, Harlem. Third Floor.

"Let us be off, Watson!" said Holmes, taking the card and tucking it into his pocket, and we, as rapidly as we could, made our way back to Manhattan, where we hoped to find Irene Adler.

*****

Several hours had passed since we arrived in America, and we had taken little time to rest or even discard our luggage. By the time we arrived at 227 Lenox Avenue, the sun was setting, and my body was tired. We stood before the three-storey brownstone. Holmes knocked firmly on the door, but received no answer. I noticed a dim light on the third floor. After a moment, Holmes opened his luggage and pulled out his leather pouch in which he stored his pins for picking locks. Then, with a great sweeping motion, the door was flung open; Holmes stumbled backwards, and I shot straight up. There, standing in the doorway, silhouetted by a light glowing from behind, was a woman. One hand remained on the door handle; in the other, a small pistol pointed down at Holmes.

"Mrs Norton," said Holmes as he picked himself up and straightened his collar.

"Adler, you can call me Miss Adler," the woman replied. She smiled at us. It was infectious. She had remained as beautiful as ever.

"I trust you are not going to have us stand out here while we discuss our business," Holmes said.

"Forgive me, Mr Holmes, Doctor. Come in," said she, and we entered.

The lodging itself felt similar to Baker Street. There was a certain English flair to its décor. We were shown into a large study, which led to a kitchen separated by a couple of French doors. The floors, though hardwood, were covered in thick fur carpets; a maroon-coloured paper with square patterns dressed the walls; lace curtains draped in front of the windows; and in the centre of this warmly lit study, just in front of the fireplace, were a comfortable two-seater sofa and an armchair with a table beside it.

"Don't think ill of me," Miss Adler said, "I would only have shot you if you were neither Holmes nor Dr. Watson."

"We have visited your house," said Holmes.

"It was in disarray," I added. "We thought we were too late, and that you had been taken or killed."

"Yes, I am not surprised. Someone is playing a game, but I do not know who," Miss Adler said thoughtfully. "That is why I left. I thought it best to hide, and therefore told the necessary people that I would be taking a holiday."

"Do you know what was being sought after by the vandals at your house?" Holmes asked.

"I'm sorry," I interjected, "but something does not make sense. Miss Adler, you believed your life was in danger, so you hid, yet you must have been at your house to leave us the clue to find you here."

"That is correct," she replied. "I saw that Godfrey was quickly buried and mourned, and decided that after his funeral, I would hide. I knew that his death was by no means self-inflicted, and suspected whoever came after him might also come after me. I did not wish to be a corpse when you and Mr Holmes turned up, so I made the arrangements to leave under the pretence that I would be vacationing. I left a reliable partner instructions to notify me if any suspicious characters showed up at my house. I was notified of this a few days ago. I knew, roughly, when you would arrive, so earlier today I donned a disguise and snuck into my house to leave you the message. When I saw what had been done to my home, for it was my first viewing of it since I took to hiding, I left Mr Holmes a clue. I knew he would notice the one untouched thing in the house. I returned here in case whoever pillaged my house returned."

"I'm afraid you must forgive Dr Watson, Miss Adler. I may be able to function and keep up on an empty stomach, but he cannot," said Holmes.

"Then let me get you something to drink and eat," our host offered.

"That would be splendid, thank you," said I.

A short while later, Miss Adler had provided us with some cold meat and a bottle of whiskey. Sitting comfortably on the sofa and feeling refreshed, Holmes began to question her.

"We shan't waste any more time," Holmes began. "Tell me all that happened with Godfrey Norton, and leave nothing out."

"I know your methods, Mr Holmes," said Miss Adler with a crooked smile. She composed herself as she pondered the events that had seen her smile quickly fade. "Godfrey and I, our marriage was good. I was happy. We have been successful since coming to New York. He was hired into a law firm, and I was welcomed back on stage and performed regularly. All was well; he kept nothing from me."

"Does his death have anything to do with the opium addiction?" Holmes suddenly asked. Miss Adler's eyes widened, and I turned to Holmes in shock.

"Opium?" I questioned.

"Yes, his clothes were riddled with the smells of an opium den. Watson, you saw me examining them in their room. The scent was faint, but it was there," said the detective.

"I had no intention of keeping that information from you. But the truth is, I cannot give you an answer. If that has had some part to play, I am not yet aware of why or how. He was not addicted to the substance when we fell in love back in London. It happened when we came to America. Through work at Morrison & James, he was asked to travel to Nevada and assist with some legal matters there; it was when he returned that he developed a taste for it. I didn't fight him over it, but told him I didn't wish to be part of it. That aside, we had no troubles.

"It was, if I recall, three days before his death that I noticed his queer behaviour. He was nervous and short in his replies. When I asked him what was wrong, he simply said, 'Problems at work, Ren. I have much on my plate at the moment.' I was preparing for a weekend show and needed to stay in the city, so I let him alone and told him I'd see him Sunday night. I was able to leave the city early and arrived back there sometime around five o'clock in the afternoon.

"I found a note from Godfrey saying he was going to be at the office for a couple of days. I found this to be incredibly strange, and without any care, I travelled back to the city to speak with him. When I arrived at the firm, the doors were locked. I picked the door, and when I went into his office he was there, shot dead. I immediately noticed that the scene was meant to look as if he had done it himself.

"The wound was on the left side of his head and the gun was just near his left hand, on the floor. Godfrey was right-handed; why would he kill himself using his left hand? It doesn't make sense. I then noticed the ash on his desk. He smokes, but never in his office, which implies to me that he is not alone. Lastly, upon his desk lay a gold doubloon bearing the year 1701. The doubloon was there for one reason only. It was a threat. The police tossed it all off as trifles and ignored my concerns. 'Suicide, clearly,' they kept telling me over and over, but it's not, Mr Holmes. Someone murdered Godfrey, and I want you to help me find them so that justice can be brought upon them."

"The ash, did you save it?" Holmes asked.

"I did," Miss Adler replied, and walked over to a desk drawer and pulled out a sealed envelope.

Holmes took it from her and sniffed. "Curious," he muttered under his breath.

"What is it?" I asked.

"A familiar scent. Miss Adler, what else can you tell me about the office? Was anything out of order?" Holmes questioned.

"His desk. The drawers, three on each side, were open but at various lengths," she informed us.

"Was anything stolen?" Holmes asked.

"Nothing appeared to be taken. No other cabinet or anything had been touched; simply his desk, and nothing inside was disturbed."

"Fascinating," said Holmes. "Was there evidence of fresh opium use?"

"None at all," she replied. I could see her eyes welling up, but she bit her lip to stop herself from shedding any tears. "I should never have dismissed his addiction, and I should have pressed harder when I knew something was wrong!"

"Did you ever follow him to find out where he partook of the substance?" I asked.

"I loved him, Doctor," said she sternly. "I was not the type of bride to hound his every step."

"And they say that love is blind," Holmes remarked. "Given the amount of time that has passed, I would assume Norton's office is no longer intact?"

"Actually, it is. I persuaded the firm to keep it as is until the day after tomorrow to give you enough time to get here and have a look."

"Well done," said Holmes with a smile. "Then tomorrow, our first line of inquiry will be to look over his office!" After some persuasion by Miss Adler, Holmes and I agreed to stay at her brownstone for the night rather than venture out and find a hotel. Near ten o'clock, we dispersed into our separate chambers and rested before the next day's outings.

I woke up around seven o'clock in the morning. I could smell the delicious aroma of freshly brewed coffee. In the study, Adler was sitting with Holmes. She lounged upon the sofa in a lovely olive dress, with her hair gathered up, and several yellow lilies pinned around her left ear. Holmes, however, was sitting with crossed legs in the armchair.

"Good morning, Doctor," acknowledged Miss Adler.

I greeted them both.

"Have some toast and some coffee. I wish to be out within the hour to Norton's office," said Holmes.

"Very well. Are you accompanying us, Miss Adler?" I asked.

"I am not. Mr Holmes believes it best to remain hidden," she replied with slight distaste in her tone.

"Surely you are not much safer here than at home?" I asked.

"I had the same question, Watson," admitted Holmes. "However, it seems that Miss Adler has taken a tip from my handbook. This lodging is known only to her."

"Are you that worried for your safety?" I asked her as I poured myself a cup of coffee and sat in the armchair opposite Holmes.

"I'm not worried about my safety. I just like my privacy. There is no harm in that," she said.

I quickly ate and drank, so that within an hour Holmes and I were wandering the streets of Manhattan, making our way towards Norton's office at 82 Park Place Avenue.

"Surely any useful evidence will have been taken by the local authorities?" I questioned.

"I'm not looking for anything that they found. If I feel the need to consult them after we have had a chance to look around, I will," said Holmes.

"Ah, we're here," said I as we turned the corner.

82 Park Place was an eleven-storey building constructed from tan-coloured bricks. We passed through an arched entrance and into the main lobby. It was a fine establishment, brightly lit with marble floors and fine wood trimmings. We made our way to the firm's floor and were greeted by a tall man with a round face and thick white sideburns.

"Hello there!" said the man with a Southern drawl as he offered us his hand. "I am Giles Penny."

"I am Mr Sherlock Holmes of London, and this is my colleague, Doctor John Watson," said Holmes as we shook Mr Penny's hand. "We are here per request of Mrs Irene Norton to have a look through Mr Godfrey Norton's offices before they are cleared."

"Oh my, yes. She was very keen for us to leave the office as it was until you got here. The police have already done their business, so there's not much left to see," said Mr Penny. "Still, she paid us handsomely for us to leave it."

"Then let us not waste that penny. Where is Norton's office?" asked Holmes.

"Right this way," and we followed the American.

"Did you know Mr Norton well?" I enquired.

"He was a good man and a damn good lawyer. A sturdy fellow," Penny replied. "Still, though, it's not uncommon for people to buckle under this job."

"Was he working on any particularly high-pressure cases at the time?" Holmes asked.

"No, not really, a bunch of minor things. Still, it seems the stress got to him. I suppose, looking back, it was clear, but what can you do?" said Penny.

"You saw signs?" I asked.

"Quite right, little things they were. The week leading up to his death, he'd been running late, getting sloppy with work, a bit forgetful, always looking like his mind was elsewhere. I thought he was having a bad week," Mr Penny informed us.

"Interesting," said Holmes.

Mr Penny pulled out a key and unlocked a door. "This is his office," said he.

"Leave us to look around. We'll call for you if we need any more information," commanded Holmes.

"Very well. I'll be at the end of the hall here."

Penny gone, Holmes walked around the room with his hands behind his back. As I followed him, I noticed a desk immediately to the right. It was large and made of oak. There were still markings on the floor from where the pistol had fallen and lain. Wrapping around the three other walls were cabinets filled with files. There was a window on the right wall that Holmes inspected carefully. I noticed that the floors in the offices were not marble but polished wood.

"The room looks clean," I said, glancing this way and that as Holmes began examining Norton's desk.

"It is far from clean, Watson," said Holmes as he took a seat in Norton's chair.

"Care to explain?" I asked.

"Several things I've noticed. Do you see there, this cabinet which was hit by the bullet which pierced Norton's head?" said Holmes, and pointed out a chip in the wood.

"I see it," said I.

"What does that tell you?" he asked.

"Other than the bullet passed through his skull and hit the wall—nothing," I returned.

"You are wrong, Watson," said Holmes. "You are missing the most vital thing about the bullet."

"Which is?"

"Where it hit!" he cried. "Here, Watson, if I were to put a gun to my head and fire it with my left hand, the barrel of the gun would be pointed like so." Holmes demonstrated. "If I fired said gun, the bullet would pass through my skull at an upward angle, therefore hitting the wall either level with my head or closer to the ceiling! The shot fired was angled down and hit closer to the floor."

"What if he held the gun at the top of his head?"

"How many self-inflicted gunshot wounds to the head aim the barrel downward?"

"I can think of a few cases…"

"Very few, Watson," Holmes interjected. "I have studied many self-inflicted gunshot wounds, and the angle is wrong. Further, having met Norton before and knowing how tall he is, I am certain he did not pull that trigger."

"So Miss Adler was correct."

"Did you expect anything less of her?" Holmes began to tinker with the desk drawers, which had been left open, as they were when Miss Adler found Norton. The desk had three drawers on each side, and Holmes pulled the top-left drawer. He would open it ever so slightly, and then close it. He repeated this motion several times before doing it with his head level with the top of the desk.

"By Jove, I think I found something!" Holmes made similar motions with the other top desk drawer and lay his head level again. "Yes, there is something here." He stood and began tapping the top of the desk and then the bottom. He walked around the front and stuck his head underneath. Standing upright, he looked at me with a smile. "Do you have your pocket knife on you?"

I pulled it from my jacket pocket. Holmes unfolded the longest blade and ran it down a thin crack on either side of the drawers. Every couple of inches, the blade would get caught, and every time Holmes's smile grew wider.

"That brass statue behind you, Watson, might you hand it over to me?" I handed him the heavy statue of a horse. "The drawers were open and yet nothing was taken," said Holmes as he took another seat in Norton's chair. "I know why."

"Why is that?" I asked.

With a sudden loud crash, Holmes slammed the brass statue upwards so it connected with the lip of the desk. I jolted at the sound and took a few steps back. Holmes repeated this several more times before, on the fourth try, the middle section of the desk lifted up and flung open on a latch.

"Good heavens, Holmes!" I cried. I could hear the sound of someone approaching. I turned to see Mr Penny barreling down the hall. I looked back at Holmes, who was stuffing something into his pocket.

"What is that racket?" shouted Mr Penny. "What in the world have you done?"

"That which was necessary, Mr Penny," said Holmes.

"You've gone and ruined the desk!" The man was red as a berry with anger. His hand held his head as he huffed.

"It was a needful action," said Holmes in a rather blasé tone. "Now, if you'll excuse us, we must be off at once."

"Pardon!" he shouted. "You can't just go, not after this. Who is going to clean up this mess?" Mr Penny huffed some more.

"Mrs Norton paid you a shiny penny to keep the office intact, now you can pay a shiny penny to clean it up, and the world will carry on," said Holmes.

Holmes and I hailed a cab and instructed the driver to take us back to Adler's brownstone.

"What did you find, Holmes?" I asked as we made our way down the busy streets of Manhattan.

"The reason nothing was taken from the drawers is that nothing valuable was in them," Holmes began. "The desk was specially made so that when the drawers are opened in a certain pattern, a secret compartment opens. In this case, I didn't have time to work it out, so I used the brass statue to break in. While you were watching Mr Penny, I was able to snatch these." He pulled out a small brown journal and a grey satin woman's glove with a crimson S stitched onto the sleeve. "It was best not to share our findings with Mr Penny and speak with Miss Adler first."

"A sentimental object Norton kept with him," said I. "What can the S stand for… another woman?"

"Possibly. The glove is certainly for a woman, but look at it. It is in perfect condition. Not worn by anyone. No stretch marks, no fading, nothing. Also, the glove is perhaps a size and a half too small for Miss Adler. She is by no means a large woman, but she is a woman. This is meant for a much younger girl. This is something else entirely," said Holmes.

"And the journal?" I asked. Holmes began flicking through the pages and let out a curious groan.

"Notes regarding clients and cases. Dates and names as well. Might be useless, but still worth holding on to. The dates seem to lead up to just a few days before his death. The most curious piece of it is this," and Holmes showed me a little slip of paper with a black circle in the centre.

"Curious," said I. "Hopefully, Miss Adler will be able to enlighten us on some of this."

"Precisely, Watson!"

*****

Upon arrival, we found Miss Adler pacing back and forth in her study. She had grown impatient in her wait and was excited to see us return.

"What did you find?" she asked.

"Two things," said I as we sat. Holmes quickly recalled the events that had taken place in the office and his speculation regarding the cause of Norton's death. There was a look of surprise upon Irene Adler's face when she was told of the secret chamber inside the desk.

"Norton was a clever man," she admitted. "I shouldn't find it that surprising. Though I am surprised that he never told me about this." She paused, as if her mind was taking her elsewhere. "Nevertheless," she continued, "did you find anything useful?"

"Well, I am certain, even more so than ever, that he was being threatened before his life was claimed," said Holmes. He handed Miss Adler the little slip of paper with the black circle.

"What's this?" she asked.

"A pirate's warning of death. A black spot," Holmes said. "I believe someone gave this to him for a reason yet to be determined, and he chose to hide out in his office. The killer arrived, smoked, leaving the ash you found, put the gun to Norton's head, firing downwards, and left the gold doubloon as a symbol. Of course, in our modern age, who thinks of the old pirate codes and warnings? This was a vital clue left unnoticed. Finally, the gun was then left to make it appear that Norton did it, again shielding the doubloon as nothing more than a piece of history. That Norton wanted to get into the secret compartment means that something inside was important."

"How do we know it was Norton?" I asked.

"Elementary! Had the killer known the compartment was there, they would have forced Norton to open it before killing him. The desk was in the process of being opened when he was killed."

"What else did you find inside the compartment?" Miss Adler asked.

"This brown journal," said Holmes, showing the book, "of unknown importance, and this satin glove with a crimson 'S' on the sleeve." Holmes handed both to Miss Adler, and she looked at them closely.

"Does it mean anything to you?" I asked.

"The journal, no," said she, skimming the pages. "The glove, yes." Holmes and I looked at her quickly.

"What does it mean?" I asked.

"It belongs to a relatively secret club here in the city," she said.

"How do you know of it?" Holmes asked.

"I did say relatively secret. I met a man at an after-party once. He had had too much to drink and was talking to me about how thrilled he was to have gained access to 'the Society'. He then showed me a grey satin glove with a red 'S' just like this. What I cannot tell you is why Godfrey had this. I will find out!"

"We will find out, Miss Adler. The mystery deepens," said Holmes. "Now, who was it who showed you this glove? Talking to him may prove useful."

"His name is Roy Oaks. He's the manager of Wilson Bank Co. on 5th Avenue," she replied. I could see something in her eyes. Her face did not express sadness or anger; rather, by her expression, I could not help but think, for a moment, that she was planning something. Perhaps, like our first encounter, she was withholding information?

"Very well," said Holmes. "I wish you to remain here while we speak with Mr Oaks. Once we do, we'll return and set another course of action."

*****

Holmes's plan for our cover story was that we were seeking assistance in storing precious jewels. In order to do this, we needed to meet with Mr Oaks, the manager, to know we could leave them in capable hands.

At Wilson Bank Co., Holmes spoke with a woman who stood behind a counter, and within a few moments she had gone to fetch Mr Oaks. We waited patiently before being called forward. The woman took us down a long hallway which was adorned with portraits of gentlemen who I assumed were the founding men of the bank. She stood before a door, and knocked gently. A voice called out for us to enter.

"Mr Holmes, is it?" said a man, rising from behind a desk. He was around my height, with a long face and pointy nose, bald and bespectacled. His dress was of the finest quality. "I am Roy Oaks." Holmes and I greeted him with a handshake before being offered a seat. "What can I do for you fine gentlemen?" he asked.

"I am the owner of a very fine stone, and while I am here in your fine city, I would like to store it in your bank," said Holmes.

"That is certainly something we can do for you," replied Oaks, leaning back in his chair with a smile.

"Before any agreement is made, I would like to see the security measures you would provide for my property," Holmes stated.

"As you wish, but might I have a look at the stone?" asked Oaks.

I paused, fearing that our game was up. Holmes, however, reached into his pocket and withdrew a cloth wrapped around something. He laid it upon the table and unfolded it slowly, revealing the emerald that Miss Adler had sent to Holmes back in London. Mr Oaks feasted his eyes upon the beautiful stone and smiled widely.

"Oh yes, that is lovely," he said. "If you will excuse me, I will retrieve a safe for you to examine." The man quickly left the room, and as the door shut, Holmes stood and looked around.

"What are you looking for?" I asked, rising to my feet. Holmes did not respond, but quickly went through the drawers in the desk.

"This will have to do," he said. He withdrew the satin glove from his pocket that we had found in Norton's office, and laid it upon the desk. "Watson, stand by the door. When he enters, close it quickly behind him." I took the position while Holmes remained on the other side of the desk. Moments later, Mr Oaks walked in with a container. I closed the door behind him, and he halted in surprise.

"What's going on?" Oaks demanded, setting the container on his desk. He caught sight of the satin glove lying exposed on the desk. "Where did you get that?" he roared, his gaze darting towards a small chest in the corner behind the desk.

"I have something for you," said Holmes as he gestured to take Oaks's hand. Reluctantly, Oaks extended his hand, and I saw Holmes slip a piece of paper into his palm. Oaks withdrew and looked at it. His face turned pale, and he began to sway. I raced over and caught the man as he fell. Holmes and I placed him in a seat, and I stood over him while he recomposed himself. Holmes walked over to the chest and withdrew an identical satin glove.

"What are you going to do?" said Oaks when he finally recovered.

"You know what this is?" said Holmes, pointing to the black spot. "You know exactly what happens when a member gets this."

"What did I do? I thought I was loyal," he whimpered.

"We'll see how far your loyalty extends," said Holmes. "If you don't tell me where the Society is, I will be forced to expose your connection to it. Further, if I am forced to expose you, you'll have to expose the Society. Pick your option," said Holmes. Oaks paused when he realised that the game was up.

"You—you can't do anything!" he sputtered.

"You may not know who I am, but I am the foremost mind in deductive reasoning, consulted by all manner of life, from kings to peasants, and I assure you I have enough evidence to reopen Norton's case and tie you to it. I'm sure the police would like to know that you both have the same satin glove that belongs to the Society. Further, I have a firsthand witness who knew you were a member when you exposed your secret one drunken night at a party. You already made it clear that the Society has aggressive tendencies by your reaction to the delivery of the black spot. I can also see from the brown stains under your fingernail that you've recently had exposure to raw opium, a substance Norton was keen on. Given that, and that you both belong to the same society, and exhibit the markings of a consumer, it is no stretch that you partook of the substance while in attendance at the Society. A very quick experiment would determine if you used the same batch of opium. So tell me, where is the Society located, and why would they kill a member?"

Oaks held still for a moment in an attempt to call a bluff. I could see him grip the handle of the seat tightly and his face begin to perspire.

"We have a private location. Sullivan Docks, Pier 4," Oaks began slowly. "The club itself is kept completely secret. Only members know of its existence, or at least it should be members only."

"And the punishment for exposure?" Holmes asked.

"You swear a life oath when you join. If you for any reason expose the club, your life is forfeit," Oaks said.

"Why is this?" I asked.

"The kind of things we do are not entirely…" He paused, taking a deep breath. "…they are not legal. Opium is a hot commodity, and many states are enacting laws that end its free use. This could have a terrible effect on our business. We have a hand that stretches across the land. Oh, the Society is but an iceberg's tip. You'll find no better racketeering in the country. From Presidents to petty shop owners, we can bribe and launder to our hearts' content. Eyes are turned when we indulge in all types of fornication."

"How does one get admitted into this Society?" I asked.

"You do not seek the Society out; they seek you out. If they believe you a suitable candidate, they will extend an invitation," said Oaks.

"The satin glove; that is the invitation, is it not?" Holmes pressed.

"It is," he confirmed.

"If I may return to the life oath," Holmes said, "would I be correct in assuming the reason the oath is taken is due to the fact that many high-profile men are members, and an exposure of them would be detrimental to their image and wealth, which would, by default, incriminate the club?"

Oaks nodded in agreement.

"Who runs the club?" I asked.

"I don't know," the banker said.

"What do you know?" commanded Holmes.

"A man called Ivory. He runs the operation. I don't know his real name. None of us do. Very few of us even see him. Just glimpses," said Oaks.

Holmes was silent a while, looking at our detainee as he cowered in his chair.

"You have been most informative, sir. You've served the side of justice this day," my friend said agreeably.

"If you go in there, you'll die," said Oaks. Holmes and I both gave him a piercing stare. "Anyone who has ever tried to get in or back at someone for revenge, debt, you name it, they get killed; and it's not very pretty."

"Come, Watson, we must go!"

We darted out of the building and hailed a cab. Leaping inside, Holmes told the driver to take us to Sullivan Docks as quickly as he could. By his expression, I could see he was deeply concerned.

"Holmes, what's the matter?" I asked, begging a response.

"Irene Adler is in great danger."

Holmes was quiet the entire journey towards Sullivan Docks. No matter how hard I pressed, he said nothing. His eyes were fixed firmly ahead like an eagle stalking its prey, unmoving. There were only a handful of times in which I had witnessed Holmes succumb to his emotions. He was indeed a caring person, but his drive for logical and deductive reasoning often muted his softer sides. However, there was something altogether different about his demeanour as we sat in this cab. It appeared to me that something else was driving him. Still, I was trying to wrap my head around this unknown danger that apparently faced Miss Adler and why Holmes was taking us here rather than back to her apartment.

The sun was setting, and I could see its rays sparkle off the water as we grew closer to our destination. Ahead, I saw two large red-brick buildings connected by a tall iron gate. The driver stopped outside the gate, above which sat a sign reading Sullivan Docks. As I stepped out of the cab, I noticed a large chain held the gate firmly shut, and I began looking for other means of entry. Holmes waved the driver on and then took a look at the blockade before us.

"How are we meant to get in?" I pleaded.

"The very same way Miss Adler did!" returned Holmes as he ran over to a pile of crates, boxes, and barrels that lined one of the red-brick buildings.

"How do you know she's here?" I asked as I followed him in climbing atop the unstable pile.

"An obvious fact, can't you see?"

"Holmes, I never doubt your powers, but I admit confusion! You must be clear, how can you possibly know she's here?"

My friend pulled something from the window above us. Once he had freed the item, he extended it towards me. It was a yellow lily.

"Miss Adler wore a yellow lily in her hair!" I confirmed.

"She did, and she's here now. She took matters into her own hands despite my telling her not to! Now we must get inside and make sure no villainy has befallen her!"

Holmes shimmied his way through the window, and I followed behind. To our luck, there was a walkway on the other side of the window to break what would have been a rather long fall. Holmes and I vacated the building and found our way onto Pier 4, where the Society gathered. The area was like a ghost town, and an eerie sense of abandonment hung in the air. No boats were docked, no workers could be seen or heard, and everything was still. Holmes and I made sure we crept close to the buildings so as not to be seen too easily.

"Look, Holmes!" I pointed ahead in the distance. I could see a small, steam-powered vessel, and on the deck was the figure of a man.

"That is Pier 4. Come, we must hurry and find Miss Adler."

"And hope that they do not already have her!"

We quickly made our way towards the building labelled Pier 4. We pressed up against the side of the brick structure, and Holmes took a quick peek at the vessel.

"They are making ready to leave, Watson." We heard a group drawing near. "Stay back!" he exclaimed in a whisper, pushing into me and signalling to kneel down. Around the corner, a group of men could be heard chatting as they hurried onto the steamboat. Holmes crawled to have another look.

"What do you see?" I asked.

"I see four men, quite rough, dressed in wide-brimmed hats, leather boots, and frock coats. They are boarding the boat."

"We must stop them!" I pressed.

"We have nothing to stop them with. They have heavy weapons more powerful than your service revolver." I could hear the sound of the steamboat powering up in the water and casting off from the pier.

"Come, let's go inside!" said Holmes. He darted around the corner and through an unlocked door.

The inside was unlike a typical docking building. It was not simply a large open workspace or factory. It was designed like a mansion. Hallways and rooms were lined with elegant wallpaper, and the floors were lined with fine hardwood. As we journeyed deep into the Society's lair, the strong smell of tobacco and an even stronger smell of opium stained the air.

"I can see how you picked up on the opium on Norton's clothes. I fear our own will smell of this stench for some time," said I.

Holmes sniffed the air a few more times. "I can smell gunpowder too. Heavy amounts of it, in fact." Holmes began to pick up speed, darting in and out of rooms. He opened up a door and paused. "We have a serious problem."

I looked inside the room and there, stored inside a vast room, were barrels of gunpowder, and in the centre of the room was an explosive device. Several sticks of dynamite were connected to a timed detonator.

Holmes raced over, and we could hear the clockwork ticking.

"Can you stop it?" I was suddenly cut off by the loud cry of a woman calling for help. "That's Miss Adler!"

"There's not much time!" said Holmes. "I will see to this explosive. You hunt for Miss Adler and get her out. I will meet you at the entrance!"

"Holmes…"

"Watson, this is no time for sentiment!"

I nodded and raced out of the room to look for Miss Adler.

My heart raced as I realised I had no idea what the time frame was. Could Holmes dismantle the explosive before I got Miss Adler out? I tried to force these thoughts to the back of my head and simply focus on finding her. The sound of her screams led me through the halls to a spiral staircase. I raced up. Once atop, I saw below a large ballroom-type area.

It was a most elegant room with seating areas, a bar, and dozens of spots for the consumption of opium. There were curtained-off areas where I presume more scandalous activities would take place. However, my gaze upon all this was quickly diverted. Down in the centre of the room sat Miss Adler. She was in male clothing: dark, stiff-looking trousers, a white work shirt, and a coat.

"Steady!" I cried, and I saw her look up towards me.

"Dr Watson!" she cried. I raced towards her.

"Are you all right?" I knew upon approach that that was a foolish question. I could see stains of blood upon her face. Her hair, once lovely and pristine, was now wild and dishevelled. Her clothes were stained with her blood. Her arms were held behind her back and I realised they were chained to the floor, as were her feet.

"Doctor, hurry! We've got to get out of here!" she pleaded. I pulled at the chains but had no luck. With no time to lose, I aimed my revolver at the chain and fired a shot. The bullet shattered the chains. I did the same with the restraints around her feet, and I helped lift her from the seat.

As she stood, she embraced me tightly. In any other circumstances, it would have seemed inappropriate, but one cannot judge another's reaction when they are saved from death.

"Come with me!" she said, taking hold of my wrist. The two of us ran out of the room and into an office-like space. Papers and cabinets were tossed and turned. Miss Adler shuffled through the papers. I saw a window and looked out to see that directly below was water.

"We really must go!" I commanded.

"Just a moment, get the window open!" she replied. I did and turned to see her stuff something into her dress. "Ready, Doctor?"

I helped her through the window. She leapt out, and I followed behind. No sooner had we hit the water than a great plume of fire rose up and spread out across the water's surface. Holding my breath and keeping my head under was difficult while the excitement atop calmed. I had lost Miss Adler in the jump, and I had no idea if Holmes had made it out alive.

I shot up to the surface of the water. The waves tossed, and debris from the exploded building crashed into me. I called out for Miss Adler, but received no response. I floated in the water in disbelief. Was she dead? Was I the only survivor? Was Holmes nothing more than a burnt corpse inside the blazing structure? I felt heavy inside, as if my grief might cause me to sink and find, for myself, a grave in this New York bay.

For a moment, I thought I could hear the sound of my wife calling my name. If anything, she was what I needed to return to. A wave splashed against me and woke me from this daydream. However, I could still hear my name being called.

It was Miss Adler! She was further out than I. We swam towards each other, then struggled back to shore. I found a ladder and let Miss Adler climb up first. She and I both lay collapsed on the ground, looking up into the darkening sky. The Society's lair was utterly destroyed, leaving no trace of its existence.

"Doctor Watson?" said Miss Adler, keeping her eyes towards the heavens.

"Yes?" I replied, doing the same.

"I'm frightened to ask where Mr Holmes is."

"He was," I paused, "inside." There was silence between us for some time. The only thing we could hear was the crackling of fire.

"When you look out at space, it all seems so peaceful and calm. Do you suppose there is as much chaos out there as there is here?" said Miss Adler, breaking the silence.

"I have no answer. I suppose from out there we, too, must look calm and peaceful."

"I shouldn't think that the universe is guided by any other laws than those found here upon this very earth," came a familiar voice. I turned my head and there, standing behind us, was Sherlock Holmes.

"You're alive!" I cried, jumping to my feet. "I thought you were dead!"

"Thank the Lord!" said Miss Adler, doing the same.

Holmes was in no better shape than we were. His clothes were tattered and burned, his face was dirty, and his hair scruffy.

"I should think a 'thank you' is in order. We have all had a narrow escape!" said Holmes.

"What happened?" I asked.

"I was unfamiliar with the explosive they used. I did my best to defuse it but failed. I was, however, able to deduce from the mechanism that we had a ten-minute window. I struggled until I was left with three minutes. I ran towards the room from which I had heard your screams, Miss Adler. Watson had fired your gun, and both of you raced out the other side of the room, and so I, too, made my own escape. The explosion knocked me over, resulting in my present state."

"It is good to see us all intact!" I exclaimed, and Miss Adler agreed.

"Let us retire to mine and clean up," said she. "The fire brigade will arrive shortly and it would be best for us not to be here."

"That would be wise," returned Holmes.

*****

Returning to the brownstone to clean up, we sat together in the study. Irene Adler lay upon the sofa while Holmes and I took to the chairs in mild exhaustion.

"Woman," Holmes began, "you have acted most foolishly today."

I was taken aback by Holmes's outburst.

"I beg your pardon?" she returned, with a sharp look towards the detective.

"You called for my aid, so let me aid. Do not go running off so childishly into the dragon's lair! We need information, and now the Society is all but a pile of rubble and virtually useless."

"You're right, I called for your assistance. That doesn't mean I'll sit idly by while you investigate; we do this together!" Holmes looked upon Irene Adler, his temper cooling. "It's not as useless as you think," said Miss Adler sharply. "Let me recount my own events. I did not intend to lead you astray; let me be clear on that. When you left to visit Mr Oaks, I started to think about the satin glove and the Society. The more I thought about my encounter with Oaks, the more I recalled him mentioning a dock. No name, but a dock. Now, Mr Holmes, if you'll notice, in my husband's journal, Pier 4 is named. I followed my hunch, and I turned out to be right. The docks were shut, which I found odd, so I climbed in through an open window."

"Yes, we found a lily," said I.

"I hoped you would. I left that for you in case things went south," she admitted. Holmes briefly smirked. "I walked onto Pier 4 and looked around. I could hear voices—men—but I could not see anyone. As I walked down a hallway, I was stopped when a man exited a room. He was tall, with a big bushy moustache and thick sideburns. He wore a nice suit, an expensive one.

"'Mrs Norton,' said he in a deep Southern voice, 'what brings you here?' I revealed my pistol, and he chuckled. 'Do you intend to kill me? You don't even know who I am.'

"'You tell me who killed my husband and maybe I'll let you live,' I replied.

"'The only person responsible for your husband's death is himself, just like the only person responsible for your death is yourself.' I cocked my gun, but was assaulted from behind. I fired a shot but it only hit the wall. Two strong men held me on each side and dragged me into the main hall, where Doctor Watson found me. I must be honest and say that I did not get a good look at the men who held me, but they did have a foul odour to them. I can imagine that they were nothing more than outlaws hired or in association with this man, Ivory."

"Ivory?" interrupted Holmes. "Who is he?"

"I am getting to that, Mr Holmes. I was chained to the chair and taunted by the outlaws for some time. They hurt me." Her eyes told a terrible story. "The man whom I first encountered came in. He slowly walked over towards me and as he did, he chuckled.

"'You see these,' he said, holding out his open palm. In his hands rested a pair of diamond earrings that belonged to me!

"'Yes, I see them.'

"'If these were real, they'd cost a fortune. Many people thought they were real when you wore them to extravagant parties, especially when you would say they were a royal gift.'

"'They were a royal gift.'

"'From whom?'

"'A King, in Europe.'

"'Well, then this King's a cheap giver.' Suddenly, without any warning, he burst out in anger, yelling in my face. 'These earrings are fake!' His voice echoed throughout, and my heart raced with terror.

"'How did you come to have my earrings?'

"The man stood up straight and brushed himself off. He withdrew a pistol from a holster hung around his waist and aimed the barrel at my forehead. 'Why don't you ask your husband when you see him?'

"I closed my eyes and prepared to face my doom, but was saved when someone entered the room.

"'Ivory!' called this other man. I took this to be my assailant's name, as he withdrew his gun and turned away. 'Just had a message from Oaks. Someone has been sniffing around and found Norton's glove. They are coming here.'

"'Oaks, you say?' said Ivory, who looked at me. 'Tut, tut, Mrs Norton.' Ivory turned towards the man who delivered the message. 'Dog, this place must burn. You know what to do.' With that, the gang of outlaws ran out of the room whooping and hollering. 'It's about to get hot in here, Mrs Norton, and you've nowhere to go.'

"Ivory laughed and walked off. He went through a door, and I saw him go into an office of sorts. For roughly fifteen minutes, the gang and Ivory yelled back and forth about their preparations. I heard him say to get the opium out of here and make ready for transfer. I heard one of the outlaws say that they sent a wire to a Homer Smith regarding their opium shipment. The outlaw, called 'Dog', told Ivory that everything was set and that all the usable opium had been made ready for transport. Ivory walked back over and stood before me after he learnt this.

"'You and your little friends have ruined this operation, and it is only a shame that I cannot make you suffer greatly before this place goes sky-high!'

"'You brought this upon yourself,' I spat. Ivory struck me across the face a couple of times. I could taste blood in my mouth and felt it trickle down my chin. He took out my earrings and threw them in my face before he crept off.

"'Good night, little lady,' said Dog as he walked by me laughing. I struggled to get free and began crying for help. That is when Dr. Watson found me, and when he released me, I ran into the office to see if there was anything I could find useful. I found this." Miss Adler handed over a wire from a Mr Homer Smith.

Holmes examined it and laid it down. "All is not lost, then," he said contemplatively.

"What do we have?" I asked.

"Homer Smith is another link in this long chain, and might be able to help us," said he. "Opium is clearly the driving force behind the Society, and Smith is in some way responsible for its delivery. See here; according to the telegram he hails from a small town in the Midwest, a town called Pendleton in the state of Indiana. Once I make a few enquiries, I will determine if this is our best course of action."

*****

A few hours later, Holmes returned. Miss Adler had fallen asleep, and I read by the fire.

"Where have you been?" I asked.

"Went to see Oaks, but he is dead," he returned. "I have bought us three tickets for Indiana. If we are to find the Ivory man and learn why they killed Norton, we must follow the drugs. We leave in the morning."

At five o'clock in the morning, Holmes woke us all. He informed Miss Adler of our next journey. We hastily packed and made ourselves ready. Quickly loading our luggage into a cab, we were off.

"Your husband did not die over a pair of fake earrings," said Holmes inside the dark cab.

"I should hope not."

"There is a larger game afoot, a devious web in which he tangled himself. I think that the earrings were a payoff of some kind. We know he was being threatened for something. Money is normally the driver of most threats, and you have been left safely out of it until now."

"Then why was my house broken into?"

"A riddle we have yet to solve."

We arrived at the station and boarded our train. Holmes had acquired a private cabin for Miss Adler while he and I sat in the main compartment with the other travellers. She came to us and asked us to join her for a while. Together, the three of us sat and conversed. I was asked about Mary and my marriage, both of which I was happy to discuss.

"And what about you, Mr Holmes, is there no lucky lady for you?" asked Miss Adler with a grin.

"The department of love I leave in the capable hands of Dr. Watson."

"Come now, is there no lady out there who is a suitable match for the great Sherlock Holmes?"

"It is not a matter of suitability, Miss Adler. I am devoted to my work and nothing else."

"Can no one share in your devotion?"

I sat there, passing glances between the two of them as they talked. When she landed upon this question, I saw a look upon my friend's face that I had never seen before.

"My dear Miss Adler, as it is, I cannot offer feelings of that nature. I should like to pass another glance through Norton's journal, so if you will excuse me I will return to my seat." He rose and departed.

"I think I shall leave you be, Miss Adler," said I.

"In another life, my good Doctor, your friend and I would have made a dynamic couple."

"Nothing would please me more than to see him partnered and falling in love, but it is clearly not his way."

"I regret the circumstances that brought us all together. I wish there was a possibility of stepping back into the past and making it different. Had I met him before…." She stopped.

"No good can come from daydreaming about what could have been. Hindsight is always clearer," I assured her. "Besides, you've already had a strong impact upon Holmes. It is true that he kept your picture in a drawer inside his study." Miss Adler smiled as I said this. "And there is no other woman for whom he has done such a thing."

"Thank you, Dr. Watson," she said with a smile.

I nodded and departed her cabin. I found Holmes sitting in his chair drinking a glass of brandy and reading through Norton's journal. He was quiet and unresponsive. I left him to his ways and marvelled at the great American scenery speeding by on the other side of the window.

What Happened to Dr Watson

The train rolled to a stop into the very small station in Pendleton, Indiana. It was seven o'clock, and our twelve-hour journey had been somewhat tiresome and lacking in any excitement. As the train pulled to a stop, the steam engulfed the long wooden platform in a white cloud. The three of us stepped out onto the platform. Holmes and Miss Adler were discomforted by the humidity which hung in the thick Midwestern air. I found myself at ease with its oppressiveness, reminded of my short time in India. Together we walked into a small ticket office. A large man with a plump belly sat inside, leaning back in a creaky wooden chair and chewing tobacco.

"What can I do ya for?" said he.

"We are looking for a local inn. Might you point us in the direction of one nearby?" Holmes asked.

The man looked at us, bemused. "Boy, I ain't never heard talk like that before!" he said with a laugh. "Where you from, Ireland?"

"England," Holmes corrected.

"Ah, ya'll sound similar, really!"

"Not quite," began Holmes, but Miss Adler put her hand on his arm.

"My friends are from out of town, clearly," she said. "We are stopping here for a few days. Where could we find accommodation?"

"Good to see you Brits have got a fine American woman to show you around!" said he. "Up that road there, take it about ten minutes till you reach the main road. You'll see a track for the local tramline. When you see it, turn right and it'll take you right into town. You ought'a be able to find something up there."

"Thanks, sir," said Miss Adler, and we left. "Mr Holmes, it might be good for you to tone down your English side while we are here," she said as we walked up the road.

"Perhaps you are correct," said Holmes in a thick American accent.

Miss Adler smiled at him and chuckled. "Yes, something like that! And you too, Doctor!"

"Do my very best, ma'am," said I.

Both Holmes and Miss Adler laughed at my failed attempt.

"It might be best, Watson, for you to remain silent," said Holmes.

"Not all the time, of course, Doctor," said Miss Adler.

We found the tramline and followed it into town. It was intriguing to see what the Americans had achieved as they colonised this new country. The difference between the great city of New York and this rural town was something quite unique.

The centre of town was made up of three blocks of brick buildings where the two main roads intersected. Looking down one street, towards a park, were a drugstore and a butcher's shop in the Chandler Block building. If one turned right, one could see a Christian church steeple. We, however, turned left. There were several horses and carts tied outside of the buildings. We walked down the street, and I saw a dental practice, an establishment called The Brownie Restaurant, Davis & Co. Undertaking, a post office, and a small medical practice.

"I wonder where the inn is?" Miss Adler asked.

"Let me go inside the restaurant and ask," said Holmes. "Watson, stay with Miss Adler."

I nodded.

Holmes passed through the swinging doors into the yellow glow of the establishment. The sound of men laughing, glasses colliding, and cutlery chiming echoed through the street. He walked out a moment later and pointed his finger back up the road. We followed him and turned left down the road towards the park.

"There's a small inn up here," Holmes informed us.

The Rose Inn greeted us warmly. A kind elderly lady with spectacles hanging on a chain around her neck met us.

"Good evening," she said in a small, high-pitched voice. "What can I do for you?"

"Ma'am, we are looking for a couple of rooms for the next few nights," Miss Adler asked.

"Hmm, let me see what we got," and she pulled out a large book and placed her spectacles upon her nose. "Yes, we have a couple of rooms. One that would suit this lovely couple." The woman paused to look up at Holmes and Miss Adler. "And one for you," she finished, and looked back down at her book.

"My good lady," said Holmes, "let me be clear, we shall need a room for my associate here and me," pointing towards me, "and a private room for the lady," pointing toward Miss Adler.

"Oh! Forgive me, sir, I thought you two were a couple!" said the old lady with a smile that creased her face. She took two sets of keys and asked us to follow her. The room Holmes and I would share was downstairs, while Miss Adler's was on the second floor. We were informed that breakfast was provided every morning at six fifty, but dinner was our own concern. We had not been in our room ten minutes, and I could see the eagerness on my companion's face.

We helped Adler take her cases to the second floor.

"Be careful with that," she instructed me.

We set her things down and she asked me to set the heavy case on the bed. She opened it and motioned for us to come over. Lifting the case's lid, inside were several handguns and rounds of ammunition.

"Quite the arsenal you have with you," said Holmes.

"I expect trouble, and we'll need these."

"I should like to get the lay of the land, Watson. Why don't you and Miss Adler get an idea of the local area, and I'll see what I can learn from the high street?"

"Besides, if you run into trouble, all you must do is shout, and we'll be bound to hear you," said I with a chuckle. Holmes turned to leave.

"Mr Holmes." He stopped when Adler spoke. "Take this," she said, handing him a loaded revolver. He placed it in his jacket and darted out.

"Well, shall we have a look around?"

*****

Adler and I explored the area, most of which was patches of woods, wild growth, and a small farmland with the occasional row of houses lit with yellow glows. Every so often, the toot of a train whistle fluttered in the air. We both froze suddenly at the sound of a boom in the distance.

"Was that a gunshot?" I asked.

"I think so!"

"Maybe it was a local farmer," I said, coming to my senses. The two of us walked up towards the park. The evening air was refreshing and cool. The sky was clear and littered with white stars, far more than one would see in London or New York.

"Wonder how Holmes has got on? He never stops, does he?"

"Certainly not," said I.

"Do you not think that he misses the beauty the world has, always being driven to solve puzzles and crimes?"

"Surprisingly, his powers of observation extend into all matters. He is a thinking machine, but he does recognise beauty and wonder when he sees it." We found our way into the park and walked along a creek until we came to a bridge built directly above the falls. We agreed that this was a good place to rest.

"Do you suppose we'll actually find these people, the man Ivory who controls the Society, or Homer?"

"I believe we will. Having spent nearly a decade with Holmes and documenting countless cases, unique in their own right, I believe in Sherlock Holmes. He will be able to track these men, even in a place as vast as America."

"I could never thank you enough for coming out to my aid."

"Holmes was determined. Aiding you was most important to him."

"And why do you suppose that is?"

"Above all, he admires you." She laughed.

"Sherlock Holmes admires me? The great detective in the silly hat," Adler returned.

"He does. He holds very few in high esteem, and you are one," said I. "You're no fool, Miss Adler. The world would be a very different place if more women were as bold and cunning as you."

"Well, maybe one of these days we'll see a world like that," said Miss Adler with a smile. "Let's get back in case he needs us."

I agreed, and we strolled back to the Rose Inn. We walked up the steps, and saw a man, wearing a wide-brimmed hat, seated in a rocking chair and smoking a cigarette.

"Good evenin'," said the man.

"Good evening," I returned cautiously.

"I hear yous are looking for a Mr Homer Smith?"

Adler and I paused and gave the man another look.

"Mr Holmes?" Miss Adler asked.

"Good work!" came Holmes' voice. He stood up and re-moved the hat.

"Where did you get that Stetson?" I asked.

"I like it better than your deerstalker," Adler commented. Holmes appeared unfazed by her remark and continued.

"I bought a couple from the small boutique. There's one for you too, Watson," he said. "I also learnt where we can find Homer Smith, but let us speak in the privacy of our room."

We came inside from the cool night air and sat in our room, which was lit by half a dozen candles and two oil lamps. Holmes stood, arms crossed, in a corner while I sat atop the dresser and Miss Adler reclined in a chair.

"Let me recount my evening's events. After I left you, I attempted to get a better sense of what was around us and at our disposal should we encounter an emergency. I stepped back into The Brownie Restaurant and approached the bar, as I did earlier.

"'Come back again?' asked the bartender.

"'I found the Rose Inn, thank you. Thought I would come back for a drink; what do you have?' I asked, putting my American accent to use.

"'We got some bourbon and beer.'

"'Give me a pint of beer.' The man pulled out a glass and filled it up. I lifted the glass to my mouth and took a sip, finding, to my pleasure, the taste to be most enjoyable. 'You serve a fine brew,' said I.

"The bartender smiled and nodded.

"'Tell me, any chance you know a man by the name of Homer Smith?'

"The bartender leaned down, resting his forearm on the counter and clasping his hands. 'Why do ya want'a know?' he asked, clearly suspicious.

"'He is an old friend of mine. I heard he was around here, so thought I'd look him up.'

"'An old friend?' he returned. 'Homer told me what to do if any "old friends" came looking for him.' At this point, the bartender had stood upright and his hands were below the counter. He swiftly lifted them to reveal a sawn-off shotgun, to which I quickly darted out of the way as he fired a shot."

"That must have been the shot we heard before we went for a walk!" said I.

"Most likely," confirmed Holmes. "I snatched the gun from the bartender, only to see a room full of pistols aimed at my head.

"'Drop the weapon!' someone roared. I laid the gun down slowly so as not to seem a threat to this trigger-happy folk.

Thankfully, a man burst through the front door. He was wearing a brown leather coat, thick trousers tucked into his high boots, a holster, and in his hand sat a rifle. I saw upon his chest a badge, and knew he was local authority.

"'What in tarnation is goin' on?' he shouted. 'All of you drop your damn guns, now!'

"The room calmed, and each man tucked his gun safely away.

"'Good evening, sheriff!' said the bartender. 'This man here is causing trouble!'

"'I ain't seen your face around here before, boy. Where are you from?'

"'I am Altamont,' said I, giving the first false name that leapt into my mind. 'Altamont Jones of New York City. I am a Pinkerton.'

"'A Pinkerton, you say?' returned the sheriff. 'Well, come with me.' I followed him out the door, and we walked up the street, a ways past the Chandler Block building, until we came to a street called Broadway. On the corner of the street sat a small police station, which we entered. The sheriff pulled out a chair and indicated that I should sit there while he walked around a desk and sat behind it.

"'So, Altamont Jones, what are you doing here?' he asked.

"'Forgive me, sheriff, but we haven't been properly introduced. You know my name, but I am unaware of yours.'

"'Name's Jesse Flood.'

"'Pleasure to meet you,' I returned, extending a hand.

"'I'm no fool. I'm not shaking that hand till I know more about you.'

"'I'm here looking for a man named Homer Smith. I have reason to believe he is involved in an underground club that deals, ships, and delivers opium into New York.'

"Sheriff Flood sat back in his chair and folded his arms. 'That's a mighty tall order, son.'

"'If you will point me to him I will be on my way.'

"'What proof do you have?'

"I reached into my pocket and withdrew the telegram Miss Adler had shown us previously. 'This note was picked up from the offices of this underground club before an explosion tore it to pieces.'

"He looked over the note some time. 'All right, Pinkerton, here's what I'm goin' to do, because unfortunately my hands are figuratively tied. Homer Smith is a powerful man and one nobody wants to deal with. So I'm goin' to give you an address and I'm goin' to give you a train arrival time. Both of these things will be important to you. If you're not gone tomorrow, and word gets out you are sniffing around about Homer, he'll have you killed. But I gotta say, if you go approachin' that house, you best have a damn good reason.'

"'What is this address and time?' The sheriff told me that if I followed the road by the park, north, I would come across a large brick house that sits just near a railway crossing; that house is Homer's. The sheriff also gave me the time of one thirty a.m. I have thus been to the train station, which we got off from, and learnt that two miles up the road is a railway yard for freight."

"What do you plan, Holmes?" I asked.

"I want you, Watson, to stake out at the railway yard. Learn all you can from this train that is soon to arrive. I will handle Homer. We should plan to meet back here no later than four o'clock. The time is just after midnight. The sheriff was kind enough to leave a stable door open for us to borrow a couple of horses."

"And what am I to do?" asked Miss Adler. "Sit here while the men go out?" She looked disapproving.

"Our situations are dangerous! I should not wish to put you in any harm," returned Holmes.

"This won't do!" she declared.

"Woman, for me, please stay behind," said Holmes in a softer tone.

She paused and looked at him a moment, blinking several times before nodding. "Be careful, both of you."

"Let us get ready!"

*****

Holmes revealed that a Stetson was not the only thing which he had purchased. He had also picked up two pairs of boots for us to change into and two sturdier jackets. His was long and brown, while mine stopped at my waist and was grey. I slipped the boots and hat on, and I admit they were not an uncomfortable fit.

With Miss Adler's approval of our new American disguises, we made our way to the stable the sheriff had mentioned. We found a small building and two horses inside. One was jet black with a white diamond on its nose, and the other was white with chocolate-brown spots dotted about. We saddled the horses, and the two of us rode off into the night, Holmes headed towards Homer's, and I towards the railway yard.

I followed the railway for about a mile. Where it came to a fork, I turned right. The stars were still ablaze above me, and the bright circular moon superbly illuminated the landscape. I carried on with great haste until I saw the rail yard. The yard itself was laden with freight cars. Adjacent to the yard stood a large brick building, which had been painted an off-yellow colour.

The building, I assumed, served as a loading bay. I dismounted and led my white and brown horse along the tracks. There was a small wood, and I decided to hide the horse in there. I tied it to a tree. As I walked down the path, keeping an eye on the rail yard, I straightened my new hat. I withdrew my fob watch and saw the time was quarter past one.

Stealthily, I crept into the yard and saw two men step from the building. One seemed to be looking at his watch, and the other was smoking a cigar. A train whistle blew in the distance. The men perked up at its sound, so I made my way closer. Dodging in and out of cars, hiding in shadows, I got nearer and nearer. The ground began to rumble as the powerful locomotive charged ahead.

In the distance, light from inside the engine room glowed, and I could hear the brakes screeching as the train began to slow down. I watched as the train drew near and stopped alongside the platform where the two men stood. The name Pemberton Rail was painted on the engine. Four men stepped out of one of the freight cars. There was something familiar about the men, but I could not make it out. Staying to the shadows, I moved forward enough to hear their talk.

"Bit early tonight," said one of the two men I saw upon arrival.

"We've had a heck of a time," said one of the men.

"We can see that. We got your shipment from New York earlier today. Everything has been stored away."

"Good work! Well, let's get this stuff unloaded so we can call it a night!"

I watched as the men went to work unloading unmarked crates from the car and bringing them into the building.

"Did ya hear what happened?" said another of the four men to one of the two.

"Nah, what's happened?" he asked.

"The whole New York compound went up in smoke. Some bird was sniffing about, apparently she had some important people on our tail after Dog here killed her husband. Saw the place explode from a boat out in the bay. Quite the sight!"

"Golly! Sounds like a pr'tty close call!"

I recalled Miss Adler telling me that when she was captive, one of the men she called an outlaw was named Dog. It was this man who killed Norton! The very men Holmes and I saw leave Pier 4 and get onto the steamboat.

"So, with all this extra opium, are we goin' to get a treat?"

"I suppose we could," said the man who had been indicated earlier as Dog. "Can't have too much though, this is our bread and butter. Ivory's already got plans for a new set-up, just working things out with the boss. And if he finds out we took some, boy, your life ain't worth spit."

Holmes was correct. The entire operation was driven on opium.

"Who's to say one of the crates wasn't damaged, right?" one of the outlaws said, and the group laughed in agreement.

"How much longer is this going to take? We got another shipment to deal with tomorrow afternoon, and I'd rather get some sleep than suck some opium," another outlaw said.

We had them! The outlaws would be here at least until tomorrow. I needed to get back to Holmes and tell him. We could warn the sheriff and bring these men to justice and hopefully be led to this man, Ivory, and learn why Norton was killed! I crept away. I placed my foot, unknowingly, onto a large iron nail. It rolled as I pressed off and I fell to the ground in a commotion.

"Who's that stumbling around in the dark?" yelled an outlaw. "State your business or prepare to get winged!"

I had no time to lose. I could not foil our plans and be caught by these bandits. I raced through the wood. The men shouted as they saw me dart off. The sound of guns firing echoed in the night. Whizzing bullets flew past me. War is the same, no matter where you are.

If I did not outrun my enemies, I'd wind up with another wound, and perhaps this time it would be fatal. I found my horse still tied. Dark figures were following after me still. Quickly I untied the steed and jumped upon its back. Coming out onto the main road, a way behind I saw two men also on horses.

They spotted me, and the chase continued. Their revolvers roared again. I withdrew my service revolver and returned fire. Ahead were two more men upon horses. Guns were drawn and shots fired. I turned the horse, and we raced into a thick wood. Four men were charging after me.

I wished for the moon and stars to be hidden. The visibility for targeting was far too easy on this night. A bullet flew right past my head. One of the men was gaining upon me. As steadily as I could, I aimed and fired one shot. The man fell from his horse. My horse suddenly jerked, frightened, and I fell off into a creek.

The water was moving swiftly, carrying me along. I fumbled for some time and eventually grabbed hold of a low branch. Pulling myself out of the water, I fell upon the bank.

Forcing myself up, I ran in the best direction that would take me back to the Rose Inn. I felt disoriented as I charged on. I came out to a dirt road, and I looked it up and down. Which way would lead me back to my companions? I thought. I could hear the shouts of the outlaws not far off. A shot was fired. Up the road I could see a dark figure on a horse. My heart began to race as the rider blazed towards me while the gunfire echoed. I crept back into the wood and watched, with relief, as the rider passed me by.

I walked back out onto the road and ran up it. Suddenly, I fell back as a horse burst from the woods. It rose on its hind legs and waved its front ones before slamming its hooves with each shaking force. There was a horseman on the creature's back, and a gun was aimed at my head.

"Hold steady," said the rider to the horse. I kept still. Under the moonlight, I could see the rider had a thick beard and moustache, their eyes barely visible under their hat. "You got yourself into a bit of old, ain't ya?" they said. "We got some people who want to talk to you. Put these on." The man threw over a pair of metal handcuffs. I didn't move. "Boy, you put those on, or you'll find yourself with the angels soon." I bent down to pick them up. A gun went off, and I fell to the ground, putting my hands over my head. There was a moment of silence, and I heard a thud. I looked up and saw the rider lying on the ground. I turned behind me to see a figure. They slowly approached.

"Get up," they told me.

I rose to my feet slowly.

"Thank you," I said, looking upon my rescuer, or captor, I could not be sure. They wore a cloth around their face and a low hat.

"Need to be more careful, Doctor," the figure told me, pulling the cloth down.

"Adler!" I said. "How did you find me?" She was disguised in men's clothing. She wore a hat to hide her long and beautiful hair.

"I followed you, in case you needed help. Silly of Holmes to send you alone, really."

"Thank God you were here."

"Do you still have your revolver?" I felt around; it had been lost in the creek.

"No, it's gone."

"Here, take this," Miss Adler handed me a new revolver.

"There they are!" cried someone in the distance.

"We need to run!" Miss Adler said.

I followed her lead, and soon I saw the familiar sight of the stone bridge which covered the falls where we stood earlier. We slid down a steep hill and rolled into the open grass. My heart pounded as we ran across the stones, over the bridge, through the park, and to the Rose Inn. More shots were fired. I could hear the bullets colliding with the ground. I turned and fired back. Miss Adler called to me, but I told her to carry on. I returned fire and followed after her, but I couldn't see her.

I came to the inn, but she was nowhere to be seen. I called out but there was no response. What was I to do, with Holmes somewhere unknown, Miss Adler missing, and a pack of outlaws on my tail? This was it.

I stood momentarily pondering these thoughts and trying to catch my breath before I continued running. Then a large carriage came out of nowhere and rattled to a halt beside me, nearly running me over. I turned, and as the door opened, I was heaved inside.

My life was over, I thought. Mary would never forgive me for dying this way. She was nervous enough regarding my adventure to America; soon she'd learn this was my last adventure. I felt discouraged. I had run all that way, was nearly killed, only to be caught right outside my haven. The carriage moved at a rapid pace. The strong hands which pulled me inside were still wrestling with me as I fought back.

"Steady, man! Steady!" someone cried. "Watson, steady!" This man knew my name. I stopped my frantic motions and was relieved by who I saw inside the dark carriage.

"My God, Holmes!" I cried. "You could have simply told me you were in here rather than make me think I was being kidnapped!"

"We have little time to lose, my friend. I am sorry for the fright." I looked around, but did not see Miss Adler.

"Where is Miss Adler?"

"Driving," said Holmes. I looked out at the driver. It was Irene Adler.

"Holmes, where are we going? I have information that is most valuable! We cannot leave!" I stammered.

A bullet shattered the back window out of the carriage. The outlaws were still following!

"Woman! Lose them!" Holmes cried.

"Hold on!" she yelled back.

"Holmes, those men! One of them killed Norton! They are unloading their…"

"Opium supplies in a factory till the Society can be re-established!" Holmes finished.

"How did you know?"

"We should worry about losing these men before we carry on with this conversation," said Holmes as bullets pierced the walls.

Holmes took out his gun and fired upon the approaching outlaws. I reached for mine and I began to return fire.

Miss Adler had steady control of the carriage and carefully guided the horses as we exchanged fire. The three remaining outlaws, however, did not seem to slow down. In fact, they gained upon us increasingly.

Holmes shot through the back window while I hung out the door. I rejoiced when Holmes managed to hit one of his targets and saw the man fall. My rejoicing was cut short; there was a bang, and I felt a stinging pain in my upper arm and fell back.

"Watson!" cried Holmes. He turned and fired another round of bullets. "Got them!" Holmes then came and examined me. I was shot.

"It's only a flesh wound in the arm, Holmes; I'll live," I assured him. I rose, but my head spun.

He poked his head out the back window and fired another shot.

"The final one decided to back off," Holmes said.

He helped me take my jacket off and get a better look at my wound. My heart was pounding fiercely. He removed his tie and tied it tightly around my bloody arm. I winced as the pain shot up and down my arm. I felt myself begin to drift, and my eyes closed.

*****

I woke a couple of hours later. The sun had risen, but the carriage had not stopped. "How are you feeling, Doctor?" Miss Adler was now in the compartment, and Holmes drove the carriage.

I now saw fully what she wore. Dark tweed trousers with brown boots; a black waistcoat, that was evidently for a young man, but was somehow flattering on her; a cotton shirt; a black velvet jacket, and atop her head, a black stetson.

"You have been asleep some time."

"What happened?" I asked.

"Holmes saw to your wound and you passed out. Likely from exhaustion, he said."

"I suppose that's right," I agreed. "Where are we going? I need to tell Holmes what I saw."

"We're getting a train soon and going further west to Nevada. All is leading there."

"How is that?"

"The station is ahead. Let us board and we can all share information."

When the three of us were comfortably sitting in a private compartment with some food and drink, I told Holmes and Miss Adler all that I had learnt.

"You must brace yourself, Miss Adler," I instructed. "I overheard the outlaws, and it was admitted the one called Dog killed your husband."

I could see Adler's face tense, her eyes lit with a concealed fire. "He may have done the deed, but he is not the man who ordered Norton killed."

"Neither is Ivory," said I.

"I know," admitted Holmes.

"Forgive me, Holmes, but what was the point in risking my life if you knew all this?"

"I didn't until last night. Both of us have had enlightening adventures," said he. "You mentioned the name of the train which carried the opium was Pemberton Rail?"

"Correct."

"Then we are most certainly on the right trail. The reason the name was familiar to you was because you saw it recently in this." Holmes pulled out Norton's brown journal and opened it. I looked and there was written the name Pemberton Rail, with a series of numbers following.

"What are those numbers?" I asked.

"Bank details," Miss Adler said.

"I believe it would do us all good for me to recount my night's ventures now that we are caught up on yours, Watson."

"Please do," said I.

"I found my way easily to the house of Homer Smith. It rests just near the tracks, as the sheriff said. It was a substantially sized lodging. I walked up the path towards the front door, and heard someone call out to me, asking me my business. I informed them that I was told that Mr Homer Smith was a provider of some of the best opium in the country, and that I was willing to pay a hefty sum if he were willing to make a deal. I was then told to stay in place, and had a gun aimed at my head, should I get any funny ideas. I waited near twenty minutes before lights began to come on within the house. A man walked out of the dark and escorted me inside. I sat in a large dining hall at a table. A glass of whiskey was offered, and I sipped it occasionally. After another ten minutes or so, a tall man with a round pale face, and beady black eyes, walked in.

"'Your name?' he asked.

"'Altamont Jones,' said I.

"'I hear you are looking to buy opium from me?'

"'I am, Mr Smith.'

"'What brought you here?'

"'I overheard your name once. From one they call Ivory.'

"Homer Smith raised his eyebrow and tilted his head back. 'You overheard from Ivory?'

"'Yes, the man who runs the Society in New York. Our paths crossed some time ago; and when I found myself in the area, I recollected him telling me a Homer Smith supplied him with fine opium.'

"'Well, Al-ta-mont Jones,' Homer Smith said, 'how much are you willing to pay if I did have some of the finest opium around?'

"'Two thousand dollars for enough opium to last me a month.'

"'Well, why didn't you just say so from the start?' he said with a smile. 'Come on, let's go somewhere more comfortable.' We rose, and I followed him into a comfortable study. He called for one of his servants and asked them to prepare some samples of opium for me to test.

"'I trust that our transaction will remain private and that there won't be any trouble with local authorities?' I asked.

"'My good man, anyone who is anyone in this town is in my pocket. You have nothing to fear,' he informed me, smirking. Smith sat down at his desk and began sorting through papers. 'I'll have some trials ready soon, but until then, shall we have a smoke? A cigar perhaps?' I agreed and walked over to his desk. It was littered with newspapers and letters, both formal and informal. He offered me a cigar, clipped the end, and lit it. With it burning in my hand, I took a quick glance at his desk. I heard the door behind open, and to my surprise I saw Sheriff Flood walk in. 'I own this town, Al-ta-mont Jones,' Smith said with confidence.

"'I'm sorry, Mr Jones,' Sheriff Flood said, his rifle extended.

"'Now, Al-ta-mont Jones, I hear you've come after me but have no warrant. I've also been told you are a Pinkerton. I don't like Pinkertons.'

"I turned my head towards Smith. 'I am neither a Pinkerton nor American,' I began, dropping my fake accent. 'I am Sherlock Holmes, a consulting detective from London.' Both Smith and Sheriff Flood looked slightly confused. 'I care little for what you do; what I want is information. I'm looking for a man called Ivory who is responsible for the death of a Mr Godfrey Norton. Ivory ran a prestigious opium den in New York City and received regular shipment of the substance from you.'

"'Have a seat, sheriff,' Smith said, then paused and looked at me. 'Holmes, was it?'

"The three of us sat; the atmosphere in the room was immensely thick.

"'Ivory, I know him only by name.'

"'How do you know him only by name?' I asked.

"'We run in the same circles, you might say.'

"'As I said, I am looking for him, and him alone. I will pay you for information and leave you be.'

"Smith and Sheriff Flood laughed. 'I told the boss that Ivory was getting sloppy. He'll probably hang for this, but not by you, Mr Holmes,' Smith said with a chuckle. 'Unfortunately I can't let you leave this room alive. You know me and you know of Ivory— anyone who gets this close dies, no questions asked.'

"'I assure you the only person leaving this room alive will be me,' I said confidently. I heard the clicking of the sheriff's rifle as he aimed at my head.

"'Is that so?' Sheriff Flood said.

"With a firm foothold on the floor, I pushed my chair back and grabbed ahold of the gun's barrel, tilting it down. In the jerk, he pulled the trigger and blew his own knee out. He dropped the gun, and I grabbed it. Homer Smith cried and fell back in his chair, scooting towards the wall. With Sheriff Flood squealing behind me, Smith began to plead for his life. 'Please, please don't kill me! I'll tell you what you want!'

"'I know all I need! I saw from the quick glance at your desk that you receive shipments from Pemberton Rail, based in Carson City, Nevada. Unfortunately, I was trying to rope you in and hand you over to the sheriff. Thus I will take another avenue.' The study door opened. I fired a shot at the ground, and it quickly closed again. 'If you come in, I will shoot Smith,' I called out to the men on the other side.

"'Stay back, damn it!' Smith yelled. 'Go! Just go! You have what you want. Pemberton will lead you to Ivory. I don't know who he is, never have. Pemberton and his gang are our only connection.'

"'What gang?'

"'The Burns Brothers Gang! They accompany the shipments!'

"I heard the sound of Sheriff Flood fall onto the floor. When I turned back, Smith was reaching into his desk and pulling out a gun. Knowing mine was out of ammunition, I swung it, and the butt of the gun collided with Smith's hand, which held his pistol. The weapon crashed to the floor. Smith yelled in pain and slammed both fists onto his desk.

"'You've lost, Smith.'

"I realised another attack was imminent. I could see through the window behind Smith that one of his men was attempting to take aim at me from outside. I judged the distance between myself and the gunman and what possible reaction Smith would have if I approached. Hearing the sound of the gun go off, I dove to the right. Smith dove to the left. I heard the sound of glass shattering as the bullet broke through. I looked over, and Smith lay dead with a bullet in his head. I took up his fallen pistol and saw the gunman running towards the house. I took aim and shot the man down. I looked out of another window to the back garden. I saw a large barn and could hear the sound of stirring animals. I scooped up several of Smith's papers before I popped the window open and jumped out, running to the barn unscathed. There was a carriage inside, so I speedily harnessed two horses and cracked the whip. We bolted towards town. As the carriage charged through the yard, several shots were fired, but no damage was done.

"Miss Adler had prepared a getaway for us in case we needed a quick getaway, and she was right," Miss Adler looked at Holmes and smiled. "Besides, the sooner we get on, the sooner we can find Ivory and end this, and Nevada is not a quick journey. Miss Adler lost you when you returned fire, so we waited in the carriage, and when we saw you outside the inn we darted out to retrieve you."

"We're both lucky to be alive!" said I after hearing his remarkable tale.

"We've made significant headway in the case. All roads lead to this Pemberton. It is no coincidence, either, that Pemberton Rail

Co. is in Nevada, the very place Norton picked up a taste for opium. All is leading to Carson City. I find these bank details most curious. I should like to spend more time with the journal and see what mysteries lie in wait."

*****

The journey to Carson City was void of excitement. Holmes spent hours poring over Norton's journal and gained few results, as there was a plethora of names but nothing to indicate who or what they belonged to. I was able to pass some time by re-bandaging my gunshot wound and making sure it was properly sterilised with some alcohol.

I enjoyed the journey through the great American West, watching the view from the window as the carriage climbed hills, barrelled through forests, and chugged along the flat plains that stretched as far as the eye could see. There were, on occasion, glimpses of large bison as they grazed on vast open fields. I noticed, though, the further west we travelled, the less civilised the world became. There was so much of this landmass yet to be claimed by anybody. So much was still wild and free and untouched by human hands.

I began to feel somewhat uneasy with just a quarter of our journey left. I found it hard to find solace being cooped up inside the train. Holmes seemed to take little notice as he kept himself busy, and Miss Adler slept the journey away. I did find pleasure in not being shot at. It seems that between my time in Afghanistan and all my adventures with Sherlock Holmes, this adventure had more bullets racing towards me than all the others combined.

I was greatly relieved when the train finally rolled into our station. The three of us stood on the open platform in Carson City. Holmes still wore his long frock coat and stetson. Miss Adler, though having changed clothes, was still disguised as a young man, and I pulled on another jacket and tossed aside the other, which had been ripped and torn with bullet holes during our frantic escape. The air in Nevada was vastly different from that of Indiana. It was substantially cooler and far less humid. It was, by my account, a welcome change.

The three of us proceeded towards the village. It was a much livelier community than that of Pendleton. As we walked up the road and into town, to my surprise, I felt someone's arm rest on my shoulder, and Miss Adler grunted as she was pushed forward.

"Make any sudden movements and the girl dies," said an unknown man behind us.

I looked at Holmes, and he nodded. This was not a situation to be taken lightly. The man quickly herded us into a nearby empty building. All the windows were closed and the shutters pulled together, masking our visibility to the public outside. We turned to look at the man.

"Do you smell that, Watson?" said Holmes.

"Keep your damn English mouth shut!" said the man.

"I know you," said Adler.

"As you should, little lady."

"This is Dog," she confirmed.

"But we left you in the dust back in Indiana!" said I.

"You took a slow train!" he said, grinning.

"Ah, I have it!" exclaimed Holmes. "Mr Dog, you are quite foolish to smoke tobacco with such a unique smell. Not only did you leave ashes behind in Norton's office when you killed him, the stench lingered inside Miss Adler's house when you and your gang ransacked it!"

"Ain't no one followed it back to me yet."

"It was but a matter of time. So tell me, what was it you were looking for in Norton's house? A bank account, perhaps?"

Dog raised his gun and pointed at Holmes. "What do you know about that?"

"I have the information you want. I suppose when you approached Norton in his office and found him opening up his desk drawers, you didn't expect him to be unlocking a secret compartment inside the desk's top, which concealed his satin glove and journal containing valuable names and accounts."

"Where is the journal?" yelled Dog.

"Hidden."

"Boy, if you don't tell me where it is, I will shoot someone!" Dog rapidly approached us. Holmes was silent for a moment as the two of them locked eyes.

"Vatican Cameo…" said Holmes coolly.

I reached for Dog's arm, which held the gun, and forced it towards the ceiling. Dog let out a grunt. Holmes, swift as ever, swept Dog's feet out from under him. He fell with a terrific thud to the floor. Holmes pinned him down with his knee firmly pressed in the man's stomach.

"Tell me where we can find Pemberton," demanded Holmes. Dog lay there, coughing. Holmes pressed his knee in a little harder.

"Ugh! The Castle! You can find him there!" Dog coughed again and winced from the pain. "You can find him in the Castle."

"Where is this Castle?"

"Up… up the hill overlookin' the lake. Three… err… fourteen miles up the mountain road!"

Holmes removed his knee and forced the man to his feet. "Cuffs, Watson!"

I dug inside Holmes's bag, and found a pair that he clasped upon Dog's dirty wrists.

"Step away, Mr Holmes," said Miss Adler, who was holding Dog's gun.

"Shoot me! Shoot me, bitch!" roared Dog.

"Did you threaten my husband?" she asked.

"Piss off!" he retorted.

"Was it you who threatened him?" yelled Miss Adler. He did not respond. Anger burned in her. She struck Dog's face.

"You killed my husband, you chained me up like an animal, and nearly killed me!"

"It was all just a bit of fun, little lady!"

"So is this!" She fired the gun, shooting Dog near the groin. He fell to the floor, screaming in pain as blood spilt out onto the floor.

"Please… please…" gasped Dog, whimpering.

"Don't kill you?" finished Miss Adler. Dog nodded furiously. "I wouldn't give you the satisfaction of a quick death, not such an easy way out for you. I want you to feel a tiny fraction of the pain you caused me before you hang." She took the butt of her gun and struck a heavy blow upon Dog's head, rendering him unconscious.

She turned and looked at both Holmes and me. "Come on, gentlemen, let's go to the castle."

What Happened to Irene Adler

We followed Miss Adler out into the street.

"We need some horses," she stated.

At a tavern up the road, there stood several horses tied to a trough. We three pushed through the tavern doors into a room full of scruffy-looking, large, bearded men. Miss Adler pulled her hat down a little low to hide her face, for even in men's clothing and her hair hidden, her face was quite recognisable as that of an attractive woman. As we approached the bar, the lanky man behind the counter asked us what we would like.

"Three whiskies," said Holmes, taking a seat upon a stool. We followed suit and waited for our drinks.

"Here ya are," said the bartender, setting three glasses before us.

"Tell me," said Holmes, continuing in his American accent, "do'ya know anyone willin' to part with a couple of horses, either on loan or permanently?"

The bartender gave us a queer look.

"Anyone in here willing to part with their horse, come talk to the gentlemen here at the counter!" he shouted. "'Bout the best I can do for ya."

I could hear the sounds of spurred boots walking towards us from behind. We turned to see two men. One was tall with a long face and a crooked nose. The other man was heavily bearded and lanky.

"What you boys looking to do?" asked the bearded man.

"We need three horses to carry us a fair distance and back," said Holmes.

"Where to?" the crooked-nosed man pressed.

"Our business is our own. I'd be willing to loan the horses, or buy outright if need be."

"I can't find you three, but I'll loan you my horse for five hundred dollars and a five-hundred-dollar deposit in case you never bring him back," said the bearded man.

"I'll do the same," the crooked-nosed man agreed. Holmes reached into his pocket and withdrew Miss Adler's emerald. The two men gazed greedily upon the stone.

"This stone is easily worth 10,000 dollars. I'll give you this for the horses. When we are done, we will return them, and the stone will remain in your possession as a payment and thank you for your service," Holmes offered. The realisation that Holmes did not accept Miss Adler's payment, but still came anyway, fell upon her face as he held the stone out. She bit her lip as the two dirty cowboys licked their own in marvel at the stone.

"Holmes…" whispered Miss Adler, but he did not turn to look at her.

"Shoot, keep the horses, we agree!" they said with big smiles upon their faces.

"Take us to the horses," Holmes replied.

The two cowboys could not have been happier to part with their beasts. Holmes and Adler, who shared a horse, and I, on my own, continued on with what felt like the final leg of our journey.

We carried on through town until we found ourselves booking a room in a local inn called The Grand Inn. It was a fair-sized establishment with a lounge and parlour. We had two adjacent rooms, which opened into one another by a door. I was pleased to be released from the burden of my luggage, as was Miss Adler. Holmes, as always, displayed no such sign of slowing down.

"If you both will excuse me, I should leave you for a short while. I suggest getting as much rest as possible," said Holmes, exiting with Norton's journal in hand. Miss Adler called after him, but when she looked down the hall, he was already gone.

"We should take his advice. The train journey has severely depleted my energy. I would like a good kip," said I.

"How can we just sit and rest, Doctor? I want to get Pemberton!"

"Miss Adler, you know better than this. You never charge in. Holmes will return with information that will be of some use to us and our future plan." She nodded and gave a half-smile. "Get some rest."

"I will try." She turned to close the door but stopped.

"He didn't use the emerald," she acknowledged.

"He did not."

"Why? It was nothing for me to leave that behind. It was a gift from the Bohemian King. For me, it was nothing to part with."

"Perhaps for Holmes, it was," I admitted.

"He kept my picture?"

I nodded.

"Will we ever know what really goes on inside that beautiful mind of his?" she asked.

"As I told you, he admires you, unlike anyone I've seen."

She smiled; her cheeks turned a shade of red. She closed the door, and I heard her collapse onto the bed. I cracked the bedroom window open to let the mountain air invade. I lay down upon my bed and drifted into a peaceful rest.

*****

I woke sometime later to the feeling of pain in my arm from my gunshot wound. While I cradled the wound, I saw the sun setting, just tipping the tops of the rolling hills. I turned and saw Holmes sitting stooped on his bed, looking at some papers.

"Four hours," said Holmes.

"Excuse me?"

"You have been asleep four hours. The woman, I believe, still is."

"What have you been doing all this time, other than timing my sleep?"

"I found the bank," he said, looking over at me.

"The one connected to the detail in Norton's journal?"

"The very one."

"What have you learnt?" I pressed eagerly.

"Firstly, I discovered that Maxwell Pemberton is heir to what is the Pemberton Estate. His grandfather and father were both gold miners. They built themselves 'the Castle' and invested their gold into the railroad. From there they built what is now the Pemberton Rail Co., which is now run by Maxwell. The company itself has an office here in Carson City. I went into the office to see what I could learn, taking the gamble that our identities had not been exposed by Dog. I resumed my identity as Altamont Jones and said that I was looking into the work that Godfrey Norton did for the company. A rather shy and nervous manager gave me everything I needed. He handed me the documents that Norton had worked on. They themselves were not incriminating, as they merely contained legal jargon regarding the purchase of a rail line from New York City towards Florida. What I found interesting was a name: Stanley's Capital and Loan. It is a small bank here. It is oddly small, though. For a large company like Pemberton Rail to use them made me curious. I left Pemberton Rail and ventured to the bank, where I presented the account number found in Norton's journal. I was shown into a private room and a lockbox was handed to me. Here is what was inside."

He pointed to the pile of papers on his bed. I proceeded to look at them.

"These look like bank transfers," said I.

"Indeed they are. Pemberton was siphoning money and dropping it into various people's pockets. All of the accounts belong to a number of political, business, and local lawmen who are established in and around the San Francisco Bay Area."

"I don't follow, Holmes."

"This is the hook that binds them all together," said he, holding up another piece of paper. "Each of the people he pays off has something to do with local shipments coming from the Orient."

"Opium!"

"Exactly! He's paid these men off in order to continue his delivery of the opium that he then sends to his hot spots all around the country. For example, the Society!"

"So Norton hid these papers, Pemberton discovered them, and had him killed?"

"I would think that is not too far off the bull's-eye, my dear Watson."

"We should take these papers to the local authorities. We can expose Pemberton; that's the case closed!"

"We are close indeed. I'd like to tell the woman what I found before we carry on." He rose and stretched before proceeding to the door which connected our room with Miss Adler's. He knocked gently but received no response. I walked over as he rapped on the door. When there was again no response, he barged through.

"She's gone!" I cried.

There, sitting on her bed, was a knife pierced through the sheets, keeping a slip of paper in place. Holmes raced over and withdrew it, reading the note aloud:

You have the information I want. Bring it to The Castle at midnight. Should you attempt to involve the authorities, the woman dies. You are watched.

Maxwell.

I felt an immense feeling of guilt fall over me. She was taken from right under my nose. How could I not have heard this, with but a thin wall between us?

"Watson, this is not your fault."

"How can you say that? I should have stayed alert!"

"Do not think that she was kidnapped, Watson. She went willingly."

"How do you know this?"

"There are no signs of a struggle. What I see is that a man stood here, over her bed, and another in the door between our rooms. There was a threat, probably on your life, so she went with them peacefully. See, there are two sets of dusty footprints: one here by the connecting door and the other by her bed."

"That doesn't help my guilt!"

"She knew what she was doing. Now come."

Holmes devised a plan to disguise us and sneak out of the inn before the sun had completely vanished. With some quick rearranging of clothes, I dressed in his long frock coat, and he took my jacket. He gave me his Stetson, and he himself went hatless. He did, however, use some cosmetics to alter his face. I was not entirely sold on this passing, but I kept faith in my friend. To our surprise, we exited the inn and prepared our horses with ease. If that statement in Maxwell's letter was true, whoever was watching our movements seemed to have missed us.

*****

We followed a rough dirt road a few miles out of Carson City, which took us up a steady incline. When we reached the top of this hill, he and I paused momentarily, and I marvelled at the beauty. The sky was aglow with red and orange as the sun set. The large, vivid green and brown hills dipped and rose across the vast landscape, and filled me with awe and wonder at the beauty that the world beheld. The road in front of us took a slight decline, but further off into the distance, we could see the majestic hills that surround the giant lake called Tahoe. It was a pity to think that our sole reason for being here was simply to catch a vile criminal and now rescue our friend. I turned and, looking behind, saw

Carson City down in the valley. It flickered with lights as darkness descended. Holmes urged us to keep moving.

A while later, under the complete cover of darkness, we came to a point where we could see the vast Lake Tahoe. It sparkled like crystal in the twinkling moonlight. I cannot recall ever seeing a more beautiful, clear lake in all my life.

"That must be The Castle," said Holmes, interrupting my thoughts.

I looked in the direction he pointed, and I saw it under the starlit sky. Built into an alcove of the hillside was a large stone structure, brightly lit. The name suddenly made perfect sense. This was no house, nor a mansion. It was indeed a castle in the hill. Directly in the middle of this structure rose a tall tower, from which I could see a balcony. To the right and left of the central tower shot off two wings with two smaller towers on opposite ends. Holmes dug into his pocket and pulled out a telescope.

"What do you see?" I asked.

"Movement in the windows. Pemberton must think himself safe; there is no visible obstruction, though I am sure hidden somewhere in the towers are gunmen." After a brief pause, Holmes turned and looked at me. "Watson, our plan will be simple. Get Miss Adler out. We can take care of the rest afterwards."

"Agreed!"

We pressed on towards The Castle. As we did, I made sure to keep to the right of the road because the left side became treacherous with a sudden, steep drop. The night air was quiet and cold as it blew across the hills. I could, on occasion, hear the sound of birds chirping and coyotes howling. As we grew closer, I could not help but think of Miss Adler and Holmes's deduction. She had done such a brave thing. I could only hope that Maxwell was true to his word and no harm had befallen her, so that I, too, could return the favour.

We approached the entrance to The Castle at just before midnight. There were two men standing by the pillars, holding lanterns.

"State your name!" called one.

"I am Sherlock Holmes, and this is Doctor John Watson. We are here as requested by Maxwell Pemberton."

"Dismount and leave the horses!" they called. Holmes and I obeyed. We walked slowly towards the two men. I could see both holding pistols. "Search them," said the man to our left. The one on our right approached and patted both of us down, checking for weapons. My service revolver was taken, as was Holmes's gun.

"This way," said the man on the left, waving us on with his firearm.

We walked up a flight of steps which led to a grand entryway with large arches. A man dressed in a fine suit stood in front of a large wooden door.

"Through here, gentlemen," he said, opening it.

A yellow light spilled out from behind the door as we passed through. The foyer we found ourselves in was vast and most elegant. The hardwood floors shone to a point that we could see our reflection in the panels. Ahead to our left was a swooping staircase that led to the balcony we saw from the outside. The doors were shut. Further along was an entrance into another room. As we moved forward, my gaze was fixed by a large bison head hanging on the wall. Dark green, textured wallpaper clung to the walls, and many more animal heads—deer, buffalo, coyotes—were displayed. There were several stuffed squirrels upon various wooden cases filled with hunting rifles, axes, and knives. There was a large painting hanging on the wall behind us, depicting miners during the gold rush.

Holmes and I were offered seats on a large curved sofa before a lit fireplace. As we sat, the man who led us in departed, leaving us with the two men we had first met. Holmes and I passed glances between ourselves, but did not speak. Instead, we sat in silence, listening to the wind blowing and the crackling of the fire as we waited.

I could hear the sound of feet on the stairs, and then approaching us. Holmes and I stood and turned to see Miss Adler walk in. She looked a mess; her gentleman's waistcoat was missing a few buttons, her trousers dusty as if dragged, and there was a fresh cut on her lip. She was led by a bulky man who was sporting a twirled moustache. He was dressed in a well-pressed white suit, and held a black cane with what appeared to be a golden hand on top. Miss Adler looked at us both and nodded.

"Gentlemen, I am Maxwell Pemberton. I am sorry to have met you under such unfortunate circumstances," said he with a smile. "I admit that this has been quite the game, Mr Al-ta-mont Jones, or should I say Mr Sherlock Holmes? Don't look surprised, I know you were posing as a Pinkerton. Did you think that you were lucky enough to get all the information you wanted so easily when you visited my office? Isn't that right, Dog!"

Looking pale and in great discomfort, Dog was wheeled in in a chair. He gave us a fiendish smile.

"You should have killed me," said he.

"You wanted to be sure I did indeed have the papers you sought," confirmed Holmes.

"And we watched you until we knew, and to make sure you did as we asked, he took your little lady," said Pemberton. "Would you boys like a bite to eat? I would. Let's move this into the dining room, shall we? Dog, you go get some rest."

Holmes, myself, and Miss Adler were seated together with Pemberton's watchmen looming behind. He sat across and looked over us with a devilish grin. Pemberton had cold meat, bread, and cheese laid before us, and a bottle of bourbon.

"So, gentlemen and lady, tuck in!" said he. "There's no need for worry: you give me what I want and I give you what you want." He pointed toward Miss Adler.

"Why did you kill Norton?" Holmes asked.

"Me? No, no, I did not. He brought it upon himself, sir."

"You killed him because he had the documents," said I.

"Funnily enough, that wasn't my original reason for going after him. See, when he stumbled on my little trade when I first met him, it wasn't too hard to shut him up. Put a little extra money into his pocket and showed him a good time."

"You got him addicted to opium!" accused Miss Adler.

"He took it of his own free will, let me be clear on that!" stated Pemberton, taking a bite of bread and cheese. "After he and I smoothed things over, I offered to set him up with my associates in New York City, the Society. Told him of the club's exclusiveness and that it'd be good networking for him. He did something nice for me, so I did something nice for him.

"Well, apparently, after a while, he found the Society to be less enthralling. Worried about his pathetic reputation or something like that. He wanted out. Of course, Ivory, who ran the club, never lets a man go for free. Norton came to me asking for money to help him. So it happened that I was in need of a favour myself. An associate of mine found himself in jail—something to do with a prostitute. The important thing was I wanted Norton to clear him. He said he wouldn't do it, and then, oh boy, that man Norton played quite the devil. He says that he has information that would incriminate me and my operation, and if I didn't get him the money, he'd release the information!"

Pemberton slammed his hand upon the table and laughed wickedly. "I told him he had a week to get me the papers or I would come after his little lady here, and skin her alive."

Pemberton's voice suddenly changed to a cold, heartless tone. "So I began sending him warnings. It was a few days later I learnt from Ivory that Norton went to him for help. We decided to bleed him dry. Ivory requested that Norton give him some very expensive jewellery—earrings of some repute, I think—in order to keep his wife safe, but when Ivory told me Norton had failed to deliver to him too, we found it best to simply have him killed. So, we staged the suicide and that was that. As a goodwill gesture, I had his house searched in case the incriminating papers were somewhere there. When they failed to turn up, we let it lie, until you, Mr Holmes, showed up and started snooping around—and that's just where things got out of hand."

"Out of hand?" said Miss Adler. "You blackmailed and threatened my husband, you drove him into a state of panic as he tried to protect me, and then you murdered him when he fought back!"

"Why tell us all this?" I asked.

"Because he does not intend to let us leave alive," said Holmes.

"That is correct," said Pemberton, grinning.

Goodnight Irene

Everything happened so terribly fast. As Pemberton leaned forward, I saw a plate shoot across the table and crash into his face.
Then I saw my own plate pulled from before me and be hurled at
the two men behind us. Holmes scooted his chair out and used it
to pin one of the men, while the other, who had recovered from
the thrown plate, was pinned by me. Miss Adler leapt atop the
table, her boots rattling the dishes with every stomp, and dashed
to the other side to apprehend Pemberton by wrapping her arm
around his neck. Holmes and I rendered the watchmen unconscious. We took their guns into our possession, and I recovered
my service revolver. Pemberton, for the first time since meeting
him, had a look of true worry upon his face.

"What're ya going to do, lady? You got the guts to kill me?"

Adler heaved the man's chair back, and he fell to the floor
with a reverberating thud. We stood over him, feeling victorious,
having brought the fiend to his knees. The kitchen maid burst in,
saw the scene, and immediately let out a piercing scream before
turning and running away.

"We should leave!" demanded Holmes, but Miss Adler began
to kick and punch Pemberton, who cowered upon the floor as he
attempted to swat away her thrashings.

We could hear men shouting, and we were rushed to get out. I
wrapped my arm around Adler's waist and pulled her off Pemberton. We ran. Dog had wheeled himself to block our exit, holding a
gun. With no time for talking, I took quick aim and fired my last
shot at the hand holding the pistol. Dog cried in pain as his pistol
fell to the floor.

"Here!" I called out to Holmes, who was without ammunition, and tossed over a shotgun which sat across the mantel. Miss
Adler and I took a couple of the rifles hanging on the walls. "I
suppose we're lucky Pemberton keeps them loaded!" said I as we
ran out.

When we approached the front door, a group of men wielding pistols burst in. Holmes turned and ran up the swooping stairs, Miss Adler and I following quickly behind. The men chased us and fired. At the top of the stair, we carried on down a hall where we split up and hid in two rooms. Holmes and Miss Adler were together across the hall from me. Quickly taking aim, we waited for our pursuers.

When the group came around the corner, we fired upon them, taking them out one by one. I looked further down the hall and saw another stair. I could hear the sound of feet and shouts as Pemberton's men raced up both stairs. We ran further down the hall, looking for a way out. We found a back stair which led up. It was the only way.

We ascended several flights and came to a closed door at the top. I kicked it in and realised we had found ourselves at the very top of the centre tower of the Castle. We ran to the edge and looked out. For a brief moment, I was able to take in the beauty of everything around. The rolling hills and stillness, with the shining stars and glowing moon reflecting on the lake, were breathtaking among the chaos.

"This way!" called Holmes.

On the other side of the tower was another door. While one group followed us up one stairway, we would be slipping down by another, I thought. Holmes opened the door and froze. To our disbelief, Pemberton was on the other side holding a pistol. Behind us, from the other door, came three more men, each holding a gun. Altogether, the four men began to surround Holmes, Adler, and me. I anticipated them to shower us with bullets and lay us to waste. But for the moment, Pemberton held his pistol tightly and grinned.

"You forced me to abandon one of my more profitable opium houses, sending it up in smoke. You then take out Dog and his gang while also killing Homer Smith, and now you come into my house like you're trying to finish some asinine crusade." Pemberton laughed. His relaxed manner set chills down my spine.

"How fast are you, Pemberton?" Miss Adler asked.

"Come again?"

"Clearly, you're not very fast at all if you can't follow a simple question. I said, 'How. Fast. Are. You?'"

"What'ya mean, woman?"

"This whole thing started with you and Norton. You and I will finish it. Let's duel; we each get one shot at the other."

"Little lady, you don't want ta do that with me."

"No, really, I think I do."

"I'm a darn fast gunman, you don't stand a chance!"

"Well, I've been dying to get my gun off, so let's see, shall we?"

"Girl, you sure like to play games, don't you?" Pemberton said with satisfaction in his voice. "Fine, everyone back off. The lady and I will duel."

Holding tight to our guns, we all stood back while Pemberton and Miss Adler faced each other to set up the rules of the duel. Pemberton's men stood behind Holmes and myself with their guns ready to fire in case any trouble broke out. The rifle she had previously held was swapped for a revolver. Pemberton and Adler agreed to take five steps before making their move.

"Are you ready?" Pemberton asked her as they stood back to back.

"As ever," she replied with the turn of her head.

"Goodnight, Irene Adler," said Pemberton.

"Speak for yourself," Adler murmured.

"On the count of three, we walk."

"Agreed." She nodded.

"One!"

I could see Adler stiffen.

"Two!"

She threw a quick glance at Holmes.

"Three!"

All I recall was the bang of the gun and a flinch. Irene stood wide-eyed and breathing heavily. Pemberton stood with his gun extended, his face contorted. Under the silver moonlight, I could see a dark patch upon his chest. He dropped his gun and coughed before stumbling back and falling, with a horrified look upon his face. His body hurled back and slammed onto the stone floor of the tower. Pemberton's men looked upon the scene, bewildered. Holmes and I made our move. One of the men fired a shot into the air as we broke out into a commotion.

Miss Adler fired another shot, which sent one of the three men over the side of the tower. Holmes and I each struggled with the other two. I laid a blow upon my man that knocked him out cold. Holmes had his arm around his assailant's neck, and the lack of oxygen quickly saw the man fall to the floor. Once his adversary was down, Holmes quickly walked over to Miss Adler.

"Are you alright?" Holmes asked.

"I'm fine," she returned with a somewhat exhausted expression upon her face. "A little shaken, perhaps."

"I'm glad you did not do anything rash and waited for us," Holmes remarked sardonically.

"I didn't want you to come back to the inn and find Watson with a bullet in his head. I assumed this way would be easier."

"I thank you, deeply, Miss Adler, for what you did," said I.

She smiled at me and nodded.

"While we can, we should leave," Miss Adler said.

"Agreed," Holmes said with a nod.

We made our way down the stairs of the centre tower, keeping our guard up. Continuing down the hall, we stepped over the bodies from our exchange before quickly making our way back down the swooping stair towards the foyer and the front door. I turned back for one final look inside. I could see Dog sitting in his wheelchair, slouched over, his gun on the floor, and unconscious; the result of further loss of blood.

We walked down the steps and along the path to where we had left our horses.

"Mind your step. That's a nasty fall on the side there," said Holmes, regarding the steep drop off the side of the road.

"Drop your weapons," said the unknown voice of a man as we passed through the gate and approached our horses. We paused and lowered our weapons.

"Ivory," said Adler, turning to look at the man.

"Is anyone left alive?" Ivory asked.

"Some."

"Pemberton?"

"No, I shot him."

"Well, at least you did something useful in this mess."

"The game is up, Ivory," said Holmes.

"You are correct. I assume you have the documents we've been looking for? Give them to me or she dies."

He cocked his pistol and aimed it dead at Miss Adler. I looked at Holmes and, after a slight hesitation, he reached into his jacket and withdrew the documents.

"Give them to her, and she can hand them to me."

Holmes passed them over to her, and she walked slowly towards Ivory.

"Do you want me to hand these to you because you think you're stronger than I am?" she asked.

"Darlin', don't you remember anything that happened at Pier 4?"

I was taken aback when she threw the papers in Ivory's face. In the moments that followed, Miss Adler reached for Ivory's gun and the two struggled a moment. The gun went off and then, with no warning, they both tumbled over and fell down the steep drop into darkness.

The shock from the commotion and firing of the gun roused my horse, and it took fright and reared up. Holmes and I moved out of the way, nearly falling down into the same abyss with Miss

Adler, as the panicked horse came down and trampled Ivory underfoot. When my horse had calmed, I rose to my feet and saw Holmes, who was still down on all fours, looking over the edge.

I placed my hand on his back. I had no words to say to attempt to comfort him. I looked over the edge and could not see. We moved quickly to salvage the documents she had thrown and began calling for her, but our only response was the echo of our own voices down into the valley. Holmes started to slide down the ledge, but I grabbed him and pulled him back.

"Don't be daft, man! The world gains nothing by having you both dead! We need to wait for daylight."

"Forgive me, Watson," were the last words he spoke that night as we rode in silence back to Carson City.

*****

We spent the next few days informing the local authorities of our grand adventure and exposing Pemberton and his grand opium organisation. Those in his association in San Francisco were all arrested based on the evidence from the documents we supplied. Wires were sent to the police in New York City informing them of our findings, the truth behind Norton's death, and that they should be aware that Mr Oaks' death was also a result of Pemberton's organisation.

We sent further information to the authorities in Indianapolis so that the town of Pendleton could deal with the factory where the opium was being stored.

During this time, we remained in and around Carson City. Holmes spent days looking for Miss Adler, but found no trace of her body. The authorities believed it to have been taken by an animal and lost forever. Thus, after a long and exhaustive search, we gave up. Miss Irene Adler was missing and presumed dead, her life having been taken at the hands of the man called Ivory.

*****

Holmes and I travelled from Carson City to New York. The journey was long and tiresome, and Holmes was not in any mood to speak. Once back in New York, we spent two more days in and around the city, residing at Miss Adler's brownstone.

"What should be done about this house?" I asked. "Is there any family we can contact?"

"I wish to leave it as is, Watson. I will make the arrangements."

As we prepared to leave to board our boat back to England, Holmes stood in her study, holding his stetson and wearing a contemplative look upon his face. I saw him lay the hat down upon the sofa upon which Miss Adler had lounged so freely during the beginning of our case. He then withdrew something from his pocket. At a glance I thought it to be the picture of Miss Adler he had received back in '88, when she became the only woman who ever beat him. I felt it best to leave him alone, and as I walked out of the room, I turned back to see him lay the picture upon the sofa. I waited for him a few moments out in the hall. He slowly walked out of her rooms and locked the door.

"The game is over," said I.

"It's never over," said he solemnly. "Back to London we go." The Return

We found London and Baker Street precisely where we left them. The day we arrived was wet and grey. From Paddington, we fetched a hansom to take us back to Baker Street.

"Didn't you miss this splendid British weather, Holmes?"

"It does have a certain appeal to it, does it not?"

I felt at peace as we rode up Oxford Street and turned down Baker Street. To see the familiar lodging of 221 made me feel that our adventure was finally coming to an end.

I stepped inside with Holmes, and we both took a rest in that most familiar study. A newspaper sat on the table next to me, which showed the current date. It was upon seeing this that I realised my sense of time had but vanished during the case. Holmes and I had been gone six weeks. Our great American adventure was ended, but not without tremendous loss.

Mrs Hudson walked in with a smile upon her face.

"It is lovely to have you gentlemen back. Shall I have the cook make some tea? And will you stay for dinner, Doctor?" she asked.

"Do stay, if you can, old boy," said Holmes. "And fetch Mrs Watson too. I should be glad of the company."

I was moved by his request. I realised, despite his not admitting it, that he was finding a way to deal with the loss of Miss Adler.

"I'd be happy to stay for dinner. I will go and get Mary and return shortly."

"Very well, Doctor."

"Thank you, Mrs Hudson," said I. She parted with a smile. I stood, grabbed my luggage, and made my way towards the door.

"Watson," said Holmes, stopping me.

"Yes?" I replied, turning to face him.

"Thank you. Thank you for coming with me and being here."

"I always will be, old man."

He nodded. He reached over, picked up his black clay pipe, and pulled his Persian slipper from his drawer.

"Holmes. She was…"

"She was a wholly remarkable woman," he interrupted. "The woman." He paused a moment. "Off you go to fetch your wife. I'm sure she is missing you deeply."

*****

I made my way home, where I found my Mary sitting peacefully in our lounge. Her eyes lit up as I stepped inside, and I embraced her.

"It is so good to have you home, John!" she cried.

"It is good to be back, dear."

"What's wrong?" My wife had the uncanny ability to know instinctively when something was afoot. I took a moment and we sat down.

"Our case was successful in that it was solved. It was, however, unsuccessful in that a dear life was lost."

"My God, not Holmes?"

"No, no. He is alive. Our client, Irene Adler, lost her life." Mary put her hand over her mouth in shock. "She fell into a gorge. Her body was never found."

"Is he all right?"

"He is silent most of the time. He has requested we come for dinner tonight. I believe it is his way of coping."

"Then we shall be there!"

I nodded, and Mary embraced me tightly as I told her my tale in full.

Epilogue

The days that followed our return to London were dull. Miss Adler's death was reported throughout America and Europe. I found that during this time Holmes did not take time to read through the newspapers. On several visits, I noticed they remained stacked and untouched. But he was not idle, keeping busy with various experiments and a few consultations for Scotland Yard. Nevertheless, Holmes was still somewhat more reclusive than usual, and if I brought the matter up, he refused to speak about Miss Adler. For a short while, this was deeply concerning but, in his own way, he worked through the unmentioned pain and slowly returned to normal.

One particularly warm day, I found myself wandering down Baker Street to call in on Sherlock Holmes. I had not seen my friend for several weeks, and wished to amend that.

I saw from the street that the windows to the study were open, which I thought was a good sign, as it helped to air the room out from time to time. I walked in and found him sitting in his chair holding a letter.

"Potential client?" I asked, taking my hat off and sitting down.

"No, Watson. It's unrelated," said he in a rather curious tone as he set the letter upside down on his table.

"Well, Holmes, how do you feel about going out for some lunch? Unless you are otherwise engaged?"

"That sounds like a good idea. I feel I have been cooped up in the study for some time. A dab of fresh air would do me good!"

"Splendid! Shall we go now, then?"

He agreed, and we rose to walk out the door.

As soon as we stepped out of the study door, I realised I had left my hat behind. I darted back inside to collect it when something caught my attention. Upon the table next to Holmes's chair was the photograph of Miss Irene Adler—the very one which I thought I saw him leave behind in New York.

When I pressed Holmes about how this photograph had arrived in Baker Street, he waved it off with little attention and changed the subject. I was baffled by the photograph's reappearance and bewildered at his oddly secretive response. Out of respect, I decided to leave the matter alone, as it was nice to see Holmes in a brighter mood—the brightest I had seen him since our adventure's tragic ending.

However, I privately speculated on the matter, and I could only reach two possible conclusions: Holmes had either kept the picture with him... or someone had sent it back to him.

The End

The Allegro Mystery

As I glance over my notes between '82 and '90, I fondly remember those early years. I, having returned to London from my Afghan campaign with a Jezail bullet as a souvenir in my limb, was by no means ready for civilian life. I will always be grateful to Stamford for introducing me to that strange bohemian man, Sherlock Holmes, whose powers of observation and deduction continue to astonish for nearly a quarter of a century.

It was in the autumn of 1885 when one of the strangest cases found its way to the doorstep of 221B. While the story received some press, a proper and accurate account of the event has yet to reach the public. I feel, also, that the parties concerned in the matter have reached a time of life where these events would be nothing more than a thrilling story of their youth—a wound long since healed, as opposed to a freshly bandaged scrape.

"I have put her away for good, Watson. I have put her away for good!" said Sherlock Holmes with a sweeping entrance into the study. I folded the paper.

"Who have you put away?" I asked.

"Miss Susan Sutherland, my dear fellow! For months, she's plagued chapels, music halls, theatres, and busy streets, pickpocketing any inattentive fool."

"Well, this is the first I have heard you mention her, Holmes."

"Yes, well, you have had your own matters to attend to of late. Though I deduce you aren't friendly with Miss Edwards any longer."

"Good heavens, Holmes!" I barked. He smiled.

"She has kept you from our work the past few months, but looking at the state of your hair—the longest it's been since you met her—and the state of your whiskers, your personal grooming says there is no one to impress."

"Not that it is any of your business, but you are, as always, correct." I rubbed my face; my whiskers had become rather unruly and were in need of a good trim. "Tell me about this Miss Suther-land."

"Right!" Holmes began as he continued through the study and fell into his chair. "Sutherland—quite the villain, I should say." Holmes picked up his pipe and filled it with tobacco from his Persian slipper. "I got word that men and women were being robbed in church services across London. And don't give me that look, Watson, the robbery was not the minister collecting the tithe. The robberies were from individual pockets and handbags! Change, watches, bracelets, and even rings were slipped off—raptured away! I discovered that each of the robberies was on the person's right side. So I was looking for a left-handed crook. Of course, the difficult thing was finding the person hiding in plain sight. I had to find the disguise among the general public facades in the crowd."

"How on earth did you catch them, then?"

"Accessories, Watson. It all came down to a simple muff."

"A muff?"

"Correct." Holmes took a deep inhale of his pipe before exhaling and continuing. "This is where I found Susan Sutherland. She always kept her left hand inside her muff."

"I thought you said the thief was left-handed." Holmes raised his finger to me.

"So I planned my trick to take place at one of her places of worship. Having disguised myself splendidly as an old woman with a monstrously huge bag ripe for the plucking, I sat and waited. Soon enough she sat by me, just to my right—her left. Then I felt it!" Holmes said, slapping his hand upon his knee. "Her hand was inside my bag. I peered over to see her left hand still in her muff. My assumptions were correct. I, too, had a similar plan. As she reached into the bag, what she did not expect to find was my hand inside. I grabbed hers, threw off my disguise, and exposed her. Soon enough one of Scotland Yard's finest came to cart her off to a cell." Setting down his pipe and pressing his fingers together, he leaned his head back and a smile of satisfaction stretched across his face.

"Though, there is no guarantee that any or all the stolen belongings will ever be recovered. Most are likely lost to the pawnbrokers."

I clapped my hands together.

"Well done, Holmes!" I paused a moment. "And I am sorry for my absence of late. I pray you won't hold it against me?"

"Watson, all matters of love I leave in your hands. While I haven't the time or energy for such commitment, I can, at the very least, understand the game you play. For love is a game—maybe the most dangerous game of them all."

There was a ring on the bell, followed by the sound of hurried steps up the stairs. A woman—my God, a woman—burst into the study. I turned quickly; Holmes slowly lifted his head. The fairest creature I had ever seen stood there, pale-faced and gasping for breath. There was a familiarity about her, I thought, as I marvelled at her tall, slender frame. She wore a long green dress and a large floral hat. Her dark blonde hair had fallen loose from under her hat. This porcelain woman, with striking rosy cheeks, darted her blue, gem-like eyes between myself and Holmes.

"I am looking for Mr. Sherlock Holmes," the woman asked in a French accent.

"I am he," Holmes returned.

"Then you must help me, sir!" she pleaded, still standing in the doorway, panting.

"My dear, won't you have a seat? You are flushed," I said. She looked at me with a blank stare before nodding quickly. She glided across the floor, her green dress flowing with every step. I called for Mrs. Hudson to bring us some tea.

"Mademoiselle Dipin," Holmes said, "what can the West End's shining star need with my services?"

"You know me?"

"I know you are a rising star, with a one-off stint at Her Majesty's Theatre performing an exotic ballet. No paper in London has missed the show."

"It is a beautiful story," Mademoiselle Dipin began. It seemed that whatever concerns she had upon entering our rooms vanished as her mind turned back to her art. "The movements, the music—oh, it's…" She pressed her fingers to her soft lips and kissed them.

"So I've heard, though yet to see," said Holmes.

"And you might never get the chance." Her face turned to stone. "I cannot say how much longer I'll survive the show."

"Is your life in danger?" I asked. She looked at me, her eyes piercing.

"For the last two and a half months we have performed and all seemed fine, but it began with letters."

"Tell me all from the beginning. Leave no detail out, no matter how trivial you might think it," said Holmes.

"Then, to tell you of recent events, I need to tell you about my past. My stage fame has inspired many devoted followers. They attend more shows than the lead actor or actress themselves, it seems. They wait outside the stage door, they bring you flowers, chocolates—many different gifts. If you miss a show they send you a card. It's quite remarkable what the fanatics will do for you. A mutual appreciation for the art brings people together.

"I love these types of people, Mr. Holmes—those who love the art and can discuss the art. But some," she paused and clasped her hands, nervously twiddling her thumbs, "they see you as the embodiment of art and assume you are the final authority on it rather than one of the many channels by which one can demonstrate its beauty. Back in France I had many admirers. Some were harmless. Some were more… forceful.

"There was a man named Jean Javet. He believed he was in love with me. He started by offering flowers after performances. I thought nothing of it at the time. I graciously accepted his gift.

That was my first mistake. Next he started sending letters. In the beginning they spoke of his love for my art and how passionate my movements were—saying how he'd never seen such marvellous style and superb technique.

"From time to time I would write very gracious letters in return, thanking him for his compliments and coming to see the performances. I started to become concerned after a rather poor review was published in one of the local papers. The critic called our performance a disgrace, scandalous, and said it should be ended now. One never forgets a terrible review. I did my best to put it to the back of my mind. Some people will always hate your art.

"A few days after that review, I received a letter. Monsieur Javet took great offence on my behalf for the review. He ranted about how terrible they were for saying such harsh things, and that the paper should know the error of their ways. I replied saying it was no issue and that we must move forward in our art. He replied with a single sentence: 'Our art will be beautiful. I will make sure no one speaks of you and our art that way again.'

"I was slightly haunted by this response. What he meant I did not know, at the time. A few days later, the paper that published the review was set on fire and burnt down! There was no evidence, no clues at all as to who started it or how it happened. It was passed off as an accident. Javet wrote me again; this time he said, 'Our art is saved'. I knew what he meant. I knew he was responsible, but I did not know if I should turn the letter over to the authorities. Would they believe me?

"I waited, foolishly. Mr. Holmes, I waited! That very night after my performance, I was the last to leave the theatre. When I left, Javet was outside the stage door. He rushed me and took me in his arms. He raved about our art and love. I pleaded with him to let me go. He continued to speak of our love and what love does to art. He said he loved me and forced a kiss on me. I was confused, frightened, and alone. I said I had no feelings for him.

"This angered him. He pushed me against the wall. My breath was taken from me. I tried to regain composure, but he held me gently and caressed my hair, saying, 'No, no, you do love me, you do. I know it. We are both artists, and we'll make beautiful art.' I dug my nails into his face and tore his skin. He fell back, holding his face, which began to drip with blood. I ran; he chased. Thankfully, a policeman was nearby and heard my cries. He stopped Javet and arrested him. He was tried and sentenced to jail for the fire and assault. That was three years ago this last July."

She paused a moment. "This brings me to now. At the end of the first week's performance here in London, I received a letter." The ballerina took out a piece of paper and handed it to Holmes. He took it and quickly read it before handing it over to me. It read thus:

My beautiful Mademoiselle, how I've missed your art. How I've missed your movements. How I've missed your touch. I am excited to see you on stage in London very soon. Keep a watchful eye, I will be there.

J

"I have been frightened terribly by this. I did not keep this letter a secret, but I was assured measures would be taken to ensure my, and the entire cast's, safety. During my second week's performance, I got another letter. It was from Javet. He said how wonderful the show was and how I am the light of London. He promised he'd see more performances and that I'd never be out of his sight again." Her eyes began to well and her lower lip quivered. But she remained strong. She straightened herself and fought back the tears.

"Two nights ago I believe I saw him in the audience. He was not seated. He was standing in a doorway. He made a nod and hand gesture at me, like an American salute. It was the only time during a performance that I have ever stumbled! The next day he wrote again, saying how pleased he was to get that reaction. Then, last night, on my way home, I was followed. A man, of similar stature to Javet, followed me from the theatre through Leicester Square. It was heavily crowded and I took the opportunity to hurry my pace and get away. I made haste to Soho, where I have lodging while I am here in London. Before I entered, I looked and took no notice of anyone else. I sat at my table and looked at the newspaper. An article in it spoke of you and your assistance to the Yard. I looked you up and thought if anyone could help me, it would be you!"

Holmes looked at the woman for a few moments.

"Well, well. You fear, then, that this Javet has escaped or been set loose from his cell in France and is here in London to watch you perform—and possibly more. Have you made enquiries with the French police to see if he is still there?"

"I have not, no," she admitted, her cheeks flushed with embarrassment.

"No need to blush. These are enquiries I will make on your behalf. If this man is in London, and intends to cause you torment, I assure you he will be found and his deeds exposed."

"Mr. Sherlock Holmes!" she cried. "So you will help me?"

"I will." Holmes handed the woman a slip of paper. "Please write your address on here. Continue life as usual. Please know I might call upon you at various times and places if need be."

She nodded eagerly as she scribbled down her address and handed it back to him.

"Tell me, the letters you received here in London—have you kept them?"

"Yes, I have."

"Good. Then I will send Watson here to fetch them and bring them back to me." Holmes looked at me. "That is, if you have nothing else pressing, my good fellow."

"Indeed, I do not! I would be happy to get them." I passed a friendly smile at the ballerina. She smiled in return. The out-of-breath and frightened creature was gone. The woman who sat before us now was different—more confident, more enticing. It was no wonder she had driven a man to lunacy.

"And you won't mind if I keep this letter until the others arrive?" Holmes asked, holding up the document she had presented to us.

"It is yours. I never wish to see it again."

"The last thing I would like to know—what does Javet look like?"

The woman swallowed and jutted her chin slightly. "He is Lucifer," she said.

"Ah, but my dear woman, Lucifer, according to the holy text, is a beautiful being," interjected Holmes.

"Then Javet is a troll who belongs under a bridge," she returned.

"Let us not get carried away with bitterness. I want straight facts."

"Forgive me, Mr. Holmes." My friend nodded and motioned for her to continue.

"He is about your height, but stocky. Broad chest and thick-skinned. He is not a fat man, though. He—last I saw—had thick whiskers on his cheeks, but his chin and upper lip were clean. He will now have three scratch marks on his left cheek from me. His hair is dark—black or dark brown. I've only seen it from under his hat and at night. I do remember him having a thin upper lip and a dimple in the centre of his chin. He is a very strongly built man, Mr. Holmes."

"Thank you, Mademoiselle." Holmes turned to me.

"Shall I retrieve those letters?" I asked.

"Yes, we can take a cab," replied our guest.

"If you will bind the letters with a thread and set them just outside your door, Watson will wait in the cab and collect them once you have placed them there. I don't want anyone to see him go inside," said Holmes.

We were off in a hurry. I sat next to our alluring client. The crisp autumn air filled the cab as we bounced down the streets. I peered, casually, out the window to see if we had been followed. Nothing out of the ordinary caught my attention. Mademoiselle Dipin sat calm and quiet, keeping her face away from the windows. I would ask her questions about the show, but her responses reminded me of Holmes when he was deep in thought—short and vague.

We passed through Soho Square before coming to a stop a few yards behind the ballerina's door. I watched as she darted out, looking back and forth, before vanishing into her building. I stepped out of the cab just as the door opened enough for me to catch a glimpse of her dainty hand leaving a bundle of letters bound together. Putting them safely into my pocket, I returned to my cab and ordered the driver to return to Baker Street.

When I did, Holmes was nowhere to be found. A note had been left which said he had gone to enquire about Javet and would return later. I did not see Holmes for the remainder of the day. What exploits he had engaged himself with were not learned until I woke the next morning.

I found my friend lying on the floor on our bearskin rug. He gazed intensely at the ceiling. At his feet lay scraps of paper, and to one side lay the letters I had retrieved. I bade him good morning. He was, as on several occasions, unresponsive. I glanced about the room for any sign of his cocaine usage, which had, at times, been the cause for his silence.

"Fret not, good fellow," he said. I turned to look at him. He remained unmoved, except for one hand extended into the air. Grasped between his index finger and thumb hung one of the letters. "I have been engaged with this. I seek solace in cocaine when there is nothing to stimulate my mind."

I raised an eyebrow at him. He finally turned his head slightly to look at me.

"What have you done?" I asked.

"Look at the floor and make a deduction," he encouraged.

"It seems like you've created a mess," I said sarcastically.

"Beyond the most obvious, Watson," his tone became stern, which I found surprising.

"It looks like you have been comparing papers to the letters, given the different makes you've laid out."

"Well done!" he said cheerfully.

"After I sent a message to the Continent to learn the whereabouts of Javet, I came back to find these letters. I immediately rushed back out after having thoroughly examined them. The letters are all written in the same hand—of that I have no doubt—even the ink is the same, as was the pen that was used. The paper, dear Watson, on which our man scribbled, is not all the same. So I scoured the city to see where these types of paper are commonly found."

"What was your conclusion?" I pressed.

"The paper is of poor quality—sold primarily through street vendors. Most vendors won't give you what you pay for, and you run out of your sheets soon."

"So our culprit is new to town and grabbed cheap paper, which is why you know this man used it so quickly?"

"The ink, Watson, is a fine ink—expensive to obtain. He is buying cheap paper from street vendors in order to avoid being recognised in more well-established retailers. How I know he's using it quickly: on two of these letters there are three droplets of ink that correspond when the pages are placed together. The man dipped his pen in the ink and it splattered, staining both pages. What I do believe is that our man has set himself up in Islington, somewhere near Angel."

"How did you come to this?"

"Street vendors!" he exclaimed, shooting up from the bearskin rug. He rifled through the papers and the letters, matching them to the blank sheets. I stood over him and looked down.

Written on the new sheets, at the top left corner, was the name of the vendor and the street where they were sold.

"It took me most of the day and into the evening, but I found them all. There are three vendors who sell these papers in the Angel area. I took their information, and once I learn about Javet from the French authorities, I will retrace that avenue if need be."

"When do you expect to hear back?"

"I sent a message to Monsieur Dubuque of the Paris police—"

Holmes was interrupted by a knock on the door.

"A message for you," said Mrs. Hudson, poking her head around the door. Taking it from her, I handed it to Holmes.

In a single motion, he leapt to his feet from the floor.

"Come, Watson! The game is afoot!"

*****

Silently we sat in the cab. My heart raced with excitement and curiosity. Mademoiselle Dipin's apartment had been ransacked during the late morning, between 9 a.m. and 11 a.m., and Inspector Lestrade of the Metropolitan Police had called for our assistance. When we arrived, two police officers stood outside. They waved Holmes and me through.

The apartment was a devastating mess. Cabinets were toppled over, clothing was scattered and torn, pillows were thrown here and there. Shreds of paper lay under every step. Inspector Lestrade stood in the middle of a small lounge near Mademoiselle Dipin. Her face was buried in her hands for a moment before she ran them through her extraordinary hair, pulling it back away from her beautiful face. When she saw Holmes and me, she stood up and approached.

"I am so glad to see you, Mr. Holmes," she said.

"Yes, good of you to come in such a hurry," said Lestrade.

"What do you know?" Holmes asked, making no time for pleasantries.

Lestrade nodded at the lady.

"Nothing seemed out of the ordinary. I did not notice myself being followed or feel that someone was watching me. I've been about my daily business. I spent most of the morning at the theatre. I came home to relax for a few hours and freshen up before I returned this evening. When I got home I found the place like this!"

"The lady here has told us about this Javet character. He seems a good suspect," said Lestrade.

"Yes, but we are not certain where he is at present," returned Holmes.

"He's certainly in London!" Lestrade said with a chuckle. "The girl told me about the letters and everything."

There was a commotion outside. Officers were shouting. We could hear the sound of several feet thumping up the stairs.

"Where is she? Where is my daughter?" echoed the voice of a strong woman. She stood in the shadow of the doorway, majestic, towering some six feet tall. Glowing golden hair was fashionably tied up and styled on top of her head. She was certainly a woman who, in her prime, would have stolen the hearts of every man. While still very handsome, she was the type of woman who now preferred softly lit rooms. Tucked under her arm was a small box which she clung to too tightly.

"Mère!" cried Mademoiselle Dipin. Her expression was of utter horror. "What are you doing here?"

"I have come to speak with you, and when I do I find you caught up in a mess!" the matriarch returned. "Tell me what has happened!"

"It seems your daughter has caught some unwelcome attention by an enthusiast for her art," said Lestrade. Her mother scoffed. "We believe he's the one behind it all."

"It's Javet, Mère."

"That man?" she roared. "This is why I came here, to beg your return to Paris at once."

"I won't leave, Mère!"

"But can't you see, this is punishment—holy judgement for pursuing such an unholy profession!"

"You're wrong!" Mademoiselle Dipin yelled.

"Come now, ladies," Inspector Lestrade chimed in. "Let's just calm down." The tension between the two women slowly eased.

"What are you doing here?" Holmes asked our new arrival.

"I am here to see my daughter," she replied.

"Yes, but why?" he pressed.

"To beg my daughter's return. Are you deaf, sir?" She rolled her eyes. "I would do anything to get her to come home where it is safe!" The ballerina's cheeks began to turn red.

"Do you know about Javet?" Holmes asked. The woman shook her head.

"Why do you have such a fervent aversion to her performing?" I asked.

"Look at it already! She was stalked and attacked in Paris, now her home has been vandalised." She turned towards Lestrade. "And what are you doing to keep my girl safe? Scribbling in your notebook!"

"Mère, please. I beg you, stop!" asked Mademoiselle Dipin.

"Ladies, calm down, shall we?" said Lestrade. "I assure you, madam, that we will do our best to find the one responsible," assured Lestrade. Holmes let out a sigh.

"Have you questioned any of the corps de ballet?" the girl's mother asked. "It wouldn't be the first time an up-and-coming dancer tried to push the prima out!"

Lestrade turned back towards the ballerina.

"I… I don't know."

"Have you noted any peculiar behaviour?" Lestrade asked.

"I have not. Well… no. It was nothing." Mademoiselle Dipin trailed off, her face blank as if she recalled something.

"Very well, then," said Lestrade. "We will get to work on this Javet character. Mr. Holmes, a word outside, please."

We left the mother and daughter in the apartment and stood outside in the cool air. The mother had made the room warm with unease. I found the brisk air refreshing.

"What do you make of it?" Lestrade asked.

"The mother is an odd character," said Holmes.

"I shouldn't wonder if it was her who did all this," said Lestrade. "What with coming here like this all of a sudden, wanting her daughter to leave. She's probably organised it all."

"Javet is very much a possibility," said I.

"We won't know until later," said Holmes.

"The young girl said you were currently looking for this Javet. Any leads?" Lestrade asked.

"Nothing that I can reveal."

"Holmes! You aren't your own authority," snuffed Lestrade.

"Do remember, I am not employed by the Yard. It was the girl who hired me. My duty is to her and her safety. If there is any information that is beneficial to both parties, I'd share it. Presently there is not. I will keep you updated, Lestrade."

Just then the girl's mother rushed out the front door and jumped into a cab. Her elegant face was distorted by a horrid expression of anger and grief. Her daughter followed, holding the box which her mother had held earlier. She only saw the back of the cab pull away.

"Your mother has quite the temper, dear girl."

"She does. She hates my work, my art," she returned.

"Has she always hated it?" I asked. She nodded.

"She has, yes."

"What did she give you?" I pressed, looking at the box. She opened it to show us two ballet shoes tucked inside.

"For someone who hates your art, I'm a little surprised by her choice of gift," said I.

"She said she picked them up from the theatre. A gift." I nodded.

"Might I have a solitary word?" asked Holmes to the ballerina. The two walked off a moment. I stood there, Holmes's back to me, watching our client answer whatever mysterious questions he posed to her.

"He's bloody brilliant, but he boils my blood sometimes," scoffed Lestrade. Holmes and the girl turned and came back towards us.

"For now, Watson and I must go. We have other business to attend." I gave Holmes an inquisitive look. Without so much as a nod or wink he took off at a fast walk. I jogged behind a moment to catch up, leaving Lestrade and Mademoiselle Dipin behind.

*****

Holmes and I arrived at Her Majesty's Theatre and walked inside. During our cab ride, Holmes told me about the brief conversation he had had with Mademoiselle Dipin. He, too, noticed her uneasy expression when her mother asked about the corps. The girl admitted that one of the fellow dancers, Esther Daines, who would be first in line to replace her should anything happen, ducked out of a rehearsal about two hours before she came home. Mademoiselle Dipin said she hadn't been close to Miss Daines and hadn't paid her much attention, but noted that she had seemed uneasy before she left.

"If ever there was a motivation, Miss Daines would have it, Holmes," said I, as we walked the backstage halls of the theatre. "Mademoiselle Dipin is a remarkably handsome and elegant woman. I'm sure jealousy follows her wherever she treads."

"Jealousy, Watson. A waste of an emotion. It spurs people and drives them to ludicrous decisions that never reveal a positive outcome. Look at David and Bathsheba, jealous for another man's wife, so he sends that man to the front line of war and he's slain."

"It is a monstrous emotion, but do you mean to tell me you do not feel it?" Holmes did not reply. "Truly, Holmes?"

"I suppose I have had my experiences with it, yes." Holmes stopped. "Ah," said he, and tapped his knuckles repeatedly upon a closed door. It swung open and a short girl with big, bold green eyes and dark brown hair greeted us.

"May I help you?" she asked. Her voice was mouse-like.

"I am Mr. Sherlock Holmes and this is my friend and colleague Doctor Watson. Aren't you Miss Daines?"

"I am, yes…"

"We are professional enthusiasts for your art and we hoped to speak with you," Holmes continued.

"Well, I, uh… are you sure you mean me and not Dipin?"

"No, no! We mean you." I stood there and watched Holmes. I smiled and nodded at the girl, who reluctantly allowed Holmes and me into the dressing room. As we followed, Holmes continued to converse with her about the ballet. I noticed no one was around. She sat at a table littered with cosmetics and a large mirror at the back. Holmes pulled a seat over and they continued talking.

"I feel you should be the lead!" said Holmes. Miss Daines blushed.

"But Dipin is a master," she replied.

"Wouldn't you like to lead?"

"Of course, it is my dream."

"Rumour has it Mademoiselle Dipin is being stalked again. Rumour has it some people aren't keen on her being here, and they want her out of town." Miss Daines frowned and laid her hand on the table. "Maybe you can take over?" Miss Daines moved her hand, knocking over a bottle of perfume. She frantically tried to pick it up. Holmes reached over and caught the bottle before it rolled over the side.

"Yes, I've heard that, but well…" she said, as Holmes handed the bottle back to her. "No. Of course I don't want her to go." She seemed startled and uneasy.

"Sorry if I have crossed a line. I mean no offence," said Holmes.

"It's quite alright."

"We really must be going," said Holmes, "but thank you ever so much for letting a couple of excited fanatics have a chance to speak with you."

"Well, at least one of you spoke. Your friend here seems shy." Miss Daines smiled her perfect smile at me.

"I am just pleased to be here…" I said. She extended her hand, and I kissed it. Holmes tapped my shoulder, and we left.

"What was all that about?" I asked as we walked down several narrow corridors.

"I wanted to see if Miss Daines did have any aggression towards Mademoiselle Dipin."

"You couldn't have possibly learnt anything from that masquerade!" Holmes pushed a door open and we came outside.

"As a matter of fac,t I did. Miss Daines has been writing letters!"

*****

We walked back to Baker Street. My friend became a silent companion as we made our way through Piccadilly, over Oxford Street and up Baker Street. Upon our return, there was a letter from the Continent. Holmes ripped it open and read it out.

Mr Holmes, I have looked into Monsieur Javet's whereabouts. He was jailed but served his sentence. Has taken lodgings outside the city. I confirm he has not crossed the Channel, nor has he in some years.

"My God, Holmes, he isn't here?" said I.

"Seems not."

"I have a few things to look over the rest of the day. I shall come to you when I need a companion." Holmes walked into his room and shut the door gently.

The next day, I was woken by a sudden jerk. Holmes had his hand pressed to my shoulder.

"Did I wake you?" he asked.

"You did, yes."

"As you are awake, might you do me a kindness?"

"Name it," I returned.

"I need you to go to Mademoiselle, tell her to end all her performing and leave at once for the Continent by the morning."

"Is her life in danger?"

"Go to her now!"

*****

I went off immediately to find our ballerina and relay Holmes's instruction. It was not unlike Holmes to keep his plans to himself. As much as he criticised my apparent romanticising of his adventures, he, too, had a flair for the dramatic when he drew a case to a close. This was no exception; Holmes was playing this so very close to his chest. But his reasons were always valid. Holmes was an endless enigma. His methods were strategic but unpredictable. What the game was rolled over in my mind again and again as I made haste to our client.

Arriving at the theatre, I found Mademoiselle Dipin. She was in mid-rehearsal. The stage was full of ballerinas in tutus, their legs bound by white stockings. They bent and twirled this way and that with impeccable timing. They flowed together, and everything was natural, like the movements of the ocean as tides come and go. Mademoiselle Dipin was glorious. She wore her outfit with pride and seduction. She was a magnificent sight to behold! Everything about her was a masterpiece. Her eyes lit when she looked out into the auditorium and saw me. She waved her hand and the production stopped. She floated towards me.

"Doctor Watson, what brings you here?"

"Holmes has sent me with word," said I. Her expression suddenly tensed. "He's said the game is over. It is best for your safety that you stop performing and leave the show."

"I demand a reason. What is happening?" she snapped.

"He hasn't informed me. He's just told me to come and tell you at once. He's asked that you pack and leave by morning."

The woman looked at me with horror. Her breathing increased. Was it panic or anger? I could not fully tell—perhaps a combination of the two. Watching this fine artist be told she must abandon her art for her safety—when has an artist done such a thing, truly?

"No!" she roared. "I won't go. I won't do it. This is what my mother wants. This is what the villain who is chasing me wants—to ruin my life." She stormed off. I began to follow her. She darted onto the stage again. She called Miss Daines over.

Our sweet ballerina looked at Miss Daines and instructed her to do something. She snapped her fingers and went off. I was taken aback by this. The woman, so gentle before, seemed tense and fierce. Miss Daines returned, looking most unhappy. She carried a pair of ballet shoes.

"I've brought these like you asked," I heard her say.

Mademoiselle Dipin took them into her hands, slipped off her old shoes, and put the new ones on. She looked at them a moment and balanced herself briefly. She clapped her hands, then the rehearsal began. She began to move and glide across the stage. She was picked up and twirled. The soft shuffle of feet could be heard against the rhythm of the orchestra. She began to twirl furiously around; the clicking of her shoes echoed as she balanced between spins. Suddenly she slipped, her legs buckled, and she fell, letting out a cry of pain. I stood. A crowd rushed around her. She was escorted off stage and taken to her dressing room. As I followed, I caught a glimpse of Miss Daines, who looked to be smirking.

I found Mademoiselle Dipin in her private room with her leg propped up. Her shoes were on the floor. I examined her leg and foot. She had sprained her ankle; at least several days' rest would be in order.

"I should have left," she said to me.

"What happened?"

"A problem with the shoe," she turned her head towards them. I picked them up.

"Heeled? Most unusual," said I.

"I wanted to try them. They are like the shoes of old."

"Looks like the heel broke," I observed. I examined it closely and sniffed the heel. I attempted to put Holmes's own power of deduction to use. I ran my finger along the broken edge. "Who gave you these shoes?" I asked.

"My mother said they were left for me here."

"By whom?" I pressed.

"Miss Daines got them as a gift."

"Excuse me," came a mouse-like voice from behind. It was Miss Daines. She looked at me with surprise. In her hand she held a letter. "Don't I know you?" she asked.

"I believe we met," I returned.

"Yes, the shy man. Your friend was very talkative."

"What do you want?" Mademoiselle Dipin snapped.

"I wanted to say sorry. The shoes—I was told they were strong, I didn't know they would do that." She fiddled with a slip of paper in her hands.

"What is that?" I asked.

"This came for her just now." She handed her the letter, which was read immediately. Mademoiselle Dipin looked at me with despair.

"Miss Daines, leave us, please."

When the girl had gone, I looked over the letter. It read:

I hope the shoes fit.

J

"It's him," she said, with an exhale.

"I must let Holmes know what has happened." She looked at me longingly, as if to say: don't leave me alone here.

I put my hand on the lady's hand.

"I will make sure no more harm befalls you. Give me a moment."

Leaving the shoes, I spoke with a young stagehand and asked him to stand watch outside her rooms and see that she went nowhere. As I walked through the theatre, I saw Miss Daines. She was with a tall, dark-haired man. Tears ran down her face, and he embraced her. A man wearing a flat cap, with a bucket and mop, shuffled past the two, bumping into them.

"Watch where you're going, geezer!" the dark-haired man shouted.

"My apologies, my apologies," the old man echoed, shuffling past me.

I exited the theatre and found a police officer outside. I begged her assistance and asked her to go inside and watch over the ballerina. When I said I was working with Sherlock Holmes, she did not hesitate. We both rushed inside, but when we got to her dressing room she had vanished. The young man whom I had instructed to watch her was unconscious on the floor. We revived him, but he had no recollection of what happened. On her table was a note that said she was leaving and not returning. My heart sank. I needed Holmes. I looked for the broken ballet shoes, but they were nowhere to be found! I took my leave and raced to Baker Street.

*****

When I arrived I ran up the stairs and into the study. I called out for my friend. Holmes came out of his room, quickly shutting the door behind him. He held a rag and was wiping his face. I took a moment to catch my breath.

"We have a problem," said I. "At the theatre, Mademoiselle was hurt. The shoes her mother brought to her…"

"They were tampered with. The heel was weak and bound by cheap glue with the intent of causing physical harm to our dear ballerina," Holmes finished. I looked upon him with utter amazement.

"Holmes! You are a magician! How can you know?"

He picked something up from his chair and tossed it over to me. It was a flat cap.

"That was you?" I asked. "Tell me what you know!"

"Let the night play out, Watson. I have a few things left to arrange. Tomorrow morning all will be revealed. Tonight, though, you and I will attend the ballet."

*****

We did just as Holmes said. The crowd was abuzz with excitement. Murmurs of Mademoiselle's departure were spoken of by almost everyone we passed. Miss Daines had finally slipped into the lead. As the performance began, she was elegant and graceful with her movements. Watching, one would think she had always been the lead. Holmes watched the stage, not as a spectator but like a hawk. He disappeared after intermission, leaving me to watch the remainder on my own.

After the show, as I made my way through the lobby, my arm was grabbed. It was Holmes.

"Where have you been?"

"Putting the final pieces in place." He smirked.

"You are enjoying this too much, Holmes!"

"Well, aren't you the detective who was meant to look after my daughter?"

I looked to see Madame Dipin.

"I am," said Holmes.

"And now she's vanished, abandoned all. I hear she's even sustained a sprain."

"And why aren't you looking for her?" I interjected.

"I told that girl this life would end her, and so it has. And I wanted to see how her replacement did."

"Some might think you ended it for her," said I. The woman's eyes blazed with anger. She puffed her cheeks and stormed off.

"Come now, Watson," said Holmes. I gave him a curious look. "Oh, dear boy, she's not our culprit."

"The shoes, though—she could have tampered with them!"

"I know who tampered with them. It wasn't her," Holmes confirmed. "I've dropped the net, and now we pull our catch in! Come and watch."

I followed my friend outside the theatre and around the back. There was a police maria and two officers. Lestrade had Miss Daines cuffed and was escorting her into the carriage. I couldn't believe my eyes. I thought back to when Holmes and I met with her—the mouse-like girl. Then I remembered her smirk when the injury occurred.

"This church-mouse of a girl is responsible for such horrible acts, fuelled solely by jealousy."

"Come, let's return to Baker Street. We don't have much time."

*****

Holmes told me to take a seat upon entering the study. He darted into his bedroom, quickly shutting the door behind him. I heard a murmur, as if he was speaking to himself. There was a sudden beat upon the door. Holmes shot out of his room. I stood. The door swung open and a dark-haired man stood there. It was the same man whom I had seen hugging Miss Daines.

"I got your note, Mr. Holmes!"

"Why don't you take a seat and explain yourself?" Holmes asked.

"Why don't you explain why you framed my darling sister!"

"Don't make threats unless you have solid evidence," Holmes said coolly.

The man pressed forward.

"You have no evidence against her, she's done nothing!" The man's face turned beet red.

"Your sister wanted the spotlight and she got it, at a high price I might add."

"She is a saint! She deserves that light, not some French prima donna!" The man lashed out and charged at Holmes. With a swift and graceful movement Holmes took hold of the man's extended arm, spun him around, and tossed him into a chair. He sat there shocked to have not caught his prey. Holmes motioned for me to stay back, but I remained ready to come to his aid.

"You will admit the truth, or your sister will suffer," said Holmes.

"Admit what?"

"This is no time to play games." Then Holmes gave three taps on the floor. His bedroom door opened and there stood Mademoiselle Dipin! Her presence only inflamed the man's rage. He shot from his chair and Mademoiselle Dipin held her hand up. Grasped in it were the letters. Suddenly the man's rage withdrew and his face turned white with panic.

"I suppose you know what's in her hand?" Holmes asked. He shook his head.

"It's... nothing."

"It's everything," she said. The man fell back into the chair.

"I... it was all done for my sister," he said.

"Miss Daines?" I questioned. He nodded.

"I got carried away. It was meant to be harmless."

"You tried to run me out of town! You tried to foil my work! You sent me letters pretending to be Javet. You followed me, you destroyed my apartment! How is any of that harmless, you… you beast!"

"This isn't over, Mr. Holmes. You have yet to prove a single thing. This is all conjecture and blackmail!" The colour began to return to his face.

"Shall I lay it out so that even you can understand?" Holmes said sharply. "You might have got away with the entire operation should you have done one thing differently." The man looked at Holmes. "Typed out the letters." Holmes paused a moment, and Mr. Daines suddenly looked sheepish. "Being familiar with the study of the written hand, when I spoke with your sister I noticed on her dresser that there was a letter on her table. I recognised the hand which had written it. I was able to take a quick glimpse at the letter," which Holmes withdrew from his pocket. "It was an invitation from you for her to join you for dinner." Holmes walked over to Mademoiselle Dipin and took a letter from her. "It's the way you swoop your L's and loop your E's that gave it all away initially when I examined the papers," Holmes paused a moment. "So, I followed your sister to her dinner date. I watched you like a hawk. I found where you live, a nice place in Angel. Inside your house I found papers bought from local sellers, all of whom remember selling to you—types of paper that match the letters received by Mademoiselle Dipin. I also noticed a particular brand of ink on your desk, which happens to be the exact ink on the letters, and a particular pen which was used to script the letters." Holmes looked at the man who now cowered in the chair. "Harmless, you say? Was it harmless when you sent the shoes to Mademoiselle Dipin with a weak heel? Your sister already said how you gave them to her, to try and win favour with Mademoiselle. Or when you placed the final letter at the front desk for her about the shoes? Oh, don't look surprised. You might remember an 'old geezer' who was mopping the floors. Yes, that was me. Give it up, Mr. Daines, the game is over."

There was a ring at the bell, and Lestrade came in with Miss Daines. She looked horrified to see her brother standing there.

"Darling, I'm sorry," he said to his sister as tears welled in her eyes.

"I didn't want to believe them, brother!"

"Lestrade, we have your man," said Holmes. Mr. Daines looked confused, as all his elaborate planning to see his sister take the spotlight had been foiled around him. In the coming months, not only would his actions ruin his life, but they would also ruin her career simply by association.

"Come now, Mr. Daines, you're coming with us," said Lestrade, taking the man by the arm and escorting him out of 221B Baker Street. His sister followed, sobbing behind.

"Mr. Holmes, I can't thank you enough," said Mademoiselle Dipin.

"It was my pleasure to assist."

"As to your fee…" she insisted.

"Why don't you treat Watson and me to your next performance when your foot has healed." She smiled and nodded cheerfully. She grabbed Holmes by the hands and squeezed.

"Until next time," said I. She touched my arm and made her way out. When she had left, Holmes walked over to the window and looked out at the street below.

"You surprise me, Watson," said he.

"Why is that?"

"She was a splendid woman, as far as women go. I gave you plenty of opportunities to be in her presence without me."

"I don't understand?" said I.

"I thought you would have invited her for a meal. I liked her better than the last one."

"Good gracious, man, were you trying to arrange something between us then?"

He smiled, reached for his pipe, and lit it. A few puffs, and smoke lifted from the cherry-wood pipe.

"Maybe we'll find you a wife with one of these cases."